City of Flame and Ash

a novel by L. Holmes

A City of Flame and Ash pronunciation guide

CHARACTERS

Sorcha:
Soar- sha

Kartix:
Car- ticks

Razan:
Rah- zahn

Senna:
Sen- ah

PLACES

Ocyla:
Oh- see-lah

Skyga:
Sky- gah

OTHER

Magik:
Magic

Hel:
Hell

Upcoming books in this series:

City of Kings and Killers
City of Death and Discontent

Look for other forthcoming books by L. Holmes including *Everybody Wants to be Loved.*

Midnight, Late Summer

The first thing she saw was a field. Wheat stirred in the still-lingering heat as the pregnant moon cast shades of silver over the vast farmland. Whispers of grass were the only sounds.

Sorcha.

That was her name. Or at least she thought it was. Her memory had yet to return.

She turned in a full circle. The humid air was perfumed with pine and wet soil. She had an urge to travel north.

But to what?

Standing in the midnight air, the young woman pondered her location. She ran a hand through her hair, the length of which she then noticed. Waist-length silky auburn strands were illuminated by the starlight above. Sorcha had yet to catch a glimpse of herself. She hoped they had not made her ugly. But then again, the Gods were not known for their kindness.

All at once, her memory clicked into place.

Ocyla, the capital of the Northern Continent.
At least she could remember where she was now.

The summer breeze sent prickles of heat across her skin. Sorcha tipped her head back, inhaling the sweet air. The yellow wheat field she was standing in gave way to a dense forest a few hundred meters ahead. The heavy canopy swayed gently in the midnight air. The Gods had told her that this world would be decimated by centuries of bloodshed and war, yet she found solace in the peace and silence.

All at once, the peace exploded into pain as an arrow pierced her shoulder. Blood trickled down in a steady crimson stream as she blinked.

What the—?

Sorcha had only been alive five minutes and already some asshole had tried to kill her.

Well, she thought, *at least I'm popular.*

Her blue eyes narrowed as she gazed ahead. Heavy fir trees were scattered in the distance, across from the grassy farmland. Just to the left was thick shrubbery. With the help of her magik, Sorcha was able to detect the barest outlines of figures. She counted twenty men hiding in the brush, about fifty yards away to her north.

Shit.

Standing there, taking in the first few minutes in this new body, had been a move of foolishness. She'd learned the hard way that complacency kills.

Cursing, the newly established creature of the Gods rolled to her right, hiding in the weeds. There was a brief pause as Sorcha assessed the wound. She gritted her teeth together, instinctually knowing what she had to do next. Heart pounding, she found a thick branch hidden amidst the brush. Sorcha bit down on it as she yanked the arrow from her shoulder. She screamed, but the branch stifled her voice, allowing her not to bite off her own tongue. Blood slowed to a halt as her wound gradually sealed, flesh knitting together with the help of her magik. The woman looked up from the ground, vengeance etched into every plane of her face.

She was going to have so, so much fun tearing these men limb from limb.

~

Just before Midnight, Late Summer

There was no debate. Kartix had been pushed to go on this mission. He was content to spend his day off reading in the Compound library, but the king had a say over all he did. So, before the sun rose, he and the King's Guard were scouting the Northern Forest, which was teeming with life in this late summer.

The library would have to wait.

As the King's Guard moved through the thick brambles of the woods, the men kept their voices low. The King's Guard were Ocyla's most elite warriors. With the exception of Mathias the head guard and Kartix, both of whom were Fae, all the men were human. Their black and red uniforms blended into the brush, allowing the Guard to go mostly undetected in the dense forest.

Whispers and hushes echoed among the men. The reason for this excursion was secret.

A few years ago, the king spiked the water supply of Ocyla with Mahoun. Mahoun was a precious metal which drained Fae of all their magik. Razan was able to harness the stolen magik, and use all the extra power to open a portal to Hel, but the Gods soon intervened. After Razan had been defeated and the portal to Hel closed, peace was supposed to have been restored to the Northern Continent. The heavenly battle had ended just hours prior. But the king, having been spared by the Gods mercy, was already hatching another plan to open another portal.

Earlier that night, the Gods had combined all of their powers into a weapon to seal the portal Razan had opened. Individually, their powers were not strong enough. But together, the Gods stood a chance.

After the king was defeated, and the door to Hel closed, the Gods broke the weapon into three parts. In order to keep the pieces disguised, the Gods chose to create the Triumvirates, the three parts of the weapon disguised to look like Fae. After the heavenly battle had been won, the Gods warned Razan that the

Triumvirates would be sent to keep an eye on him, although the king would not know who they were or what they looked like. Despite the king having tried to overtake the entire world, the Gods somehow allowed him to keep the Compound, and maintain control of Ocyla.

A few hours after the heavenly battle had ended and Razan was back in his throne room, he began sensing upticks of magik around the kingdom. These upticks of magik were the Triumvirates being sent to earth to keep their promises to the Gods; They were to watch over the king and report any missteps to the Gods. But once Razan started sensing the women arriving on earth, he turned to his surviving advisors and said quietly, "Now, it is time to locate the Triumvirates, and drain their magik."

Razan had detected a large uptick in magik around this area. The king had quickly sent his most trusted platoon to the Northern Forest. Now the men were all gathered in a wooded clearing, cleaning and sharpening their swords as they took shifts looking out for a Triumvirate.

"Shoot her," Mathias whispered in his ear.

Kartix, red in the face, turned toward the head guard. He felt small as he questioned him. "My father said to keep the Triumvirate alive."

And instantly he knew he shouldn't have pushed. Known for his alcoholic rages in the barracks, Mathias towered over him.

"Alive, not unharmed." Spit flew from his lips as Mathias sneered. "You don't have daddy to save you now."

A chill ran down Kartix's spine.

Pick your battles.

With no other option, Kartix slowly drew an arrow from the quiver on his back. The two men looked back at the young woman, now standing in the middle of the field, taking in her surroundings.

Here goes nothing.

There was a twang just before the arrow found its mark. It lodged deep in her shoulder. Something like dread filled Kartix's gut. But just as quickly as she appeared, the young woman was suddenly nowhere to be found—she was no longer gazing across the starlit field. There was no trace of blood either. For several moments, all twenty men took in one collective breath. For most, it was the last one they ever took.

Kartix did not hear the bones breaking until it was too late. Necks snapped and the King's Guards fell limp in rapid succession where they all stood around the clearing.

Kartix had just enough time to twirl around, armor digging uncomfortably into his back, to notice the last of the King's Guards dropping to their knees, dead.

And it was the Triumvirate who was the last one standing in the wooded clearing, alert and upright. She was not finished.

Kartix understood he should be afraid. He knew he was as good as dead as she met his eyes. He knew he was in such deep, unrelenting shit, especially when the young woman picked up a sword from one of the dead King's Guards and shifted her attention to him. The woman had used her own hands and magik to kill the men, but she wanted a weapon to face him. Kartix just froze, even as some distant part of his brain was begging him to move.

She swung the sword up to rest on Kartix's golden chest plate. He noticed she had a full mouth, soft and plush, set in determination. Her thick lashes brushed her cheeks as she blinked. Smooth, fair skin, stained with a blush was aglow in the moonlight.

She cut the leather straps attaching his armor to his shoulders and it fell away. Her sword slashed his shirt, exposing his chest, then cut into the delicate, tan skin of his clavicle, a trickle of blood staining his cobalt undertunic. He smirked as the crimson liquid bloomed across the fabric. She was grimacing slightly from where she stood before him with the sword still in hand. She was strong, powerful. The Triumvirate looked like she was ready to conquer the world. Kartix couldn't help but be a little turned on by her sudden show.

"Run back to your king."

She was so thin, he wondered how she could be holding up such a heavy weapon. Kartix expected himself to be afraid, but rather, curiosity got the best of him. "Who are you?" he breathed, his voice low but not weak.

~

Crickets and the whispers of wheat were the only sounds in the darkness. A warm breeze sent strands of dark hair across her face. She noticed his big hands and shivered with arousal. Sorcha realized then that he was years younger than her. The Gods had told her during her creation just hours prior that she appeared twenty-five years old, not that she would age, her magik having slowed the aging process down to a mere trickle. If she had to guess, the Fae male before her was around twenty. The young man's tan skin was smooth, his jawline angular, the planes of his face strong and sure. He had a powerfully built, muscle-clad body.

The head guard groaned, coming back into consciousness from where he lay on the forest floor.

Sorcha whipped her head around to him. "We don't have much time." Once again, her eyes turned toward the man before her. For several moments, they took each other in. She couldn't kill him, but she could give him something to remember her by. Her sword cut a thin line into Kartix's upper chest, just below his clavicle.

A bloody "S" now marked him permanently, a warning to all those who crossed her.

~

She stalked up to the man on the ground, gripped his golden hair, and yanked his head back. Kartix could see the thin chains of light which bound the head guard. His jaw dropped, but he quickly closed it. An image flashed across Kartix's mind; The Triumvirate, this beautiful woman, licking the blood off his hand, her soft, warm tongue scraping his skin, looking up at him with her wide, blue eyes.

Kartix shook his head, blinking quickly, a blush staining his cheeks. He glanced back up towards the Triumvirate.

She whispered something in the head guard's ear. Smiling softly, a look of pure serenity crossed her face, despite the violence etched into every single inch of her body as she held the guard against his will. Kartix had never seen Mathias look afraid, but as she spoke to him gently under her breath, his eyes went wide and wild with terror.

What had she said to him?

She spun around and froze. Her eyes narrowed in on Kartix from where she stood over Mathias, who was still bound in little golden chains of magik. With a snap of her fingers, the head guard fell unconscious, his head sagging on the forest floor. She cast a wicked glance at Kartix, a feral grin lighting up her sharp features. "I had to keep a few of you alive to deliver my message to Razan."

Kartix was still backed up against a large oak tree when Sorcha stalked up to him. This time she did not use the sword, but threw it at his boots. "Take your sword and run." Her face was set in determination.

He didn't move.

Sorcha rolled her eyes and sighed, her hands on her hips—not a very aggressive posture considering she had just killed most of Kartix's men. "Are you deaf or just dumb? I said, run." Fire sparked on her fingertips now, lighting up her face in the dark, the magik dark and strange and wonderful.

Kartix sucked in a breath. For such a formidable woman, she was the most stunning being he had ever seen. Her jawline was sharp and angular. Her pale skin perfect and smooth. He was not afraid of her. Somewhere deep down inside, he knew she would not hurt him.

And he was right.

"Why are you here? Where did you come from?" Kartix pressed, pushing off the giant oak and coming closer to Sorcha now.

Sorcha was caught off guard, taking a step back as Kartix straightened to his full height. Her breath quickened as he crowded her space. When she wouldn't answer his questions, his brows furrowed, sending wrinkles across the handsome planes of his face, onyx hair falling into matching dark eyes.

He noticed her withdrawn expression and felt a pang of sympathy echo through him. "I am not here by choice," he said. "I did not shoot you by choice either." He motioned to Mathias, who was still lying on the ground, unconscious. "The head guard made me do it. He threatened me."

Strangely, Sorcha nodded, as if understanding. "Wouldn't want to upset the king, now, would we?"

Kartix glowered and lowered his voice to a near whisper. "Despite what you may assume, I can think independently from the crown."

She looked thoughtful for a moment, and Kartix swore he could see her tucking away that bit of knowledge for later. Her eyes swung back to his.

"Well, we've had fun here tonight, haven't we? Alas, the festivities must come to an end." She bowed deeply, then straightened, locking eyes with him. "Goodbye."

She vanished before he could open his mouth.

Kartix was left with eighteen dead guards and one unconscious asshole who he now needed to drag back to the Compound.

The night had *not* gone according to plan.

Ten Years Later

Reid paced the foyer, his jaw clenched tight. The soft padding of his boots on the plush rug was the only sound in the otherwise silent space. Kartix was not back yet, and he was desperate to see him.

As the prince's half-brother, Reid was considered a bastard by most of those in the High Court. His mother had been the king's slave. She'd died while giving birth to him, and the king loved to remind Reid of that fact any chance he got. Kartix's mother was still alive, having been spared execution only because she came from noble blood. But the prince rarely saw his mother, seeing as she cared more about opium than her children.

At last, Reid heard the sounds of guards approaching. He straightened up when he saw his brother. After finally being freed from his captor's massive bed, bloodied and bruised and naked, Kartix was hauled through the Compound and thrown into his room. It took all of two breaths before he collapsed in the foyer. Reid turned to his half-brother.

"Bath. Now."

~

Reid's tone was nonnegotiable.

Kartix was still lying on the floor of the foyer, but he managed to pick himself up and cross to the bathing room. The prince was tired. *So, so tired.*

Clear, icy water was immediately heated with one lick of his magik. Kartix slid into the gold waters of the now-warmed bath. Reid lay curled up, his back against the tub, guarding his wounded, broken brother. Reid twitched at each sound that drifted from beyond the bathroom doors as he listened intently for any threats.

From beneath a layer of gold bubbles, Kartix sighed. The hot water did nothing to soothe the memory of what Senna had demanded from his body hours prior.

His captor was third in command to the king. Kartix was surprised that Senna was at the right hand of Razan, given that she was a woman, and women in Ocyla were not treated with respect. But then again, he supposed, Senna was incredibly manipulative when it came to men. *She probably has the king wrapped around her little finger.*

Having come from the distant city of Sykga, Senna was the definition of trouble. Raised by noble parents, she had been orphaned during the Seven-Years War, which had ravaged the land decades prior. After the fighting ended, she'd been sent to live with a distant cousin in Ocyla. Her cousin lived within the Compound, so Senna had quickly been exposed to the High Court. Once it was revealed that Senna had magik, Razan recruited her to work for him on the King's Council.

That had been years ago, when Razan had allowed humans to intermingle with Fae. All Fae had magik, and Razan loved that he could use his power to enslave humans. Recently, the king had ordered all humans to be servants. Some even went into slavery when their villages were burned, if the King's Guard thought that they would fetch a high price.

Senna had been a servant in Skyga once, and she fought her way to the top to become Razan's third in command. Apparently, she'd set her sights on Kartix. After Kartix had spoken up against one of his father's decisions, and he had been brutally punished. Razan betrothed his son to Senna, as punishment for rising up against him, knowing full well that Kartix hated Senna.

And thus began Kartix's torment—every night, Senna would call him to her bed, then have her way with him while he was tied down.

And there was nothing Kartix could do to stop it.

He had begged his father to choose someone else, any other female to wed. But Razan had stood firm—Senna would be the only one for him.

From where he lay under a thick cloud of gold bubbles, he shook his head, black strands aglow in the dying light of day. Reid glanced up toward his half-brother, concern etched into every plane of his face. Kartix could barely speak. Another shudder racked his body. He would not allow Senna to break him. Not completely.

But he only had a few minutes of silence to try to piece himself back together before Hel began all over again.

Reid's golden eyes slid back to the prince. "They're here."

With his brother's warning, Kartix dared to use what little magik was left in his reserves to speed up the scrubbing of his muscled body. Gold soap melted into his skin. As the sun cast its last rays into the gilded bathroom, Kartix looked like a falling star. A prized possession. A trophy.

Just the way Senna liked it.

"I'm ready." The prince allowed one last glance toward his brother, whose body was still tense. If not for Reid, he would have ended his own life some time ago.

As the sound of metal armor on marble approached, the prince swallowed. Kartix had just enough time to lean back in the tub and gaze out the large window, so when the Imperial Guards opened the gold doors to the bathing room without announcement, his handsome face appeared disinterested, gazing out toward the Eastern Mountains, hundreds of miles away.

A guard named Lenon cleared his throat. "It is time for the execution."

Reid and Kartix tensed at the same time. The prince slowly stood, water dripping from his pectorals. He eyed the guards with suspicion as he stepped out of the bath and wrapped a towel around his waist.

Reid stood as well, stretching to his full height as the guards took a step back. "Who is being executed this time?"

The guard looked nervously between the two Fae males. His eyes found the ground and refused to meet their stares. His voice was whisper soft as he said, "Your cousin."

Back and forth, the dirt was flung across the withered stones. Thin stalks of wheat scraped like claws through muddy remnants. The wooden broom chafed what skin was left of Sorcha's blistered palms. No matter how many times she swept this particular spot, the damn dirt wouldn't go away.

Sorcha briefly thought of how her friend Meg would often complain, years ago, about how sweeping was degrading to women.

A few years after being crafted by the Gods and sent to earth, Sorcha had grown tired of living alone, surviving in the wilderness. So, she had enrolled in a local school, posing as a higher-educated human woman. It wasn't unnormal, in those years following the heavenly battle, for women to achieve a higher education. King Razan had shut down the schools a few years later, however.

Sorcha had managed to befriend a classmate, Meg. Once, offhandedly, the Triumvirate mentioned that she didn't have anywhere to live during the summer break. Meg immediately told Sorcha to come and stay with her parents in the countryside. After a few years, Sorcha had come to spend all her holidays with Meg and her parents. For years, Sorcha considered Meg and her parents her adopted family. Until, they were killed by Razan's soldiers, and Meg sold into slavery.

The king had ordered Meg's village to be burned down years ago, as punishment for harboring people who rebelled against the reign of Razan. Sorcha had watched Meg's parents be slaughtered, and Meg carted into a wagon to be sold into the slave trade.

Shaking off the memory, the Triumvirate unraveled from her hunched position. The men in the stock room, when asked, had given her a broom that was too short, and the bastards knew it. She could practically feel their eyes, all seven pairs of them, roving over her body as she bent down. Sorcha had to stick out her ass to reach the dirt with the short broom, to finish yet another one of Senna's mindless chores. And the men certainly enjoyed the view.

Sorcha and all the other servants had gathered silently in the early morning mist for the first morning's prayer. Apparently, one had to pray to the Gods every morning in order to be a servant in the Compound. Ever since the heavenly battle, Razan decreed that every morning citizens of Ocyla were to pray to the Gods. Sorcha bit her lip. The king only made everyone pray because he was afraid of the Gods taking away his magik. His control. His power over the people.

Sorcha almost rolled her eyes. Ocylan society was too religious for her taste.

Senna, a woman slightly older than Sorcha, took to the raised dais at the center of the courtyard. She was Razan's third in command, and she also oversaw the servants. Despite her youth, Senna held herself as if she was the king himself. She shook her long, wheat-colored hair in the early morning air. Her features, albeit plain, were set in determination as she led prayer.

Senna was the woman whom Sorcha had influenced with her magik in order to get this job. Sorcha could still remember the gleam in Senna's eye after her interview for the servant position. Sorcha had crept into her mind, letting magik work its way through her blood, convincing Senna that she was perfect for the job.

If the fate of Ocyla weren't on the line, Sorcha might have cared. She might have questioned the morality of altering someone's mind. In general, she had a policy of only entering someone's head as an emergency, or if someone truly deserved it. But this was her only chance to get close to the king. She had no other connections and knew no one else in the Compound. And so, Sorcha let herself influence Senna's mind, if just for a moment, just in order to gain access to Razan.

In the end, Sorcha was selected for the entry-level servant position despite having zero references or experience.

And so, they had let a lion into the sheep's den.

It had been half a year since being hired. Sorcha kept her head down and began to crave—even love—the excruciating routine. Every morning, she awoke before the sun to light fires around the

Compound—except for the tenth floor. She was never to go as far as the tenth floor, because that was where the King's Court began.

Sorcha sometimes wondered, like all servant women, what it would be like to live among Razan's court, falling asleep on plush beds, never wearing the same dress for weeks on end, with bellies full of food.

However, the Triumvirate needed to keep focused on phase two of her plan for taking down the king. Razan began slaughtering villages again five years after Sorcha and the other two Triumvirate woman had been sent to earth. Sorcha needed all the help from her sisters she could get, but not even the Triumvirates knew who their sisters were. Sorcha had no idea where her sisters might be, or if they were even in Ocyla. So when the king started plundering villages again, Sorcha knew she had to take action, with or without the other Triumvirate women. Phase two of her plan would be to find close to Razan, and use them for information.

Despite her scheming, Sorcha had other priorities as a servant.

After lighting the fires, it was the kitchens for the next ten hours. Sorcha's body was put through all kinds of toil. Scrubbing dishes, polishing floors, cutting potatoes—whatever it was, Sorcha did it all. No one noticed that her hands did not become red from the scorching hot water. No one noticed that a thin layer of golden light covered her hands, sunk deep in the tubs.

She knew using her magik wasn't truthful. She felt horrible as servant women triple her age, with knobby fingers, scrubbed the floors all day, backs bent, knees sprouting long-established bruises. Sorcha's heart had shattered at that. What was still left of her heart, that was.

So, despite having to reserve her own magik, Sorcha did what she could to take away the other servants' pain with her magik. As the soothing powers threaded through the old women's bodies, their leathery faces wrinkled even more as broad smiles lit them up. For some, it was the first time in twenty years they hadn't felt pain.

One afternoon during their breaks, Sorcha had sat near the old servants. As she'd pretended to be focused on her bread, she'd listened to the elderly marvel about their joints.

"Why, I feel like I did when I was forty!" Handfuls of belly laughter erupted as tears slightly shone in their eyes.

Sorcha almost let her tears slip out as well, yet Senna would notice—she always had a habit of noticing Sorcha's actions, since Senna took breaks with the servants. So that's why Sorcha didn't socialize, didn't go out. Didn't do much of anything except work, sleep, and plan.

Every night, she would set aside an hour to hone her magik. Asleep in their dirty quarters, the other servants would not hear a thing, exhausted from a full day's work. Her fellow servants did not notice how easily they fell into a deep slumber and had peaceful, joyous dreams, which left their eyes bright and clear the next day.

Sorcha was storing up her magik for Razan's death blow. She figured if she could absorb more magik than the king, she could use it to take his power away. So, Sorcha listened to rumors and whispers around the Compound. When the king had spiked the water supply of Ocyla with Mahoun and drained all Fae of their magik, he had stored that stolen magik somewhere. Sorcha's mission was to find where Razan had hidden the citizens magik, and give it back to the Fae, restoring balance to her city.

Sorcha thought of her sisters, the other two Triumvirate women. When the Gods had crafted Sorcha, they had told her during her creation that she was not allowed to know who the other Triumvirates were.

Arena, one of the most powerful Gods, and Sorcha's favorite, had said that Sorcha was not allowed to know who her sisters were in case Razan was to capture one of the Triumvirates.

"If the king captures you, you won't be able to reveal who your sisters are, because you won't know their identities. You couldn't give them away if you tried."

The few hours after Sorcha's creation, before she was sent to earth, was a blur. She barely remembered it. She had remembered in her final moments, what Arena had spoken to her.

"There will be a link between our minds. I can hear your thoughts and you can hear mine. That way, we can communicate about your mission."

Arena would often, in the first few years of Sorcha's life, send the Triumvirate visions of the future. Now that she had installed herself as a member of the court, Sorcha had access to more information than ever.

The Gods would have been proud, but she hadn't heard from them in years, her connection with Arena had been severed.

However, her plan was set in motion; Sorcha had installed herself as a spy in the Compound. With the help of the Assassin's Guild, she was to battle Razan to the death once she had absorbed his magik.

If Sorcha was going to hone her magik, if her massive plan was to succeed, she needed all the training she could get. If she had to train, then she could kill two birds with one stone—she could restore life to Ocyla by slowly healing the people who needed it most, while strengthening her magik for the king's deathblow.

Sorcha blinked her eyes as Senna cleared her throat, snapping her back to the present moment. The tittering servants, some a decade younger than herself, whipped their heads toward the overseer, giving her their undivided, acute attention. This meeting was taking too long. Then again, she always liked having everyone's eyes on her. These morning meetings were all dramatics.

Sorcha lingered toward the back of the group. She didn't attempt to cover up her yawn—not that she made it obvious or let anyone hear. A few younger servants, perhaps no older than seventeen, let out a small chuckle. She caught their eye and winked. Everyone was tired of these gatherings. But if they wanted to keep their heads and still have a warm bed and hot meals, no one dared utter a word against their overseer. Besides, Senna would probably throw another one of her fits if she thought someone was drawing the attention away from her.

Senna lead the servants in chants, songs, and prayers to the Gods. Sorcha's overseer mentioned and prayed to Gods by name. Arena's name was even mentioned.

Sorcha bit the inside of her cheek. She hadn't received a vision from Arena in years. The Triumvirate was so close to giving up on the Gods.

After prayers had ended, a second delicate clearing of Senna's throat had the small crowd silent within a few seconds.

Her lilting voice filled the courtyard, cold and unforgiving. "As all of us know, the use of magik is forbidden under the reign of King Razan."

Murmurs laced their way throughout the crowd. A sharp look from Senna was all it took to silence her servants. She tucked one strand of silken, golden hair behind her ear.

It was said that Senna had been betrothed to a Fae male in the high court. The Triumvirate bitterly thought of the poor man who had to suffer through a lifetime with her overseer. Senna was said to not respect consent when it came to men: human or Fae.

Sorcha's fingers dug into her palm as she clenched her fists. Senna continued, "If you are caught using magik, you will be subject to the King's Council—or death."

A shiver went through the crowd at that. The members of the King's Council were the highest-ranking members of the court, second only to Razan himself, meaning that the Council was above Senna. The council was composed of Fae who held immense power. Razan believed Fae to be better than humans, and Ocylan society was modeled after such. Razan recruited Fae to work for him, to use their magik to do his bidding. Sorcha would rather die than help the king. Gods knew what Razan would do to her if he ever discovered that she was the Third Triumvirate.

Senna's speech came to a close, but not before the overseer turned toward Sorcha and locked eyes. "Oh, and Sorcha?"

Ice shot through her veins.

"Come find me after this meeting."

~

Thankfully, she kept her head.

Senna had assigned Sorcha to be a server for the Harvest Banquet. Stunned, Sorcha had only bowed, carefully keeping her face neutral. When she asked why she had been selected, Senna slowly looked her up and down. "Razan likes pretty women," she replied. She patted Sorcha's cheek, perhaps a bit too hard.

So, with that dismissal, Sorcha switched from lighting fires to preparing food. She was looking forward to a change in stations. Serving at the banquet would provide the ideal place to overhear gossip from the High Court. Fae of all ages in Razan's Compound were invited to the feast. Customary as it was, Sorcha found it strange that Razan enjoyed gathering with his subjects at all. She would have thought that evil dictators did not care for entertainment, but she supposed that showing off the Compound's opulent wealth was one form of power and control in itself.

Sorcha sighed and headed toward the kitchens. The banquet was one day away, and she was sure the cooks needed all the help they could get. Not that she had a choice in helping—she would be put to work regardless of her will.

She swung open the wooden doors to the kitchen, spices and aromas assaulting her nose within seconds. Preparation for the feast was already underway. She headed toward the nearest sink and rolled up her sleeves, plunging her hands into the dirty water, a stack of plates already piling up before her.

It was going to be a long day.

Kartix tried and failed to unclench his fist as the woman's scream was cut short. Tried to move, to do anything but stand next to the man who had just murdered his cousin.

As the last remaining echoes of Harar's screams faded from the gold-lined room, Kartix refused to show even a glimpse of emotion. He knew his father was a murderer, but he had never been a witness to one of his killings. He refused to acknowledge this monster of a father. His mother was a doped-up addict who barely left her rooms, so he was left to stand guard at his father's side. Always.

Harar.

Kartix's tongue was lead at the bottom of his mouth.

But, like the rest of the King's Council, if one was to interrupt his father, their heads would be joining the one now rolling across the hall. The

King's Council followed the same rules that Kartix was following.

A laugh, ancient and laced with malice, echoed throughout the otherwise silent space.

"No loyalty, even from my niece."

Blood, crimson and fresh, still warm from her arteries, dripped in a steady pattern onto the marble floor. Razan's jet-black hair gleamed in the morning light, seeming to swallow up the sun. His jaw was gritted with anger. Drunk on power, Razan's nose wrinkled with distaste.

Kartix wished he was dead for the millionth time that morning as he plastered a fake smile across his features. "Excellent work."

No one else spoke.

"I never did care much for her." Hands in his pockets, he gave his father a shit-eating grin as he stalked up to meet him in the pool of blood. He smiled and his teeth gleamed white, blinding, and brilliant as he met his father's cool stare. "It is a relief." Kartix couldn't help but to shift his eyes to the line of observers along the wall, catching Felix's wince before his face smoothed over again. Every word sent fire through Kartix's veins.

Traitor, traitor, traitor.

His rage was nearly capable of incinerating him.

"This is what happens to spies," Razan hissed, spitting on the decapitated corpse inches from his black leather boot. "Her other-half though..."

The entire hall turned to face the cowering young woman, kneeling in a pool of her mate's blood. She was no older than twenty, ten years younger than Kartix. Her black hair stuck in strands to her perspiring skin, her frame trembling and small. A terrible bile threatened to coat Kartix's tongue.

Anna. A healer.

She had grown up on the castle grounds with Harar. She'd first been assigned to be her playmate in youth, and, as the two girls grew into women, only then did something develop between them.

It had been late summer when Harar, breathless and wild, had run into Kartix's rooms. "Make fun of me all you like, but I think I love her."

Kartix didn't even have to look up from the book he was reading to ask who the subject of his cousin's emotions was. It had been obvious enough, over the years, seeing the way Harar gazed at Anna. It had taken every ounce of his strength not to shake his cousin and demand she break the tension that had been building and building for years.

With quiet joy, Harar had whispered, "I love Anna, and I'm going to tell her." A joyous, strangled thing of a laugh choked out of Harar's throat. "I'm going to tell her tonight."

And then, one night later, their bond had clicked into place.

According to law, the death of a human wife or husband was painful, but eventually, the remaining spouse would be healed. They could find a new spouse. But for Fae, other-halves were a different situation altogether. Other-halves were as different from humans as the ancient beasts which prowled the Northern Mountains. Legend had it that before the Gods trapped their magik in the Triumvirates, Fae were crafted from power itself. When the magik was too intense for one being to handle, the Gods split each of them into twin pairs.

Fae spent their lives—eternal unless killed—searching for their other-half, their equal in every way.

And now Harar was dead. Joyous, brilliant, wild Harar was *dead*.

Kartix was falling, falling deep into the core of himself. And he did not particularly care if he found his way out. Then again, he'd been lost for years. Perhaps his entire life, if he was being truthful. He could not imagine what Hel it was to lose one's other-half. There was no greater pain, for they said that the bond followed one beyond the grave, eternal even in the afterlife.

As Razan stood in front of Harar's surviving other-half, the young woman said nothing, did nothing, but stare and stare and stare at her slaughtered mate. The flame that had once been in her eyes had been permanently extinguished. Anna at last slowly met Razan's ancient, cruel gaze.

"Do it."

Razan slid his blade in between Anna's ribs, and the woman did not make one sound. As she bled out on the floor, the pool of her blood mixing with Harar's, she did not once look away from her other-half.

A sharp laugh echoed off the gold-lined walls of the massive chamber. "No one clean it up. I wish to savor my kills." Razan's dark eyes seemed to swallow up the sunlight which was streaming in through the floor-to-ceiling windows.

Kartix did not hear the rest of Razan's speech. He did not hear his dismissal, but merely turned and strode out of the King's Council room. He was too stunned, too shocked to feel anything but pure terror as he managed to make it out before betraying the mask he wore. The rest of the Fae were still mingling behind in the massive chamber. Kartix was already moving, his feet mechanically taking him somewhere. And he didn't care where he went, as long as it was far away from Razan.

He fled down passageways, torches lighting his way, stumbling into the servants' part of the Compound. Kartix turned down a decrepit hallway.

L. Holmes

What seemed to be little more than a broom closet appeared to his left. He didn't care when he stumbled into the strange, cramped room. He didn't care as he slumped against the stone wall, sinking to the ground. He didn't care as he hung his head, the memory of Harar and Anna dead still burned into his mind. Kartix didn't even care as tears, hot and quick, slid down his cheeks.

He didn't care about anything.

Anything at all.

She was exhausted after a long day's work
and the thought of bed practically made Sorcha's legs
tremble. Only five more minutes of sorting through
the winding passageways of the Compound's
underbelly to her room. She wondered if she would
have nightmares that night. She had long ago given
up on the idea of having a peaceful night's sleep.
Memories of her family being sold into the slave trade
and Meg's cottage going up in flames haunted her
most nights. All Sorcha wanted was to sleep
peacefully, without dreams of the fucked-up world.
But restful sleep, just like everything else, seemed
impossible.

The door to Sorcha's room was ajar when she
rounded the corner. Every hair on the back of her neck
stood at attention. She slowly crept forward, her
magik sparking to life at her fingertips, fire dancing
at the ready. But as she peered into her room, she
beheld a Fae male, head in his hands, crying, against

the far wall. He had sunk against the cobblestones, and his massive frame was shaking with the intensity of his sobs.

The boy from the clearing, all those years ago. I branded him with my sword.

This was the *last* thing Sorcha was expecting to find.

The male looked up suddenly, having noticed he was not alone. The two locked eyes. He sat up, as if embarrassed, and quickly made to stand. Once the male had regained his footing, he finally stretched to his full height. He was massive compared to her.

Sorcha took a step back unconsciously, biting her lip, as she took in the heavily muscled Fae.

A look of anger flashed across his face as if annoyed she interrupted him at such a private moment. Violence was promised in his dark eyes.

But all thoughts of the handsome male blinked out when she realized fire still danced on her fingertips. She quickly clamped down on her magik, once more curling it into the pit inside her.

His eyes narrowed. She tried to scream as he approached, but nothing came out of her mouth.

"You have magik." Kartix's voice was soft.

Sorcha's heart sputtered as if it had forgotten how to function. As the figure, cut in all black silks, approached her from where she trembled just inside the doorway to her room, his onyx hair slid over smooth, tan skin, and despite the trouble that would soon come, Sorcha wondered how someone could be so stunning, and how one of her last thoughts could be about a hot guy.

Great.

Sorcha, embarrassed beyond belief, wished for the thousandth time that night she could die. She could go to Hel for all she cared. It would be good to die. To feel no more.

One would be an idiot to *not* consider the option.

Whipping the emergency vial from the folds of her ragged cloak, Sorcha chugged its midnight-colored contents.

Oh Gods, oh Gods, oh Gods. Spirit, end me now.

Gasping for breath, the concoction trembled down her windpipe, which was scratched from heaving up the contents of her breakfast earlier. Sorcha would die within half an hour. Luckily, being a skilled poisoner, she also carried with her the cure— a time-sensitive lavender paste concealed in a thin vile, folded into her skirts. She had no issue enduring a bit of a stomach-ache. That was, if she managed to escape this stranger. She could only imagine the violent symptoms she would have if she was unable to ingest the paste. Any delay was a dangerous act.

A woman was singing in the courtyard. The melody was haunting and strange. Sorcha realized with a start that the words were in the foreign tongues of Vaas.

How cruel it is, she supposed, *that the taunt of beauty remained in this dismal place.*

As instantaneously as it had come, the thought of music was ripped from her mind as obsidian eyes met hers. Sorcha could no longer hear the pretty song, for it was but a simple thing compared to the pristine, heart-wrenching beauty that were his features.

She felt an ancient creature awaken somewhere deep in her core.

Who was he?

And why the *fuck* was he in her chamber?

~

Even though he could practically read the thoughts racing across her beautiful face, all privacy dissipated as Kartix took a few hulking steps forward. "What did you just take?" he whispered quietly, but not gently. His black and red cloak, edged with gold, gleamed in the dim firelight.

"Poison."

Kartix dared a glance to her generous mouth from which black liquid now dripped. She smiled wide, teeth soaked in the deadly concoction. He focused on her lips as his breathing hitched.

What causes a woman to be this...empty?

Shaking his head, Kartix's eyes flashed in anger.

~

Without even realizing what she was doing, Sorcha reached into her pocket and tightly squeezed the tiny vial of antidote.

His eyes. That's all that ran through her mind as the stranger closed the last few yards between them and entwined his fingers with hers, forcing the antidote bottle to her lips. The powerful male growled, "Drink."

Her breathing quickened as he came closer. Sorcha had forgotten that she'd taken the lavender paste out of her skirt pocket in haste. She ripped her hand out of his warm grasp, flinching away until her thin dress bit into the cold stone wall. "I don't take orders from males."

She wished she'd hid the trembling in her voice. Wished she hadn't flinched. Her magik shook inside of her, threatening to undo the control she had on herself. If she wasn't careful, she could send her dress up in flames. She needed to control her triggers if she was supposed to get to phase two of her plan for taking down the king. She'd already needed to blow off some of her magik today.

Like an animal assessing its prey, the Fae male tilted his head to one side, like he could practically hear her thoughts screaming inside her skull. Jet-black hair obscured those eyes much to her relief.

"Why?"

"What do you mean?" Hissing through clenched teeth, Sorcha assessed every inch of air, laced with tension, which lay between their bodies. No, she wouldn't let fear or panic take over. It was a game. This was all just a game. And she was its master.

Sorcha did her best to will her features into cool dismissal. She dared herself to let her eyes lazily roam over this handsome male, crossing her thin arms. She smirked as she finally dragged her eyes up from his broad chest to meet his piercing stare. "You know," Sorcha said, inspecting her dirty, food-crusted nails, "for a pretty court boy, I wouldn't take you for the type to force his way into a woman's bedroom."

Lowering her voice to a husky, almost gentle tone, Sorcha plucked an invisible piece of dust off his jacket lapel, flicking it over his shoulder. "Stupid as you may be, you and I both know that you aren't naive enough to not have noticed the guards at the end of the hallway. I could be screaming assault within the next ten seconds, and Brannon and Jesse would come charging in seconds after that."

"I promise I'm not here to hurt you." His eyes flashed as something like restrained rage writhed back and forth inside him. The powerfully built Fae stalked to the now-trembling Sorcha, closing the space she had carefully placed between them. Enormous hands planted on either side of the wall, surrounding Sorcha with his massive stature. His midnight sky colored eyes widened as her breath caught in her throat. He once again growled in her face. "I am not here to cause you harm."

Sorcha allowed her magik to poke through his mind, unbeknownst to him. After a few brief moments of sorting around, she found that this male was indeed not lying.

Sorcha moved tentatively, still within his arms, chugged the lavender paste as quickly as she could, ingesting the antidote with mere minutes to spare.

~

"You talk a lot for a thin girl who won't let anyone touch her."

She went eerily still, the color draining out of her sallow cheeks, which were already ashen from all her time inside.

Kartix realized immediately he had struck a deep chord. With a deadly quiet, the young woman whispered softly, but not gently, "Back the *fuck* up." And suddenly, with surprising strength, she managed to flip him onto his back.

Kartix had been so focused on the poison that he had not noticed her slowly positioning her feet between his wide stance. He was strong, but she was faster. With a flurry of curses that would make the ladies of court flinch, he groaned in pain as Sorcha glowered over his frame.

As much pain as he was in, as all the insults poured into his head, Kartix managed a glance at her shoulder, exposed from their scuffle. Despite the raging pain which coursed through his veins, every cell in his body froze. The long, ratted, well-worn cotton sleeve of her dress had been ripped as Kartix had flung his arm out in the fall, latching onto her arm. Because her servant clothes were such shit, so used, the white sleeve of her gown had torn from the shoulder hem to her elbow, exposing the smooth alabaster skin where her best-kept secret lived: her half-sleeve tattoo. The colors of her intricate tattoo turned and twisted like ink dropped into water.

What light the fire provided seemed to dim, sucked out of the room as Kartix took in her tattoo from where he sat on the floor, amazed.

She noticed his gaze, her eyes slowly lifting from the marks on her arm to Kartix's obsidian stare.

Kartix whispered, "You're a Triumvirate. You're *the* Triumvirate."

Everyone in Ocyla knew the legend of the three Triumvirate sisters.

Sorcha's blood turned to ice in her veins. There was no turning back now. He'd seen her tattoos, her magik on her arm. She had to come clean. Or wipe his memory.

But strangely, a small part of Sorcha, growing larger each day, wanted someone else to know about her powers. It would help her to feel less alone, less alienated from all these humans and Fae.

Silence echoed all around the room. Sorcha and Kartix both slowly lowered their eyes to her right arm, now exposed. Glowing faintly in the firelight, the design of her tattoo shifted from flowers to vines to foreign languages. The wide-eyed Fae dragged his eyes up her body.

"The Third Triumvirate was fabled to have power so immense, they needed to let off a bit at a time in order to not be overwhelmed. They quite literally needed to *blow off steam*. To *release the pressure*. Razan declared all Fae state-owned property. I assumed, therefore, that all the Triumvirates had been drained of their powers." He got to his feet. "But you survived. How?" He breathed. "How are you still alive? How did you escape?"

Sorcha's eyes suddenly went somewhere far away, glassy and unfocused. She thought of her adopted dead parents, and Meg who had been sold into slavery.

"I barely survived. I had help." That was all she offered. Then Sorcha snapped out of her trance, out of her memories. Grunting, she crossed her arms. "Don't ever get that close to me again."

He shook his head. "I didn't have a choice. You ingested poison to avoid me finding out about your tattoos, which, by the way, are fascinating."

Sorcha's cheeks heated. "I don't care about compliments. I care that you know. And not only do you know about my magik, but now you know I'm a Triumvirate. I can't have that."

A slow cold crept into Kartix's limbs. He said softly, "So what do you plan to do?"

"Have you ever heard of a curse bond?"

Kartix nodded his head, black hair sliding into his eyes. He remembered his studies as a child.

"Curse bonds are established between two parties, usually as a means of controlling someone. The bonds show the truth always. Bonds can only be broken when the maker allows it to be."

She tilted her head, impressed. "Looks like someone's been studying. Essentially, yes. I would like to make a bond between us in order to keep you from giving away the fact that I'm the Third Triumvirate."

Easy enough, Kartix supposed. He expected himself to be more afraid, but he wasn't. "How do we create this curse bond exactly?"

"I read your mind, cipher through the information I require, and then if you pass my inspection, our minds will be linked. I will be able to hear your thoughts, and you, my own, but only if we have our mental shields down." Sorcha rolled her shoulders and strode over to her bed, pulling her sleeve up over her tattoos once more. She sat down, not daintily, collapsing into her bed. "Come here."

He noticed her dress riding up while she moved, how her waist-length auburn hair shifted like silk over her shoulders.

Kartix's face heated. "Why?"

Sorcha sat up on her forearms, annoyance written all over her face. "Because I've worked all day and can barely stand, I'm so exhausted. And now I have to concentrate extremely hard so I can properly sort through your mind to make sure you're not going to turn me in to the king for being the third and final Triumvirate."

Kartix snorted, but made his way to her, dropping down across from her at the edge of the bed. "I won't tell anyone. This is the first fascinating thing to happen to me in years, to be truthful." He met her eyes and nearly looked away because of their beauty. "Go on then. Establish the curse bond."

"This shouldn't hurt. You won't even know I was there."

Kartix nodded. "Do your worst."

Sorcha smiled. "You really don't want to know what my worst is." And then she dove into his mind.

Sorcha, thankfully, had trained enough to recognize the spaces in someone's mind to leave alone, to only sort through information she needed.

She took nothing, gave nothing. That was her rule. She only shattered the minds of those who shattered others. Those who deserved it.

Eyes flitting open after several minutes, Sorcha took a deep breath. "I believe you."

Kartix arched a dark eyebrow and rolled his eyes. "I told you I wouldn't tell. And now that you can hear my thoughts indefinitely, you have to understand you can truly trust me."

And so Sorcha told him everything. They stayed sitting on her thread-bare cot until the morning doves cooed, awakening from their alcoves, and the firelight dimmed into embers. Neither had any idea of the tremendous shift which had just occurred in their reality, but as her past was revealed, Sorcha felt an immense weight being lifted off her shoulders.

After a few minutes of silence, despite the hours of talking that had rubbed both of their throats sore, Kartix turned to Sorcha. "How did you get through it?" A frank, open question. No judgment, never from him.

"Through what?"

"Your creation. Living on your own. Razan."

Sorcha was quiet for a moment. "It wasn't living. I was surviving. And those are two very different states of being." She turned to him with a start. "I don't even know your name!"

The handsome male paused, then tipped his head back and let loose a great boom of a laugh. It echoed around her small stone chamber and startled the doves into morning flight from their perch outside her window. Sorcha whacked his massive bicep, marveling at how it hurt her hand *more* than hurt him, his strength that immense. "You break into my room, attach yourself indefinitely to my mind, yet I don't even know your name."

"Kartix. My name is Kartix." He didn't give her a last name.

"Kartix." Sorcha pronounced his name slowly, the foreign sound of it rolling off her tongue. Why was the name so familiar to her? She recognized him from ten years ago, when she was first sent down to earth. Even then, however, she still hadn't learned his name, since she had been a bit preoccupied with her plan for taking down the king.

"What is your name?" Kartix's soft voice cut through her thoughts.

"Sorcha. My name is Sorcha."

Purple shadows bloomed beneath Sorcha's eyes. Bright as they were, he could tell she was fading fast. "You can't seriously be sleeping here." Kartix glanced around her dismal room.

"Too used to silk and velvet up there, living in your fancy quarters? Have you forgotten that the rest of the world lives like this?"

He paused as something like fear flickered briefly across his features. "I wouldn't call it living." He wasn't stupid enough to think directly about Senna, about his captor. Thinking about her would be equivalent to shouting his secret through the curse bond, directly into Sorcha's mind. Kartix would prefer his torment to stay a secret. He was too exhausted to explain his relationship with Senna.

Despite the distant expression on Kartix's handsome face, Sorcha wasn't stupid enough to ask if he was alright. Clearly something bothered him about his living situation. Tired as she was in the early light of dawn, Sorcha couldn't help but wonder who his parents were, just who he was *exactly*. Taking in his silky shirt, in contrast to her filthy rags, she saw Kartix came from money alright. From whatever rank, however, she couldn't decipher.

Stifling a yawn, the male unfurled his legs, and made to bow. From where she sat on the cot a sudden abruptness awoke her from their lengthy conversation. Right. They had jobs to do. Well, at least *she* did. Gods only know what useless task Razan had court boys like him partake in. From the considerate size of him, however, Sorcha would not be surprised to learn that he often trained in the legendary fighting rings. Maybe he was a mercenary for Razan.

Shrugging, she carefully unwound her legs and stood on cramped feet. Shit. She hadn't slept— and today was the fucking Harvest Banquet. Groaning, Sorcha carefully eyed her door. Senna could come by any moment. With him in her room, the Hel her overseer would unleash would *not* be worth having a hot male in this close proximity. Rushing to tie her ragged apron behind her back, Sorcha felt like she'd been run down by a cart.

Multiple times. She was running on no sleep. But it was worth it, she realized with a start. It was worth having someone know her secret.

Her anxious glance toward the door made Kartix shake his head. "I apologize for any inconvenience I caused you. I'll take my leave now. I know you must have a busy day ahead of you."

Sorcha met his eyes one last time as he strode to the door. "Don't make me regret forming this curse bond. I'll know if you attempt to deceive me."

A smile tugged at the corner of Kartix's full lips. "Then I will never deceive you."

Her heart fluttered.

And with that, he disappeared around the corner, into the corridor. As his footsteps faded away and the sounds of servants awakening all around her rose, Sorcha felt numb.

What have I done?

6

Sun scorched the top of Sorcha's head, despite the wide-brimmed straw hat.

She was so tired.

Breakfast had provided no energy as the stale bread and bruised apple rolled around in her mostly empty stomach. A sharp stab of pain echoed in her abdomen, her body angry at the lack of fuel. Last night, she'd stayed up with Kartix and hadn't slept a wink.

After he left her room, Sorcha had managed to wash quickly with ice-cold water. The water had rushed over her skin, cooling her body and mind so that she was able to think clearly. Well, as clearly as she could, given the fact that she was running on no sleep. Paranoia had shot through her veins then—someone *knew*.

"Idiot," she murmured to herself.

Ice shot through her veins again, despite the already-muggy morning temperature. In the vast garden, late-summer heat scorched the abundant earth. The near-tropical climate of Ocyla gave some of the most bountiful harvests. Landscapers quietly clipped away at hedges bordering the herb garden. Behind them, the Compound jutted up out of the soil, alabaster stone, faded due to many centuries in the wind and rain. When it was foggy, the Compound blended right into the mist.

The only thing keeping Sorcha grounded in her panicked state was the feeling of damp, rich soil beneath her. She was used to working with her hands. The herbs and flowers she studied had slowly evolved over time. She had planted them the very first day she arrived at the Compound, and now the seeds had burst into a small garden, all due to her meticulous attention to detail.

Each servant in the kitchen also had the responsibility of taking care of one plot of the garden. When she wasn't working in the Compound, Sorcha could often be found on all fours, weeding, and sometimes singing to the plants—that, she only did when she was alone. Foolish as she knew it was, she liked to think that it helped them grow. Plus, the songs of the Gods were often said to have healing properties. That was, when magik was still around. Before Razan poisoned the water supply of Ocyla with Mahoun, Fae and humans had lived in peace.

However, another secret that she had not yet revealed, that was still completely hidden, was the nature of the herbs she tended to. Beneath her, growing in the soil, was a concoction of some of the deadliest plants on the whole damn Northern Continent.

In the Southern Continent, Zia was the capital of scholars. Sorcha marveled at their knowledge, famed to be powerful enough to keep Razan from their shores—as well as having some of the best poisoners in the world. She wondered what different plants they had, what she could learn from Zia. She ached for more knowledge.

Because she had swallowed her poison last night when Kartix had first approached her, Sorcha would need to make more of the toxic paste and its accompanying cure.

In order to avoid suspicion, she had planted ten herbs and flowers. Some combinations can be used to flavor food. Others, to add fragrance to a dish. What no one suspected was that if all the herbs were combined, it would form the most toxic poison known to man.

The Fae, on the other hand, had superior senses and would likely detect the poison.

A light peal of laughter sounded across the vast garden. A certain type of light filled Sorcha's heart. Marie and Facim rounded the corner.

Taller in stature than Marie and Sorcha, Facim's gold silk skirts brushed over the pebbles as she walked. Her hair brushed her lower back, gold woven throughout her dreadlocks. Her dark skin was aglow in the light of day. Facim held herself with a sort of quiet confidence Sorcha only hoped she could emanate one day. Facim's full lips, painted red, parted in a wide smile as she finished her joke.

The woman at Facim's right was Marie. Her hair matched her straw-colored gown. A parasol cast patterns of lace over her fine features. She was still mid-laugh as the pair came toward Sorcha, still kneeling in the grass. Her friends were so beautiful, sometimes it made her insecure. To feel that way was ridiculous, she had to remind herself. They were her friends. They didn't want to harm her. It was stupid that she even thought like that. Then again, Sorcha supposed she needed to work on her trust issues.

At last, Facim approached Sorcha, her deep voice echoing inside Sorcha's mind as she stood up to face the oncoming pair. *Hey.*

Sorcha smiled wide as she beheld her friends in the early morning light. *Hey.*

The group of women laughed, this time out loud. Facim and Marie had also made a curse bond with Sorcha, so all of them could communicate in their minds. It was easier for them to talk telepathically, but they could not get away with having silent conversations too often. Guards were abundant anywhere one went in Ocyla, ordered to kill anyone on sight if a citizen displayed a show of magik—or worse, bring them to Razan and the King's Council.

The two women had long known about Sorcha's magik, themselves being Fae. A few months ago, Sorcha had stumbled into the Compound grounds late at night. She'd been drunk as ever, and on her way back from the fighting rings when she'd accidentally used a bit of her magik to slip through a locked gate at the back of the Compound. She'd bumped into Facim and Marie, who'd been attempting to sneak out that night as well. The women had bonded instantly when they realized that they all had a deep-seated hatred for Razan. It had taken all of two weeks before Sorcha revealed her Triumvirate status and asked the two women to join her at the Assassins Guild.

Facim smiled sweetly. "What are you doing?" What she really asked in Sorcha's mind was, *What are we doing tonight?*

"Oh, something very exciting." Sorcha wiggled her eyebrows at the pair, and they all broke out into expectant but nervous laughter.

"Is that so?" Marie asked both out loud and in their minds.

Midnight. Assassins Guild. Meet me there. Sorcha locked eyes with Facim and Marie as the two women silently nodded.

"Well, we'll leave you to do your gardening!" Facim made sure to raise her voice so that the nearest guard could hear them. "Good luck with your basil." The group smiled, as they all knew the plant Sorcha was tending to was definitely not basil, but a type of poisonous plant that looked almost identical to it.

As her two best friends walked away arm in arm, Sorcha dared a glance back at them. Months ago, when she had first arrived at the Compound, she'd had no idea that there would be women like her who despised the regime, that there would have been rebels inside the Compound, even then.

Sorcha, when she'd first entered as a servant, hadn't known where to start. Sure, she was the head of the Assassins Guild, but without any direct ties to Razan himself, the Guild and Sorcha were as useless as paper against a sword. There was no way to directly attack Razan, not without a massive advantage.

So, when Sorcha had discovered Fae in the High Court who were opposed to Razan, she had quickly befriended them and made a curse bond, as well as invited them to join the Assassins Guild. And that was how Facim and Marie had gained Sorcha's coveted trust. She had taken the women to the Guild, shown them the humans and Fae who were willing to fight for justice. It had taken all of one night before Marie and Facim were committed to the rebellion and promised to provide insider information.

That agreement amongst the women had been made months ago. Now, they were more than accomplices to Sorcha—Facim and Marie were her best friends. It was dangerous in their world. It was dangerous to care for something, because that something was just another thing to be taken away, another thing to lose. Sorcha had realized months ago, if caring for Facim and Marie was a liability for her, then so be it. It would be worth it to burn in Hel if it meant that her time here in Ocyla was spent with them.

A small smile bloomed on Sorcha's lips. She was tired, and sleep was hours away, but strangely, she felt alright. Better than alright, if she was to be truthful. Perhaps it was the warm summer sun on her back, but when she stood up and brushed the dirt off her knees, she felt happy. Or at least, the closest thing to happiness she could feel.

She had been sent by the head cook to gather herbs for the banquet. She'd been allotted two hours to tend to the plants before she had to make her way back inside. The rest of her day would not be so leisurely, as preparations for the Harvest Banquet would be well underway.

As Sorcha made her way back into the Compound's cold corridors, she carried the feeling of the sun, warm and comforting, inside her bones, as if she could cling on to whatever remaining happiness she had found.

Despite his tanned skin, the overnight meeting had left him pale. As he gently shut the wooden, cracked door to Sorcha's room, Kartix could barely detect the early rustlings of the servants, hallways down.

Shit. He had stayed too late.

He only hoped, if spotted, that the guards wouldn't report Sorcha's movements to his father. Kartix had to be an idiot not to consider the consequences for her. "Associating with the scum is beneath you," Razan would claim. If his father knew Kartix was spending time alone with a woman other than Senna, Sorcha's head might wind up impaled on a spear—so it went in the reign of Razan: guilty until proven innocent.

Sighing, Kartix shook his head as he trudged up the winding staircase. He used what little reserve of magik he had left to distort his features. To any person passing by, Kartix would appear as another servant, unassuming. He wished he could live in this state forever. He wished that no one knew him. Kartix longed for a world in which he could start over. Where he wasn't chained to Senna and his father and this ridiculous city of flame and ash.

It was at least a twenty-minute walk back to his corridors, on the tenth floor. How Sorcha managed to walk the halls of this vast Compound day after day he had no idea.

Finally, Kartix reached the High Court. Having barely stumbled back to his rooms, as soon as he opened the double wooden doors to his suite, his brother met him on the other side. "Where the *Hel* were you?"

Reid had been known to be a little more than overprotective. A few years older than him, Reid had been at Kartix's side since they were children, the brothers inseparable.

Sighing, Kartix made to shrug off his jacket, tossing it on a velvet-embroidered chair near the fireplace. He was stiff from all those hours spent with Sorcha, talking, listening, pacing on several occasions. He did not know or care how long it had been since he'd last closed his eyes. "I was out."

"Out?" Fuming, Reid crossed his muscled arms, dark skin illuminated in the morning light. "You do not get to just *go out*. You fucking scared me to *death*."

Kartix was so tired. "Can you not yell at me right now? Our cousin was just fucking executed. Is it so impossible to think, I just needed some Godsdamned time alone?"

At that, Reid winced. "I haven't forgotten about Harar and Anna." His voice was gentle. No one spoke for a few moments. "It's because of their execution that I was so concerned." Sighing, Reid shook his head. "You are right. I'm sorry I yelled. I just— Next time, tell me where you go."

Kartix shook his head, body going numb. He sat down on a chair close to the fire. "After she was executed, I didn't know why, but I just left. I just walked and walked until I didn't know where I was."

A dark eyebrow shot up to Felix's hairline. "And where exactly did you spend the night?"

"In the courtyard." The lie was smooth and rolled off his tongue. "I needed some fresh air. And the night was warm enough. I couldn't sleep."

Liar.

Kartix paused as Sorcha's gentle voice filled his mind. He was hearing voices now. He must be delusional from lack of sleep.

Reid sighed and rolled up his shirt sleeves, his muscular forearms flexing in the firelight. Although Kartix had magik, Reid had the strength and could beat his ass any day in the fighting ring. Which he had, on several occasions. Kartix had the bruises to prove it.

"I couldn't sleep either." Felix's dark eyes went flat and dull. "I keep picturing her face. How the light in her eyes went out."

Despite sitting next to the roaring fire, Kartix shivered with cold. Sorcha had been the girl in the clearing that night ten years ago. He remembered her. How she'd snapped the necks of all those King's Guards and marked him permanently with her sword. Kartix hadn't told Sorcha that he recognized her. He didn't want to scare her off. Kartix pressed a hand to his throat, the scar she'd made raised against his skin.

His eyes flitted closed briefly as he recalled when they first met. She looked so fierce and proud standing before him, having just slaughtered most of his comrades. She had been trembling with rage holding the sword in front of her, her blue eyes wide and focused on his.

He thought she was the most beautiful woman he had ever seen. Kartix had nearly dropped to his knees at the sight of her.

Now, years later, she'd appeared before him again, but this time in the Compound. Kartix knew he should feel lucky to have found her, but he was terrified. The Gods only knew what horrors Razan could inflict upon her if his father knew just how much he liked her.

Kartix clenched his hands into fists. His heartbeat picked up as he remembered the time he spent on Sorcha's cot just hours prior. He remembered the way her dress shifted higher up on her thigh when she'd climbed onto the thin mattress, how her auburn hair shifted like silk in the light.

There was no safe distraction—he had no other way to escape reality. He needed to hit something, anything, to get these emotions out. Kartix blew out a breath he didn't know he was holding. He had to get a grip on his own desire. He couldn't allow Sorcha to consume him, no matter how quickly he was falling for her.

As Kartix looked at Reid, he realized just how sad and hurt he felt. The only thought he had was of the fighting ring. Razan had cleared Kartix's schedule for the day due to the Harvest Banquet which was due to take place later that evening. There were no King's Council meetings to attend or visiting entities to entertain. So, the training grounds it was.

Kartix met Reid's concerned gaze. "Would you care to have a duel?

Reid grinned, the gesture lighting up his handsome face. "I thought you'd never ask."

And as the males made their way out of the Compound and into the bursting light of day, as they wove their way through the gardens to the training grounds, Kartix could swear he heard Sorcha laugh, the sound bright and joyous, from somewhere far off in the distance.

How strange, he thought, *that so much joy can live amongst such sorrow.*

She struggled with the massive copper pot.

Sorcha, climbing up the winding staircase which led to the main hall, cursed softly under her already-labored breath. The damn thing was too heavy. With this many servants around, she didn't dare risk using some of her magik to lift the weight. So, she was stuck heaving the twenty-pound pot from the kitchens up, up, up to the great banquet. Besides, the overseers of the Compound were already on edge. She would do well to keep her head down, especially after what happened with Kartix. How she—

A guard bumped into her shoulder, nearly sending her and the copper pot's contents flying. "Watch where you're going," Sorcha hissed through clenched teeth. That had been a mistake.

"What did you say to me, you little bitch?" Instantly, Sorcha regretted her quick tongue. The guard, no older than twenty but twice as muscular as her, turned around where he stood in the stairwell and stalked toward her.

Sorcha was quicker than that.

Just as the man reached out to try to grab her by the throat, Sorcha disappeared. Empty space greeted the guard's fingers where the delicate skin of her clavicle should have been. When her magik had her reappear in an empty broom closet all the way across the Compound, she cursed herself. Why was she so quick to anger today? Ever since Kartix had been in her room, her magik had been all jumpy. She had nearly set her hair on fire when she'd first seen him. She needed to have better control over her powers. The lack of control was already starting to fray her nerves. She could have sworn she was hearing a voice inside her mind. Maybe she just needed sleep.

As Sorcha exited the broom closet, still clutching the copper pot of stew, a young girl came around the corner. No older than ten, the girl was fine boned, her delicate features highlighted with makeup. She was dressed in red fabrics held tight against her slim frame.

The two stared at each other.

"Why did you just come out of a broom closet with a pot of stew?"

"Why are you dressed like someone twice your age?" Sorcha asked, a question for a question.

The young girl put a dark hand on her hip. "Because my master chooses my clothes."

Sorcha cringed at the word *master*. So that was what she was. A slave. Sorcha's knees threatened to wobble, bile coating her tongue. She was so young, *too* young.

"What's your name?"

"Why did you come out of a broom closet?" The girl was clearly not giving up her interrogation.

Sorcha sighed, shifting her weight from one foot to the next, anxious to get to the banquet hall. "Because I was avoiding a creepy man and needed somewhere to hide."

The child snorted, humor lighting up her face. "I would do the same if I could," she said with a sweeping motion down to her clothes. "Don't think I like dressing this way."

It felt wrong. It *was* wrong for Sorcha to just walk away and leave this child behind. All she could offer this girl was magik.

Sorcha said quickly, "Who is your master exactly?" The word *master* tasted like ash on her tongue. A plan was already forming—a plan to get this child away.

The ten-year-old shook her head. "His name is Devonshire, but he is new to the Compound, so not many people recognize him. I can point him out to you at the banquet if you'd like."

Sorcha raised an eyebrow. "How did you know I was going to the banquet?" The damn copper pot was really starting to be heavy, and if she didn't hurry, she might just *have* to use magik to help.

"Because you're carrying a massive pot of stew? And the only place to go with a pot that big is the banquet which starts, by my calculations, right now."

Sorcha cursed softly under her breath. She was late and needed to go.

"Lucky for you I'm also going to the banquet. So, join me." The girl turned and walked daintily down the passageway, her high heels clicking against the marble floors. Sorcha marveled at the fact that a ten-year-old was in heels. She knew it hadn't been the girl's choice to wear them. It disgusted her, the exploitation of young girls on this fucking continent, plucked and preened and groomed for the wealthy men of Ocyla.

Bile coated Sorcha's mouth as the girl disappeared around the bend, and she struggled to keep up. This pot would be the death of her. When Sorcha finally caught up to the girl, they were getting closer to the banquet hall. "What's your name?"

"Lyra. What's yours?"

Sorcha debated giving her a fake name, but she was too tired to lie. How could she deceive a child whom the world had already deceived so many times?

"Sorcha."

"Well, Sorcha, it's nice to meet you."

"It's nice to meet you too." For once, Sorcha meant it.

The banquet hall loomed before the pair. The room was an opulent show of wealth, designed to impress whatever visiting company attended these stupid parties. Sorcha had to admit that Razan had good taste in architecture. The space was beautiful. Flowers bloomed from hundreds of different vases, and the air was perfumed with an intoxicating mix of foreign spices. Alabaster marble pillars held up a roof painted with Ocyla's most famous battles. The artwork which captured Sorcha's attention the most hung right before the throne, which was raised on a dais at the north end of the room.

The tapestry took up most of the wall, massive compared to any other art in the room. The inscription beneath it read, "The Creation of the Triumvirates."

Sorcha shivered as all warmth left her body. Her vision spotted with black, and her knees almost gave out beneath her. Without warning, a vision overtook her.

All she could see was blood. The battlefield had long been soaked with carnage. Blood ran down Arena's face from a large wound in her forehead. Her side was slick with it too. She knew she was dying. But she didn't care. She didn't care about anything but sealing the portal.

The battle had raged long into the night and swiftly into the next day. Now the sun was setting once more, and still the portal to Hel remained open. Too many Gods were dying.

On a rocky outcropping overlooking the barren desert of the battlefield, demons still slithered through the open portal, black, monstrous creatures flew, crawled, and stalked through the door to Hel.

"Fall back!"

Arena could just barely hear the shout of the commander over the clamor of battle. She grimaced under her helmet. She hated to retreat, clearly having sown a path through the enemy already, but Hextor was right—the Gods needed to reconvene.

Another demon met the tip of her sword, its black blood spilling out, soaking her fighting leathers. Arena had to rely on her body now, sheer strength for defensiveness, her magik having long since failed her. She was said to be one of the most powerful Gods, but now, after fighting for days on end, even her strength had been nearly depleted.

She made it to a cavern cut into the side of a mountain where several of the main Gods awaited. Hextor snarled to the lot of them, "We have to seal the portal, but individually, our magik is not enough. However, when combined, we can possibly close the portal to Hel that Razan has opened." The God raised a white eyebrow, in contrast to his dark skin. "Does anyone object to combining our magik?" His voice boomed off the great walls of the cave.

Not one God raised an objection. Everyone had grown so incredibly weary. The war was nearly lost. Desperate measures needed to be taken.

Hextor nodded then. "Then it is decided. We shall combine all of our power into one weapon to seal the door. Let us continue."

Snapping out of the vision with a jolt, Sorcha suppressed a shiver. She hadn't received a vision or any word from the Gods in years. Why did she just have this vision? Was Arena finally sending her visions again? Sorcha shook her head, too confused.

The great tapestry which loomed over the entire banquet hall was depicting the very moment she was crafted—the Gods looked down from the heavens as three women fell to Earth, unconscious. The tapestry was threaded with gold and silver, using rubies and pearls to accentuate the details. Its rich colors were vibrant and bright against the dismal space that was the banquet hall.

As creepy as it felt that Sorcha was staring at a depiction of herself, she couldn't help but be disconcerted. This painting and the placement of such showed that Razan was very much aware of her and her sisters. That their power had caught his attention. Good or bad, they had caught the eye of the most powerful male in the world.

She smiled. Razan had no idea what was coming for him.

At last, Sorcha staggered over toward the main banquet table, trying hard not to trip over her ragged dress. She plunked the pot of stew down at last and groaned, rubbing her sore biceps, then stepped away and joined the other servants who were lined up against the wall.

Occasionally a Fae called out for a glass of wine, which one of the servants would refill. Besides that, Sorcha and the rest of the humans were made to wait on the Fae as they dined and drank to their hearts' content.

The first hour wasn't so bad. Sorcha felt quite entertained by the High Court and the visiting parties who dined before her. It was interesting as she used her Triumvirate hearing to overhear conversations.

Did you hear Phelonious gambled away his family's fortune?

Devonshire has a new niece in town.

Leonard left Katherina! What a scandal.

Bits and pieces of random conversation snagged Sorcha's thoughts, but one conversation stood out in particular—that of a white man who looked like a pig embodying a person, who was seated at the far right of the banquet table. Candlesticks illuminated his pudgy and sweaty features. She locked her eyes on the man dressed in velvet and silks.

"Devonshire, do tell us about your niece." A blonde woman dressed in pale blue turned toward the man, addressing him with a bat of her eyelashes.

Godsdamn, Sorcha thought. *Devonshire really had to be loaded with money if pretty girls wanted to lower their standards to be with him.*

Sorcha's entire body froze as she saw Lyra standing against the opposite wall, behind Devonshire. The two locked eyes. A hollow sadness filled Lyra's eyes as she smiled at Sorcha. So, this was the man who enslaved her.

Without hesitation, Sorcha grabbed a pitcher full of wine from the nearest servant. They protested, but Sorcha didn't hesitate or look back as she began walking around the large banquet table. Her grip on the handle of the pitcher tightened as she closed in on Devonshire. She reached into her skirts, careful not to give away the poison in her hand.

She paused, looking the ugly man up and down before he caught sight of her. "More wine, my lord?" A saccharine smile slowly crept over her face.

Devonshire, the hog that he was, dabbed the sweat off his brow with a stained handkerchief. "My dear, yes, please."

Sorcha was surprised the pig had manners. Then again, she had to remind herself, he was only nice to her because he wanted to fuck her. To him, she was nothing more than a pretty girl on a serving platter.

Sorcha bent down slowly, her dress not revealing, but she made sure to hover close to Devonshire as she made to refill his glass, but at the last moment she whispered, "Get fucked, pig." She tipped the wine pitcher and every single drop of its contents into the slave owner's lap. Devonshire's head jerked up, his eyes latching on to hers, alarm clearly painted on his features.

Devonshire stood up, gasping, surprisingly sounding exactly like a squealing hog. He was dripping with the crimson liquid from the waist down, forever staining his luxurious clothing.

The entire banquet had gone quiet.

Sorcha stood up, straightening her spine. "Take me away, boys." She held out her wrists as the guards rushed toward her.

It was at that exact moment that Sorcha locked eyes with Kartix, who was seated right next to Razan. This time, it was her turn to gasp. Her blue eyes went wild with fear. He was seated next to the king, in a seat reserved only for family members. The two Fae males looked at her at the same time.

Dear Gods. Kartix is the prince of Ocyla.

She could see it now. The two males both had jet-black hair and eyes the color of the midnight sky. Both had a sharp jaw and were powerfully built.

Sadness crept over Kartix's handsome face as if understanding her sudden realization.

Before she could respond, the guards reached her. Bruises and cuts were formed as the men scuffed her up. Meanwhile, Devonshire was whining in the background about his expensive suit, and the lady in blue was attempting to dab handkerchiefs on his silks, to no avail. Lyra was barely containing her smile. Sorcha laughed as the guards dragged her off.

What an awful night this had turned out to be.

9

As soon as she was tossed into her room, Sorcha started planning her escape.

I need to look for Meg. I need to search the slums.

She recalled her adopted family with a grimace. She remembered how her Meg, who had been sold into slavery when captured, and how her parents had been killed by those soldiers. It had been four years since her family was torn apart. So every night, Sorcha hunted in the illegal fighting rings in the slums for information.

The southern fighting rings on the mainland were legal and aboveground, sanctioned by the state. However, the most fun was had on the slum island where the illegal fighting rings were held. Knives and weapons were not out of the question.

Soldiers liked to gossip on the outskirts of the rings, drunk on whisky and cheap ale. It was almost too easy for Sorcha to eavesdrop for information. She had to find out where the soldiers were keeping her sister. She couldn't afford to waste time locked in her room.

She waited until the Compound had gone to sleep, the banquet having ended hours prior. She used her magik to slowly bend the metal lock on her door. Since the servants' quarters were so incredibly shabby, the wooden doors were worn with decades of use. The metal slid free immediately and the door swung open. Sorcha peered down the hallway, after her magik cast her invisible.

She managed to make it out of the Compound without being detected. As cut off from her magik as she had been, she still was able to use *some* of her powers. It was easy, almost too easy, to escape to the slums. She quickly found the entrance to the underground tunnel. She quickly ducked inside, the dampness of the tunnel greeting her within seconds.

The tunnels were magik.

One only needed to open their mind to the tunnels. They would not let anyone through without first examining their desires. If you tried to barge through the entrance, you would be perpetually lost in a maze of darkness. If the tunnels did not want you to find your way out, you never would. Even though the tunnels liked Sorcha, sometimes they did not let her through if she was in a bad mood.

"I wish to go to the Assassins Guild, please." Her whisper faded into the darkness, then, she felt a breeze blow her hair off her shoulders. It whooshed through the tunnel, past her, bringing with it the scent of the slums—ash and burnt flesh.

"I have important information I need to share with the rebellion," she whispered again, her voice growing more frantic.

Nothing happened. The tunnels stayed the same before her.

Sorcha felt an ever-growing panic rise inside her. She tried again, gritting her teeth. "I have information pertaining to Razan's son. I wish to utilize him and the information he can provide to the Guild. I have no intention of crossing to the island except to bring an idea which could lead to peace."

The tunnels and the darkness before her shifted, the scent of the slums growing stronger. At last, Sorcha could see through the damp mist a light at the end of the tunnel. "Thank you," she whispered into the darkness. "You've always been my favorite." She smiled as the tunnels shifted in response to the glowing praise. The air warmed around her, brushing and winding itself through her legs as if a cat were rubbing up against her in pleasure.

Sorcha took a step forward into the tunnel. Then another. Then another. It took her a few minutes of walking to reach the exit, but when she did, the slums greeted her.

Broken buildings, half-destroyed by fire, surrounded her. The old beams of the ramshackle buildings pierced the sky like daggers. She sucked in a deep breath and kept walking until she found the building she was looking for.

The headquarters of the Assassins Guild was hidden away in the northwestern part of the island in an old, abandoned warehouse. The space had once been used for storing hay, but after the fires came, the building had collapsed in on itself when the hay caught fire. However, this was partially good news for the rebellion, since the crumbling of the building had exposed a long-forgotten basement. Once cleared out, and after months of renovations, the cavernous space had been ready to be utilized for training grounds, offices, and an armory. Sorcha was especially proud of the vast expanse of weapons at the Guild's disposal.

When she strode in the doors of the Guild, all the young trainees in the fighting pits stopped what they were doing. Women, Fae and human, of all kinds greeted her with a slight nod of their heads as she passed through the main aisle to the back of the hall. Sorcha returned the greetings with a nod of her head as well. The women resumed their training as soon as she passed by. At the back of the hall, the main room greeted her. It was less a professional office and more a crumbling pile of stones caused by the collapse of the building, but there were Marie and Facim, playing cards on an old pile of rubble as if this space was theirs to own, which it was.

Sorcha strode up to the pair. "We've got a problem."

The two women whipped their heads up toward Sorcha, immediately standing. Facim growled, "What is it?"

"I made a curse bond with the prince."

"You *what?*" Facim and Marie yelled at the top of their lungs. The trainees out in the cavern went silent.

"Resume your training!" Marie's annoyed tone echoed off the stone. The sounds of punches and kicks soon resumed.

Sorcha lowered her voice. "I had no choice. He saw my magik. He knows, not just about my powers, but that I'm...." Sorcha didn't need to finish her sentence. Facim and Marie both knew that she was the Third Triumvirate. Sorcha had told her best friends her innermost secret months ago.

Facim shook her head. "How? How did this happen?"

"It's complicated." Sorcha's cheeks slightly heated. "I found him in my room. I tried to escape, but my magik flared up to protect me. I had no choice but to go inside his mind and make that curse bond, therefore prohibiting him from telling anyone. He won't be able to say anything. To anyone. Especially not Razan."

Marie looked dazed. She took a step back and sat down on a rock. "Sorcha. This is bad."

"He agreed to give us information, to be our spy."

Marie shot back up to her feet.

Facim straightened. "Did he willingly come under our command, or did you force him under your curse bond?"

"He hates his father. I saw it in his soul. We can trust him."

"Okay. He can give us information on Razan and the High Court—but there's one rule."

Sorcha raised an eyebrow. "What is the rule?"

Facim continued, "Kartix is your responsibility alone. If he even steps out of line, you'll need to be the one to correct him. Marie and I have too many responsibilities to juggle on our plate as is. We need to step back, just this once."

The pair had been overworking themselves training the new recruits as of late. Sorcha nodded, agreeing to the terms, even though the thought of being alone with the male once more made her sick to her stomach with dread.

"I'm exhausted. We need to close up shop, send everyone to bed."

Most of the women at the Guild stayed at the Guild. The headquarters had transformed into a safe haven for the women. The bedrolls had already been pulled into the corners of the room, and girls and women of all ages sectioned off into groups as the Assassins Guild settled in for another long night surviving the slums of Ocyla.

Sorcha made her way back out into the cool night air of the slums, Marie and Facim on her heels. "I'll update you when I get new information. I have to get to bed, though. I'm exhausted."

Facim clapped her hand on Sorcha's shoulder. "Good night. Don't do anything too reckless, again."

"I'll try." A small smile was all Sorcha could muster in the dim light.

As Sorcha walked away, back to the entrance of the tunnels, Marie called out to her. "Oh, and Sorcha?"

The young woman turned to look back at her friends.

"Be careful."

10

The next night, Sorcha stood hunched over a large basin of soapy water, alone in the kitchen. All the other servants had retired hours ago, and now pushing the midnight hour, Sorcha was groaning with exhaustion.

Senna, her overseer, had heard about Sorcha's "incident" at the banquet. To everyone but Devonshire and herself, it had looked like Sorcha had spilled wine accidentally. She still remembered the terror on that bastard's face when she'd whispered her threat in his ear. Could still feel the fear radiating off Lyra at her lord's closeness. Could still remember how she had spiked the wine with poison as she'd carried the pitcher around the table.

When Sorcha had been out planting herbs earlier that day, she had replaced her thin vial of toxins and folded its contents into her skirts. As she'd made her way to Devonshire, pitcher in her hands, she had spiked the wine with her homemade poison. He would be dead within a few days' time. Even though he had not ingested it, this batch of toxins was so potent, contact with skin was enough to kill.

Then, after Devonshire was dead, Sorcha planned to free Lyra and bring her to the Assassins Guild. She already planned to ask Facim if she could help to train Lyra in self-defense.

Lyra was strong, and training with the Assassins Guild would be a drastic improvement to whatever Hel she was currently entangled with.

Sorcha used just a bit of magik to shield her hands from the scalding water. Soap dissolved around the dishes, taking grime and food off with them and tumbling down into the large sink. She scrunched her nose. Doing dishes was her least favorite activity. Senna knew that, thus why she'd been put on dish duty for the "foreseeable future."

The only sound now was the running water. Senna had assigned Sorcha to wash dishes after the servants' meal every night. She had made sure to serve everyone extra portions of food, therefore creating more mess for Sorcha to clean up. Usually, a few women would be assigned to the dishes, cleaning and scrubbing until at least the tenth hour. Yet because of her unfortunate incident at the banquet, Sorcha had been assigned dish duty, alone.

Bitch.

Dirt coated her fingernails and she gritted her teeth. Just as she was about to start on a new pile of dishes, she heard footsteps. She whirled around to find Kartix—*Kartix,* of all people—standing in the doorway, leaning against the frame of the open door.

"Hey."

"Don't do that."

"Do what?"

"Pretend like I have no reason to be completely pissed at you."

"Sorcha." Kartix took a step inside the doorway, coming into the kitchen fully now. He moved with such unnatural grace, she wondered how he was not already king. His black clothing was threaded with silver and red threads. She swallowed, her cheeks blushing slightly.

He shut the door behind him.

She tensed, bringing her hands out of the soapy water and putting down the dish she was holding. "What?"

"I didn't tell you because I figured you would never agree to let me be part of the rebellion if you knew Razan was my father."

Sorcha crossed her arms. "You're damn right. I wouldn't have involved you in the first place. Even if you *are* on our side, how can I trust anything you say?"

Kartix tapped his thick head of hair. "Because of this. The curse bond ties us together."

Sorcha rolled her eyes, seriously regretting the fact that she'd made the damn thing in the first place. "Fine. You're right. I suppose I can go inside your head and control every molecule of your being."

Kartix winced. "I won't give you a reason to do so."

From somewhere far away, the great clock tower chimed the midnight hour. Even in the kitchens, far away from the courtyard, one could still hear the great boom of the clock.

L. Holmes

The soapy water sloshed over her apron as Sorcha started on the last stack of filthy bowls. A pair of large, strong hands dove into the sink next to hers. An innocent brushing of their fingers under the water had Sorcha hyper aware of how close Kartix was. She eyed the prince out of the corner of her eye as she felt her stomach flutter. She clamped down on her mental shields to keep him from feeling her attraction.

"What are you doing?" Humidity clung to every pore and crevasse of her body, the air still warm from the fires of dinner.

"What does it look like? I'm helping."

"Don't you have somewhere to be?"

Kartix tensed, quickly putting up his mental shields so she couldn't hear his thoughts.

Does Sorcha know about Senna? How she calls me to her bed most nights? That the only reason I'm in the kitchens is the fact that I was not summoned to her side?

Eager to change the topic, the male suddenly asked Sorcha, "Tell me about your life."

114

Sorcha peered at Kartix, whose massive
frame looked laughable compared to her small, lithe
body. "I was forged ten years ago, but you know the
folklore. You know how my sisters and I were crafted
during the Heavenly Battle." She shook her head,
hands once again submerged in the soapy water.
"After the battle was won, the Gods sent my sisters
and me to earth, to preserve magik. The Gods dropped
me in the middle of nowhere. My first memory is of
a field. Nothing more."

He rubbed his chest as if he could still feel the
searing "S" that had been carved into his skin ten
years ago. Kartix turned toward her. "I remember
you." He could barely breathe. "I saw you fall to Earth
that night. I was only twenty then. I didn't tell you I
remembered you that first night we met, since I didn't
want to scare you off."

Sorcha turned off the running water. Her
memory flickered back to the day she and her sisters
were made, how they had been dropped off at
different spots across the world. How she had found
those men hiding in the brush, waiting to attack. How
she had killed all but two men.

A dish slipped out of her grasp and shattered on the floor, breaking the stunned silence. Sighing, she bent down to clean up the mess. She kept her head bowed as she picked up the materials from the floor. She kept her dignity, Kartix noted, even while doing the most laborious tasks. The way she habitually held her chin high, no matter who ordered her about. Her icy gaze, stiff back, and impeccable hips proved that she cut through space with staggering accuracy.

"Where did you live?" Curiosity got the best of Kartix.

He could barely hear her over the clatter of plates as Sorcha whispered, "After the battle, I was alone in the wilderness for years, until I found a family who took me in, until Razan came and burned our village. They slaughtered my parents and kidnapped my sister."

Sorcha went quiet. No one spoke for a few moments. "The night our village was attacked, I chose to save a group of young girls instead of my sister. After that night, I took the children to Ocyla. There, I created the Assassins Guild with the surviving girls. We train women so that they are never defenseless.

'*Never again*' is our unspoken motto. What the girls don't know is that almost every night, I search for my sister who was taken from me."

"What is her name?" Kartix refused to use the past tense. He couldn't dare suggest that Sorcha's sister might be—

A sad smile broke out across her face. "Meg. Her name was Meg. I loved her. I loved them all." She continued, "I finally found a family after years of living in the wilderness, attempting to develop my powers myself. Meg and her parents took me in and raised me as one of their own. I finally had people to come home to at the end of the day. All I wanted to do was spend holidays in front of the fire together, watching the snow fall."

Kartix didn't take his eyes off her back. Not once. Despite her rigid spine, her shoulders melted a bit as she sighed. "It sounds stupid. I know."

"No." He rushed to cut her off. "Everyone needs someone."

"I agree. But I'm not human. All I am is power in a shell. I'm not Fae, or human, or a God. I'm the Third Triumvirate, nothing more."

He closed the space between them in two strides. Her heartbeat quickened as he crowded her space, and she realized she liked having the prince this close, no matter how dangerous it might be.

Tilting his head, Kartix's eyes lit up as he smiled. "You look pretty human to me."

Sorcha's voice was flat and dull. "I am not human—*ow*!"

Rubbing the spot he had just pinched, she shot Kartix a death glare as he smirked, "You feel pretty human."

She tried and failed to keep a perverted thought from entering her mind as she slid her mental shields into place.

Touch me again.

Damn.

Maybe it was the fact that she hadn't been touched in more than a year.

Then again, she thought, *when you're trying to save the world, sex isn't really at the top of the priority list.*

Then she remembered Meg. She remembered the bloody, broken bodies of her parents. And nothing, nothing, nothing was enough to save her then. She looked at Kartix, sadness and desperation lighting up her eyes. Despite her sadness, he thought she was devastatingly gorgeous.

"My parents were murdered. I can't sleep most nights. I see them in my dreams. Their faces. Their screams."

Kartix could have sworn a memory, drenched in blood and carnage, flitted through the curse bond. He quickly sent up his inner wall, keeping her out of his mind for now.

Silence weighed heavy upon the space. "I need to finish these dishes. It's best if you go."

Kartix had more questions than answers and, if he was being honest, wanted an excuse to be around her for longer. "What about a last name? Surely you have a last name."

"No. The only name I was given was Sorcha. That was when the Gods still spoke to me. Now I've been cut off from communications, and most of my power drained. I cannot figure out what happened."

"Maybe you finally got your wish to be human."

"My wish was to never be crafted in the first place."

Kartix blinked. *That implies she does not wish to exist.* His heart cracked open at that.

Throwing him an exasperated expression over her shoulder, Sorcha turned back toward the large sink. "I'm nothing more than power in a shell."

"Then why are you still here? Why haven't you—" Kartix couldn't finish that sentence.

"Because I'm going to burn this city to the fucking ground." She turned to him, smiling. He sucked in a breath. Her smile was a thing of wild beauty.

"I'm going to kill your father for all that he took from me, and you aren't going to stop me." She looked at him then. *Really* looked at him. Kartix was powerfully built, all sleek muscle and sharp angles. *His body was crafted by the Gods themselves*, Sorcha thought. She swallowed her desire. "It's getting late." She motioned to the stack of clean dishes. "Thank you for your help."

Kartix nodded. He walked with her out of the kitchens and into the hall. She took a left, heading to her room. He fell into step beside her.

"Can I help you?"

Kartix blinked, his thick lashes brushing his cheek. "I'm escorting you to your room." He raised a dark eyebrow. "Or is that a problem?"

Sorcha smirked. "I think I can find my way back by myself."

He shrugged, the movement graceful and unhurried. "Suit yourself." He bowed, his eyes never leaving her face. "Good night, sweetheart," he purred.

Sorcha, red in the face hissed, "You're such an—" But she got no further. One moment Kartix was smirking, his handsome face the definition of male pride, and then the next, his powers had him disappearing in front of her in an instant.

She had forgotten that the asshole was Fae. That he had probably reappeared in his bedchambers. She could practically feel his rumbling laughter, a thing of dark, cruel beauty, through the curse bond. She shook her head.

Kartix would be the death of her.

11

Two weeks later, after yet another late night of scrubbing dishes for Senna, Sorcha burst into tears the moment she entered her room. She was desperate to escape, to scrape off all remnants of this life. She wanted no part of it. Of any of it. This wasn't her.

Sorcha slumped against the stone wall of her chamber. Thick, charcoal-rimmed lashes began to leak in streams of black down her cheeks.

Lashing out never ends well.

She froze where she was, ice lacing through her veins. Kartix's voice reverberated in her skull.

She stared blankly into the darkness. Sorcha had a curse bond with Marie and Facim, but this damn bond with Kartix, things were different, only because she was attracted to him. He could read her thoughts if she accidentally left her mental shields down. The thought of someone being able to read her thoughts was just another stressor piled on top of an already fucking awful night.

Sleep. She needed sleep, but Sorcha couldn't stop thinking about Meg and her parents.

"My Gods, I am going insane," she said out loud.

Sorcha ran, half-stumbling to the small window in her room.

Air, she needed air.

Peering over the ledge, she saw that the crimson city was ablaze in the pitch-black night. The fires were a new tactic to drive out the citizens who still dared to survive in the slums. The rich gathered at the river's edge, which separated the city into two divides. Binoculars were drawn out of petticoats and silks.

To these people, it was entertainment to see the "others" burning alive. From the distance, no one could smell the flesh burning, or hear the hissing bodies dissolving into ash. It was better this way, they said, to not smell the dying.

A shiver ran down her spine. The full moon slanted its silver rays over her fine features. Swaying jasmine vines perfumed the air.

She vomited over the edge of the window. Again, and again, even though she hadn't eaten all day.

Sinking against the cool stone, curled into a ball, Sorcha suddenly felt choked by the beauty of her surroundings.

Children are dying. And I'm surrounded by flowers.

~

She did not know when she fell asleep; Sorcha groaned in pain as nausea ripped her from consciousness. Panting heavily for a few seconds, she could barely register anything but the flush of blood in her veins.

Sorcha did not recall when she remembered to start breathing. Time was not a concept as the late-summer air raked over the thin clothing that was left. For in her rage, her magik had burned through her dress. Ash coated her in a thin layer.

At least the burnings were finished. For the night.

Trembling, Sorcha gathered herself, now shaking in anger. She wanted to see the damage. She needed to check on her city. The Gods had chosen her since birth. This was her mission, her purpose for living—to lead the rebellion. Restore order and equality to an otherwise Godless planet.

Her body groaned from the multiple hours she had spent unconscious on the stone floor of her room. Hugging herself, she stared at the now-quiet city. In the full moon, silver light cast its net across the water, the buildings, the courtyard below her. It was as if the entire world was holding its breath. When had violence become the new normal?

This anger was capable of incinerating her. She quickly turned and punched a hole in the wall. Over and over and over again, not stopping until the searing pain felt *good*. It was better than hitting her head. Too close to the brain. She had learned from last time. Besides, the constant headaches were not worth it.

Blood seeped from her knuckles. But it wasn't enough. She was still burning up. Burning alive. Sorcha's blood trickled in a steady stream down her arm. She was so tired of crying. Sorcha knew it wasn't worth it to hurt herself. At least, not in this way. If she was going to be self-destructive, there were far, far more interesting ways.

Stalking towards her dresser, she quickly shed what remained of her clothing. In front of the floor-to-ceiling mirror, she dared a full-bodied glance.

At least donning her costume was a thrill. Sometimes the anticipation was more exciting than the actual adventure. Onyx leather clung like oil against her skin as she slid into the full-bodied suit. Pale in the moonlight, she quickly braided her long auburn hair, pinning it into a tight coil. Sorcha had learned from fights long past that a braid, bun, or ponytail were excellent ways for an attacker to grab her. Cloaks were as well. However, because of where she was going, the young woman needed to be dressed as a male. If she wanted to live, disguising her frame was the only option, which was why she opted for a thick and immensely heavy cloak.

The last step was her mask. She pulled a silky black fabric from the deep pockets of the skintight suit. Showing only her sapphire eyes, pupils rimmed with emerald, she was a terrifying nightmare of androgyny. Bending over, partly to reach her shoes and stretch, Sorcha at last laced up her thick leather boots.

Eyeing herself one last time, the once-trembling girl assessed the ambiguous figure staring back in the mirror. Through her mask, she grinned.

She was going to have so, so much fun.

She is more reckless than usual, Kartix thought to himself.

Sorcha had picked the fight too easily. Perhaps that was why she requested backup. Well, backup was a strong word for what had recently occurred. Awoken in the middle of the night by violent banging on his chamber door, Kartix had been more than annoyed when Sorcha threw him a black wool cloak.

"I need cover," was all she offered as an explanation.

Turns out, Sorcha's idea of backup was a guard to watch her back if worse came to worst in the fighting pits. That's right. She had so much anger that the thing she most enjoyed was beating men into a pulp. Perhaps Sorcha dragged Kartix along to remind the prince of that fact—to be careful, especially around her.

Back in his room, Kartix hurried to put on his boots and cracked a smile.

Of course, he could have said no tonight. Slammed the door right in Sorcha's face. Called the guards. But after all these weeks spending time with her, some deep part of him knew that Sorcha had knocked tonight because she knew Kartix would not refuse the adventure. Or her.

Besides, nighttime seemed to be her favorite time. Lucky for Sorcha, it was his as well.

So, turning on silent feet, she guided him down, down into the passageways which led beneath the Compound. Kartix could not help but feel as if an old life was ending, and a new one was just beginning.

Through the tense journey in the dark, the tunnels beneath the city seemed to close in on the pair. Kartix did not recognize where the tunnel resurfaced until Sorcha let go of his hand, now no longer in the underground mazes which connected the two parts of the city. His hand was cold where hers once was. Her touch had been warm and reassuring. Sorcha had told him that he needed to hold on to her before they entered the tunnels.

"The darkness likes to play games," was all she offered as an explanation.

Walking briskly for what seemed like an hour, the pair reached a broken-down storefront. The structure could easily be mistaken for an out-of-business antique store. With a few short knocks, the wooden door swung open to the heavily cloaked pair. How it had opened, Kartix had no idea. There was no one standing in the doorway.

Sorcha turned to Kartix in the drizzling rain. Her smile lit up the dark as she turned toward him. "Welcome to my happy place." And just like that, Sorcha descended into the dark.

13

Hours later, Kartix was exhausted.

He had been front row when Sorcha had challenged the fighting pits' undefeated champion. Had seen her dance, fluid, sure movement with carefully placed blows, which had her opponent unconscious after a few breaths. Her body moved through space with staggering accuracy. Her body was impressive, Kartix noted.

It was not a surprise, her victory. As the crowd swallowed her figure after the match, medics rushing toward the former champion, Kartix silently surveyed the dim, cavernous space. Muggy, hot air clung to his lungs. Even at night, the sea air did nothing to cool the slums of the coastal city.

Watching her fight like that, there had been no joy. No light. Sorcha was just another captive who had come to love her cell.

As the clamor of the underground tavern rose with boisterous laughter, he searched the crowd for her. Sweat trickled down the back of his neck, his eyes straining to see anything in the dim light.

Kartix wasn't aware Sorcha was next to him until the barmaid stopped at their tucked-away booth. "I'll take whatever brandy is the cheapest." Sorcha eyed Kartix. "Actually, make that two."

The barmaid nodded and disappeared toward the bar. Kartix and Sorcha had settled into the booth, far from the fighting pits. She was sporting a bruised lip and swollen eye, yet Sorcha managed to pull off the look. Kartix glanced away as the barmaid brought them their drinks. Sorcha flipped her a gold coin and the woman smiled before fading once more into the crowd.

A burly man was standing in front of their table. The weapons strapped against his chest gleamed in the lantern light. "You deserve to die, wench, for how you fought tonight."

Sorcha realized with a start that this was a man she had fought earlier in the night. She had needed to blow off steam. To be truthful, all the faces of her opponents blurred together. But she remembered him now. The man stank of ale and dried blood. Sorcha's lips curled back from her teeth as her fingers wrapped around her glass of brandy. She was getting really tired of drunk old men who wanted to fight her.

"Go home, old man. You're drunk," Kartix growled from where he sat across from Sorcha. He eyed his partner, her shoulders tense and eyes hollow. He could tell that she did not want another fight that night.

The man leaned over the table, sneering in Sorcha's face. He got within inches of her before she promptly grabbed her brandy and soaked the man in liquor. He sputtered as the alcohol soaked into his clothes.

Kartix launched up out of his seat. They were turning heads in the fighting pits, and attention in the seediest part of town was never good.

Before the man could come back with a punch for Sorcha's head, Kartix grabbed her by her collar and hoisted her out of her seat. "I'm really not in the mood for more fighting tonight," he growled in her ear.

Kartix rolled his eyes as he shoved Sorcha out of the fighting pits and into the alley.

She would be the death of him.

14

The rain was still pouring buckets from the midnight sky as Sorcha stormed into the dark streets of the western slums. She sank against the stone wall, not caring what or *who* was smeared across the disgusting, grimy surface of the alley.

"What the *Hel* was that?" Kartix closed the distance between himself and the thin woman, both thoroughly soaked in the downpour. He stood over Sorcha, rage threatening to overtake him completely as the prince whispered, "You want to tell me what the fuck happened back there? We should have just left instead of soaking that man in brandy."

"He was an asshole," Sorcha muttered from where she hunched on the ground. Tears streamed down her face. She was exhausted. She didn't have enough strength to make it all the way back to her rooms. More tears leaked out. Sorcha was so tired of Kartix seeing her get emotional. As the shaking overtook her frame, the rain seemed to blend with her tears as the young woman lifted her chin to the sky. She just let the rain wash over her. Trembling, Sorcha managed to whisper, "I just need to feel something good. For once in this Godsdamn life, I want to feel *good*."

How could Kartix argue with that?

So, for what seemed like hours, the two stood silently in the dark. Well, Kartix stood, and Sorcha remained hunched over her knees from where she sat on the ground.

Kartix didn't make a move to touch her or say what minimal comforting words crossed his mind. Sometimes it was better to just listen. Not provide any ideas or tactics to stop the onslaught of heavy emotions. To just let Sorcha cry, to release the weight she had been carrying for months, years. He was wise enough to understand nothing he could do or say would reach that endless dark pit inside her. If he could reach it, he knew it would be beautiful.

Drenched in the rain, Kartix did not tear his gaze away from Sorcha once. He kept track of her breathing. Badass as she was, hypothermia was no match for her already drained magik reserves.

Just as the sun's crown began to crest the sea, sending its beams across the drenched city, her trembling finally ceased. Sorcha said nothing to Kartix as she tore her stare from the sky. She stood, forced herself to take a step, then another, toward the Compound. Her thin legs were barely able to carry the weight of her thick, sodden cape. She couldn't make it all the way to her room. She had picked too many fights that night.

So, with a heavy sigh, Kartix uncrossed his arms and strode to Sorcha's side. A strange, hollow girl had taken Sorcha's place. He could barely feel the curse bond. It was a dark and cold thing within his chest. She was such a stark contrast to the ruthless woman he had seen just hours prior, fighting men twice her height and size.

"Is it alright if I touch you?" Kartix's words were soft, gentle, as if speaking too loud would shatter her completely. Spook her, like some type of wild animal.

Hollow, lifeless eyes locked onto his. A small nod of her chin was all it took for the prince to softly lay his hand on her thin shoulder. "Let's go home."

Home.

Sorcha's legs buckled underneath her fighting leathers. A shuddering breath broke from her exposed throat. He scooped her up in his arms.

Sorcha was quiet for a moment as they made their way through the tunnels, back toward the Compound. She nestled into his chest for warmth. Sleep was hovering just over her shoulder, but she managed to hold on to consciousness as Kartix used the last remnants of his magik to transport both himself and the woman in his arms back to her room in the servant quarters.

Kartix set her down a few feet away from her bed. He stepped back. "Your training is in a few hours. You better get cleaned up."

Sorcha nodded slowly, still in a daze. "Thank you. For coming with me tonight."

She barely felt it, barely registered it, but as Kartix came close, bent down, and pressed a feather-soft kiss to her cheek, Sorcha felt something like heaven.

She was too tired to stop a smile from breaking out across her face. Kartix's eyes went wide, and he felt like he'd been gutted. "Do that again," he breathed.

So Sorcha gave him her biggest smile, letting him see her full, wide lips and straight white teeth.

"You're perfect," Kartix whispered.

She breathed in sharply, her gaze going to his lips, but Kartix only huffed a laugh and turned away from her. "You have work to attend to." And then, the bastard left her alone, walking out of her doors, to greet the coming day.

15

A few nights later, Sorcha tumbled out of the pub, stomach heaving with laughter, tears streaming down her flushed cheeks. Marie and Facim were right behind her, covered in blood but eyes shining.

The three women could still hear the crowd hurling death threats. A drunken man yelled from the balcony just what he would do to Sorcha if he ever saw her again, along with a string of very diverse curses. Wine bottles were thrown from second-story windows, shattering against the cobblestones. The girls shrieked with laughter as they clung to each other, sidestepping the broken glass.

The fights had gone well. Each woman had tumbled out of the tavern with several new coins to line her pockets with, much to the dismay of their opponents and the poor souls who had bet on said opponents. They had done so well, fought so hard in the ring, that the women had completely swindled the crowd out of their money.

Apparently, the men were not too pleased with having their asses handed to them by a bunch of young women.

As the money jangled in the women's pockets, Sorcha couldn't help but grin like a fool. It had been almost too easy, finding a place like this. The women had snuck out of the Compound to the slums at half past midnight. Senna had worked hrt late into the day again, still pissed at Sorcha for her antics at the banquet. She supposed her superior would be angry with her for a while. It wasn't every day that a servant embarrassed herself in front of the king.

They picked a fighting ring on the outskirts of the slums, far away from the Compound and prying eyes. They had made a plan to split an ounce of hawthorn root to smoke, far from wanting the night to end. It was convenient, since the dealer often frequented the pub.

The fights had chased away the shadows in Sorcha's eyes. She'd allowed her muscles to burn with adrenaline as she collected more coins, more winnings.

It wasn't until Sorcha spotted Kartix, brooding in an alleyway, that her laughter came to a halt. The male stepped out of the shadows, his heavy wool hood obscuring most of his face, yet she could tell from his stance and preternatural stillness that he was pissed. She swallowed her desire as he came closer.

"Sorcha?" Marie looked over her shoulder to where he was standing, just outside the glow of the lanterns.

Sorcha didn't respond, but rather crossed her arms as the handsome male came closer. "Are you stalking me?"

"If by stalking you, you mean keeping an eye on you, then yes." His voice was low and threaded with violence.

Facim and Marie inched closer, their hands clenched into fists, ready to fight if necessary. Sorcha waved them off. "I know him." She took a step further, the alleyway now quiet in the late hour. The drunken tavern members had dissipated, no longer interested in heckling the women who had taken their money.

Most of them anyway.

The man that Sorcha had dueled second to last stalked out of the doors of the tavern, clearly unwilling to let his loss go. He staggered toward the group of women, completely and thoroughly intoxicated. The burly man pointed a fat finger at Sorcha. *"You little bitch."*

Kartix tensed at the words.

Sorcha's lips curled back from her teeth, not quite a smile but all the more deadly. "Is that so?" she purred.

The man swayed where he stood in the middle of the broken glass, clearly unable to feel it through his thick leather boots. Sorcha noticed a flash of silver on the inside of his coat. He was armed.

Marie and Facim slowly took a step forward.

"Give me back my money."

Sorcha tilted her head, the move purely predatory. "Or you'll do what?" She tossed the bag of coins into the air and caught it, weighing it in her palm. "Seems like I beat you fair and square. Better luck next time." Sorcha made to turn away, head down the alleyway, and do anything to avoid escalation, but clearly the drunken fool did not care to see her leave. His arm lunged toward her, intending on hurting her.

The moment the man made to grab her, everything changed. Sorcha had thought she was the strongest fighter in the alley, but that idea was quickly destroyed when Kartix—*Kartix* of all people—had the man up against the wall, choked out, in a matter of seconds. His grip on the man's collar was strong and sure, his face unflinching. He growled in the man's face, quietly but not without aggression, "Walk away."

The man choked out, "*Fuck you.*"

Kartix grinned. "I was kind of hoping you would say that." And then he punched him. The drunkard went down immediately, slumped against the alleyway wall. Kartix hauled him to his feet, punching the man again. And again. And again.

Sorcha had a feeling he was holding back. No matter how turned on she was at the sight of Kartix

defending her, she strode up to him, laid a hand on his
shoulder. "Enough."

The man was whimpering like a child,
nursing his already-bruised face. Kartix still stood
over him, panting in uneven breaths. He bared his
teeth as the man stood and stumbled back to the safety
of the pub.

Marie grinned from where she stood ten
paces away. "Looks like Sorcha isn't the only one
who needs to blow off some steam."

Kartix turned toward Sorcha, raising a thick
brow. "Is that so?"

Sorcha nodded, a sudden jolt of pain racing
through her cheek. In the last fight, she had taken a
punch to the face. She hadn't felt it then, but unless
she got ice on it—or used her magik to stop the
swelling—the injury would bruise horrendously.

She grimaced against the onslaught of pain.

Kartix caught her hesitation, but still thought,
despite the marks, how sexy she was. His eyes briefly
flitted down toward her lips.

"I'm not going to ask if you're alright." The male turned toward Marie and Facim. "The three of you look like you've been dragged through Hel."

Facim was ringing the blood out her dreadlocks, the crimson liquid dripping onto the cobblestones, while Marie was rotating her arm. She had dislocated her shoulder in the fights and screamed while Sorcha had put her shoulder back into its socket. The latter of the two grinned. "The night is far from over."

"Oh?"

Sorcha smiled. "We are rich with winnings, so why not have a little fun?"

"Don't you have work in the morning?"

"Senna can go fuck herself." Sorcha's grin widened as she pulled out another, smaller bag from her deep pockets. With their Fae sense of smell, they could all smell the pungent odor of the bag.

Kartix wrinkled his nose. "What is that?"

Facim tilted her head back and howled with laughter. "It's like he's never smelled hawthorn root before!" Even Marie raised a brow at Kartix. "Is that so?"

The male shook his head, his black hair glistening in the light of the lanterns. "I grew up under strict circumstances."

"Strict is one word I'd use," Sorcha grumbled. "Have you ever even wanted to try?" A devilish light lit up her blue eyes.

Kartix smiled hesitantly. "I have, yes."

Sorcha looped her arm through his as she smiled wide, letting him see her bloodied mouth. "Then let's go."

~

An hour later, Sorcha was high as a kite. She never wanted to come down.

Kartix had invited them all to his room on the tenth floor. Facim was passed out on the purple, lavish pillow across from the raging fire, and Marie and Kartix were staring at a chessboard, as they had been for the past ten minutes, without either of them making a single move.

Sorcha looked up from her rolled cigarette, the earthy smell of the root mingling with the scent of jasmine from the terrace. "You know, you're actually supposed to move the pieces in order to play, right?"

Kartix met her eyes, a slight haze across his vision. "I'm too high to move."

Sorcha sat up, concern etching her features. "I'll get you water."

"No, I'll get it myself." Kartix stood up, wobbled on his feet, and then promptly sat back down. "On second thought, I might take you up on that offer."

Sorcha laughed and rolled her eyes. "First-timers." She fetched the water pitcher. The water pouring into the crystal glass was the only sound in the room besides the crackling of the fire.

"Are there any burnings tonight?" asked Facim suddenly.

Sorcha looked up from the glass. "Why do you ask?"

Facim shook her head. "I can't tell if the smoke I smell is coming from this fire or the slums."

Silence echoed throughout the room.

"What a sad fucking thing we have to ask ourselves. What type of world do we live in where we smell the burnings of the damned?" Sorcha gave the glass to Kartix and then began pacing in front of the fire, continuing on with her speech. "This is bullshit. Absolute *bullshit."*

Sorcha cut herself off as she realized just who she was speaking in front of. Their alliance being newly formed, it was fresh enough that she still was hesitant to talk about her blatant disapproval of the king.

Kartix sat in a brown leather chair, his dark hair reflecting in the firelight. His white shirt was stark against his tan skin. Sorcha did not know why she noticed those tiny details. She did not know why she liked the image of his shirt sleeves rolled up, exposing his muscled forearms.

But she did. She noticed.

"Do you want to be king?" Facim asked, point-blank. It felt like the air had been sucked from the room. For a few heartbeats, no one spoke. Sorcha glanced at Kartix, and he met her eyes only for a moment.

"I want to heal this country," Kartix said evenly. "I have no intention of being king if that means continuing on with the current political system." Anger, raw and wild, flashed behind his dark eyes. "How many have died under my father's reign? How many families had been torn apart irrevocably? Too many. Too many to count." He launched out of his chair and stalked to the fireplace.

"What would you do if you were king?" Marie tilted her head, assessing him as if expecting him to shy away from her question. Instead, the male met her stare.

"I would kill my father, burn down the Compound, slaughter every one of the King's Council members, and restore magik. Perhaps not in that order."

Marie smiled. "Well, this is all too convenient then."

Facim grinned as well. "Kartix, let us make you a proposition."

He raised a dark brow. "I'm listening."

The women met each other's eyes before Facim continued. "Have you ever heard of the Assassins Guild?"

Kartix nodded, confusion starting to etch into his features.

"Well, we are all members of the Guild." The women waited for Kartix to be surprised, but a composed calmness was written all over his striking face.

"And?"

"And we would like you to give us information."

"You want me to be a spy for the Assassins Guild?"

Facim nodded. No one spoke for a few moments.

"My only regret is that you didn't ask me sooner." A devilish grin lit up Kartix's handsome face. "Of course I'll do it. Any excuse to fuck the system is good enough for me."

Facim and Marie laughed, but Sorcha furrowed her brows. Even though it was stupid, she was worried for Kartix. She blushed at her concern for him. There were rumors amongst the servants that Razan had murdered his niece and her other-half in cold blood. Family meant nothing to the king. If

Kartix was caught, execution was one option on the table. The thought sent a tremor through her legs despite the fact that Sorcha was sitting down.

After they discussed the details of their plan, Marie and Facim slipped out to their rooms yawning, the high of hawthorn root having faded off already.

As she left a few minutes later, Sorcha caught Kartix by the sleeve. She pulled him close, keeping her voice down. "You need to be careful. Don't put yourself in any unnecessary danger." She shook her head. "Death is almost certain if you fail." She didn't bother softening her words as the truth hung in the air between them.

Kartix met her stare evenly as he said, "You do not need to worry about me." His eyes suddenly went distant.

"Yes, I do." Sorcha's brows furrowed further.

"Well, you shouldn't." Something like annoyance threaded Kartix's voice.

Sorcha let go of his arm, realizing now that she had been touching him the whole time. "Fine."

"Fine."

Sorcha turned down the hallway, not bothering to say good night. No guards stopped her as she walked from the tenth floor back down to the servants' quarters. She crawled into bed, exhaustion weighing down her limbs, but couldn't help but picture a prince, lonely and lost, drowning in a sea of blood.

~

Kartix threw the doors to his bedroom open and stalked inside, throwing his overshirt onto his bed.

A fire roared in the hearth but Kartix was covered in a cold sweat.

She cares about me, clearly, so why did I push her away just now?

Sadness weighed upon him as Kartix stumbled into bed, not even bothering to take off his boots, he was so tired. He whispered through the curse bond, *Will you forgive me?*

A voice, soft and distant, brushed against his inner wall. *I already have.*

Thank you, for caring.

Good night, Kartix.

Good night, Sorcha.

And somewhere far away in the Compound, in her own bed, Sorcha smiled.

16

It was a nightmare.

She knew it was.

But Sorcha couldn't wake. She was paralyzed, a helpless victim to her unconsciousness.

The night her parents were murdered, Sorcha had been kissing a boy in the stable, like the fucking idiot she was. That night, she had just been about to get on her knees when the screaming started, miles away from the barn she and John were hiding in. Sorcha had gathered her skirts while he'd gathered his pants, then they ran down the road to their village.

It was all in flames.

A few yards away, hiding in the woods, Sorcha and John could see their houses from where they crouched, protected. Nothing in all her years could have prepared Sorcha for what she saw next: her parents and Meg were dragged out of their cottage and thrown to the ground by a pair of soldiers. Sorcha marked the guard's faces, memorized their frames.

Even as tears blazed down her cheeks, she would not forget them. She would never forget.

It was then that the soldiers slit her parents from groin to sternum, their intestines spilling out in the village square. They sank to their knees and fell over, one final time, onto the pavement. Neither one moved again.

Then the guards hauled her sister to her feet.

"*Meg!*" Sorcha bellowed at the top of her lungs.

But it was too late. By then, Meg had been shoved into the back of a covered wagon, her arms and legs shackled.

John held Sorcha back as she screamed and screamed and screamed. She sank to her knees as his arms restrained her. She fought him, fought John so that he would let her go, let her run to her parents and Meg. So that she could try to save them with whatever magik she had left. John only held her as she cried. "Sorcha, you have to be quiet. They haven't found us yet. If they do, Razans' guards will kill us."

She swallowed her screams at that. All they could do was sit, trembling, in the woods, watching everyone they loved burn into flames and ashes. Her and John then caught sight of a group of young girls, some as young as four, running to the outskirts of town. They could see a group of soldiers begin to follow the children.

"John, forgive me for this."

"Sorcha, *no!*" But he couldn't stop her. Sorcha had already begun to run.

She had to rescue the kids.

Hot tears streamed down her face as she approached. The village had burned quickly. As the straw roofs went up in flames, the screams of the villagers cut off. And all at once, the only sound were the burning structures cracking in the heat.

Razan's soldiers slaughtered as they went, dragging the young women off to the edge of the clearing. No men were spared. Sorcha could hear the soldiers raping the women. She could hear the soldiers calling out for the children. They wanted the girls.

She emptied the contents of her stomach, vomit staining the pristine white of the birch tree she hid behind. A voice, a thin thread of golden light from somewhere deep inside her, seemed to sway her conscious.

Run.

She needed to move.

This was war.

These types of situations were unavoidable.

As she turned away, Sorcha gritted her teeth. It was an impossible decision, but her magik could not strengthen in time to do what she really wanted to do. As much as she hated to think it, saving those children topped saving Meg. She used what little magik she had to blur the outline of her frame. Not completely invisible to the eye, but enough to go unnoticed, Sorcha ran around the outskirts of her village, sticking to the tree line, keeping her steps silent and quick as she made her way through the underbrush.

There, the voice whispered to her again.

Sorcha's eyes caught on a group of soldiers who were stalking close to the spot where the children were hiding.

And just as she was about to catch them, torture them with her magik, Sorcha woke up. It took several heartbeats for her to register that she was alive.

The nightmare disappeared in an instant, leaving a terrified woman in its wake.

She curled up and cried herself to sleep.

~

Kartix awoke with a start. He tried to move, but he realized that he was still tied to Senna's bed. He had been tied up since he had fallen asleep. He pulled on his restraints. Not even his magik could undo them. He silently looked at Senna then, in the moonlight that was streaming in through the floor-to-ceiling windows. His captor was sleeping beside him, curled up, her back to Kartix. Senna's blonde hair was a stream of gold that flowed over her shoulder, yet she was not beautiful. There was nothing remarkable about Senna.

Perhaps that's why she wants me—so she can feel powerful.

She'd claimed him tonight because Kartix had evaded her last time. Senna had not found him in his bed the night before. When she'd inquired about his whereabouts, Kartix had said he'd been out in the Compound's gardens and would have sought her out had he known she would be looking for him. Senna seemed to buy his lie.

But last night, Kartix had really followed Sorcha and her friends through the tunnels, all the way to a seedy tavern in the western part of the slum island. He had seen her fight, duck, twirl, punch, and jab her opponents, all with staggering accuracy.

Senna sighed in her sleep, and Kartix pushed every thought of Sorcha out of his head. It was too dangerous to think of her next to Senna. It felt like a betrayal of sorts. A betrayal to Sorcha. If the Triumvirate knew what Senna did to him, what bargain Razan and Senna had struck over him, over his body, Sorcha would probably set the entire world on fire. Some part of him knew—perhaps it was the curse bond—that Sorcha would go to the ends of the earth to save those she—

He almost thought it.

Almost thought the word he dreaded most.

Almost admitted to himself that she cared about him.

Kartix had given up hope a long time ago, somewhere during the first six months that Senna had tied him to her bed every night. How she had taken advantage of him, riding him over and over, even as tears streamed down his face.

Kartix looked away from Senna, counted the hours till sunrise, until he could be free of these restraints and go to wash off every trace of this horrible, evil woman.

Some small part of Kartix kept him awake. Kept whispering to him in urgent tones.

Something's coming.

Kartix stilled as a cold wind blew past him.

Hurry.

He pulled once more on his restraints, and surprisingly, they came free, as if whatever entity that surrounded him had freed him. As if it wanted him to escape.

His magik awoke as soon as he was free. The shackles which had chained him to Senna's bed were made of Mahoun, a precious metal that drained all of one's magik. Now, Kartix had his full strength back.

Quietly, he picked his clothes up off the floor. Dressing silently, he stalked toward the door, his magik muffling any sounds he might have made. Trembling, he reached the door, pulled it open gently, and stepped into the hallway. He let out a breath he hadn't realized he had been holding.

Relief washed over him, even as that silent but steady voice urged him.

Move.

A torch lit suddenly to his left, from where it hung against the stone wall. Then the torch after that was lit. So on and so on until every single torch down the hall to Kartix's left was aglow. They were lit by magik, not of his own. It was as if the Compound was trying to signal him.

So, he followed the lights.

The torches flickered out when he reached a familiar hallway: the entrance to the servants' quarters. There was only one servant who held any interest to him.

Kartix stalked to Sorcha's room. Her door was open. He smelled another male's scent in the room. He smelled something else, a huskier, deeper scent. Kartix realized with a start that that was the scent of Sorcha's arousal. She had had a male in her bed, only a few hours prior.

He ground his teeth together. A cold, calculating calm settled over him, a primal rage that threatened to send him to his knees.

But where was Sorcha? She was not in bed. He had not seen her in the hallway. And it was far too late to still be working in the kitchens.

All these thoughts were shattered as an alarm blared to life in the servants' quarters. Humans and Fae alike rushed out of their beds as red light filled the entire compound. Kartix's entire body locked up. There was only one alarm that sounded like this: it meant that a Fae had been discovered in the Compound. A lockdown would soon go into place. Magik would seal everyone in their rooms until they were questioned. Until Razan found the being who still harbored magik they had not yet given to the state.

Kartix could hear the slam of doors as the servants began to shelter in place. He waited a few more minutes, but Sorcha was nowhere to be found. Cursing to himself, Kartix ran out of the room.

Where was Sorcha?

17

The tavern was seedy and ruinous and wretched, but that was just the way she liked it.

Sorcha had run from her room hours ago in search of the fighting pits, needing to burn off her anxiety. The nightmare of her village burning, of losing Meg, had kept her from sleeping. She was afraid to sleep most nights. The reason she escaped the Compound that night was Meg. Every night she could, Sorcha stole out into Ocyla. Hunted every strange pub and tavern and whorehouse to gather any information about Meg. Every night she could, she searched for her sister among those still enslaved in the slums.

Every night, she heard nothing. Every night, the soldiers who'd taken Meg, who'd murdered her parents, were nowhere to be seen. She only heard whispers, rumors. It had been years now that Sorcha had been frequenting these pubs. All she knew was that Meg was in Ocyla. Nothing more.

Sorcha's ears pricked up at the mention of Kartix's name.

"Prince of Bastards," a burly man laughed from across the room. Her hands clenched into a fist. She heard other rumors, too, but for some reason, when the man mentioned Kartix's name, it caught her ear. The stranger was tall in stature but short in intellect, she noted. *What did the man mean when he said 'Prince of Bastards'? Was that Kartix's codename amongst the enlisted men?* Sorcha pondered this, ducking her head lower, pulling her cloak over her head to obscure her features.

Men loved to gossip in taverns. These places were abundant with insider information, especially since Razan's soldiers often frequented this pub. The lazy bastards would get piss-poor drunk. All she needed to do was stand in the corner, drinking, hood over her face, listening to the men for information. It was what Sorcha was doing now—she stood near the bar in the back of yet another stomach-churning tavern. The memories of her parents' murders were still seared into the back of her mind, unable to be chased away. She had fought in the fighting rings for hours, taking money from the crowd. She gambled away her necklace, and every night, she won it back. The men were pissed, to say the least. But she still couldn't shake her nightmares.

Sorcha felt a heavy gaze land upon her. It didn't move. Her eyes slid over to the source of the suddenly focused attention. A striking young male was leaning against the opposite tavern wall, a mirror image to her own position. Both were reclined against the stone walls, arms and legs crossed, watching each other with a predator's focus. The male was broad-shouldered, rugged, and, Sorcha realized with a start, familiar.

Adonis.

Right. This was the Captain of the Guard. Mathias was still head guard, but Adonis was his second in command.

Sorcha's lips parted in a saccharine smile as she locked eyes with him. *Oh, what fun she could have, using him for information. He could prove to be an excellent source of intelligence for the Assassins Guild, to aid the rebellion.*

Sorcha didn't trust him. Not one bit.

However, he was attractive, and had enough sway with Razan.

She tilted her head, allowing her hood to fall, her long, auburn hair washing over her shoulders in a waterfall of silk. She noticed Adonis's breathing hitched, uneven, as his pupils narrowed. Every inch of him seemed focused on her. Sorcha made her eyes go wide, made her lips part as if she was breathless with anticipation as well. She smirked, leaning back against the wall once more, tugging her hood up and turning away from the male to order another drink.

She played hard to get. Males always loved the game, the chase, anyway. It was lucky for Adonis that Sorcha loved the game as well.

So, only when Adonis appeared to her left, a few inches from her shoulder, did she turn her attention to him. They locked eyes. She took a long sip of her drink, finished it, all the while looking up at him through lowered lashes. Adonis had a serpentine smile on his handsome face. Sorcha placed her mug back on the bar. Wiping her mouth, she let him see her straight, white teeth as she smiled wide.

"Can I help you, captain?"

"You most certainly can."

18

She didn't know how late it was, only that the sun had not yet risen. She was slurring some words, yet the ground remained steady underneath her feet. The alcohol was slowly leaving her system, thanks to the magik surging in her veins. Even still, Sorcha was fully intoxicated.

Adonis's soft laugh sent shivers up her spine. "We should get you to bed."

Right.

Senna would be knocking on her door in a few hours.

She was so, so tired. Her body felt like one big bruise. Sorcha was lucky she didn't have a broken bone, the way the fights had escalated earlier that night.

"Fuck me..." Sorcha groaned as she hit the thin mattress.

Sorcha was just faintly aware of his voice as he muttered, "I would love to." Adonis's large frame filled the doorway as he shut her door behind them.

She managed to sit up on her elbows, fighting leathers still clinging against her skin, along with crusted blood of her opponents. "That's not what I meant," she hiccupped, tasting the alcohol on her breath. She grimaced in the moonlight that was streaming in through the small window. "As attractive as you are—" Drunk as she was, Sorcha managed to grimace at her own honesty— "I shouldn't."

"So, you find me attractive." A statement, not a question formed on Adonis's full lips.

"Whatever I feel has nothing to do with anything."

He shook his head, laughing quietly in the small chamber. His shoulder-length golden curls brushed against the collar of his thick wool cloak. "So, you don't want me to fuck you then?"

Her mouth went dry, tongue sticking to the roof of her mouth as she forgot how to breathe. Her heartbeat a wild, thunderous thing in her chest, Sorcha managed to meet his eyes, tilt her chin up, and take in the male standing before her.

Why did he even want her in this way? Her makeup was smudged, although a bit of charcoal still rimmed her lashes. Her clothing reeked of blood. She held her carnage-soaked hands up to him, exposing the tender underside of her palm. Adonis gripped her hands in his warm ones as he sat next to her on the bed silently. Time trickled by, and slowly, so, so, so slowly, Sorcha realized how lonely she was. How she needed to feel something other than this empty silence, the endless void inside her. It has been years since someone's bare skin had met hers. *How nice it would be*, she thought, *to feel something good, for once in this Godsdamned life.*

She slowly turned to him, her hands still in his. She met Adonis's eyes, her chin barely at the level of his chest. All Sorcha could do was whisper, "Okay."

He was on her a heartbeat later, the thin mattress biting against her back. Their joining was a clash of teeth and hands tearing at clothing. His fingers raked red marks down her spine, and she groaned in ecstasy as the pain centered her. His mouth met hers. Every second spent touching him sent thrills up her spine.

She wasn't supposed to feel this good. It was impossible for this happiness to exist solely with another being. Yet here she was, trying to suppress her moans, utterly naked before someone she barely knew.

She tried to be quiet when he entered her. She really, truly tried.

"You feel so fucking good." She trembled as he whispered against her neck, still unable to take in the sheer size of him.

She arched her back as his teeth raked over the delicate skin of her neck. Hot breath sent shivers up her spine.

A wind blew in from the high sliver of a window, cooling her flushed skin. She closed her eyes.

I want to get lost. To feel nothing.
Nothing at all.

19

Sorcha awoke with a start, breathless and exhausted, but fully on alert. Adonis had left hours prior. She was alone, but her magik writhed and screamed inside her chest, her very soul. Sorcha vomited over the side of her bed.

Something was wrong.

She pulled on the curse bond, asking Kartix for any information, but his mental shields were up, as if he didn't want her to see where he was, what he was doing. Sorcha swallowed the lump in her throat. Was Kartix in trouble? Were Facim and Marie alright? Was it the Assassins Guild?

Oh God, the girls.

Sorcha tumbled out of bed, every hair on her body sticking up straight.

Go, go, go, go.

Her magik was begging, crying out to be let loose, to protect her. So, she let it come out in a stream of gold, her powers settling over her skin, her bones, her blood. It wove in between every molecule and cell, and it felt so right, so fucking right, for Sorcha to release the pressure which had been building under her skin. When magik was not used, it manifested as pain. One always had to let out a bit of magik regularly so as to not be overwhelmed with their powers.

Sorcha was finally able to break free of her restraints as she used her magik to become invisible, a shield fitting around her body, covering her scent. She threw open the door to the hallway and bolted down the stairs at the end of the hall, all the way to the bottom of the Compound. She found the entrance to her tunnels.

Run.

That voice inside her, that bond of golden light buried deep within her chest, pushed her forward to the tunnel. She placed her hand on the wall. "Something's very wrong. I don't know what, but please let me through. I—we might be in danger."

The tunnel warmed and shifted its walls before her, a light appearing at the end of the passageway. Sorcha kissed her palm and then pressed her hand to the wall. "Thank you, friend." The tunnels warmed even further in response, as if pleased with her praise.

Sorcha, without hesitation, sprinted into the darkness. Her magik pulled her toward the slums, as if it wanted her to get as far away from the Compound as possible. As if she was being hunted.

All of the sudden, an alarm blared out behind her—an alarm from the Compound. It all clicked into place. Last night, when she had taken off her clothing, she had been too drunk to hide her magik from Adonis. She had probably forgotten to hide her half-sleeve tattoo. He had probably told the king himself about her magik.

Sorcha skidded to a halt. Horror curled in her gut as bile coated her mouth.

Holy Gods, Razan knows about my powers.

She was so fucked.

~

Kartix gritted his teeth and swore as he sprinted down into the tunnels. He had managed to follow the pull from the curse bond down to the tunnel entrance, but now that he was in the slums, he had absolutely no idea where Sorcha was. He tried to track her scent, but it was as if she was covering her trail. He tapped the curse bond, but any message he tried to relay faded away, as if she was too far away to receive even his messages.

The alarm still blared on the main island. He needed to find her, and fast, before Razan did. The thought of Sorcha winding up in the hands of his father was the only thing that raced through Kartix's mind. It would either be the gallows or the King's Council for her. There was no in-between for those who harbored their gifts from the state.

He flew down an alleyway, desperately clinging to whatever remnants of the curse bond remained, which still pulled him forward, as if an invisible hand lay on his shoulder.

This way, the soft voice seemed to whisper.

Kartix didn't hesitate as he swiftly darted through more broken buildings, dodging fallen beams and piles of rubble as he went. The slums really had gone to shit.

His mind flashed back to what he had left behind: Reid was probably already up, searching for him, frantic with worry. Senna would wonder how he had escaped his bonds. He could worry about his brother and captor later. Right then, every single cell of his body narrowed in with a predatory calm. He had to find Sorcha before anyone else.

He dove somewhere deep inside himself, letting his magik settle over his blood, his bones, sinking further into the core of his body. From that state, where his magik was settled and calm, in his mind, Kartix gently lay two hands on the curse bond and gave it a tug. He let the curse bond go taut with tension, giving it a pull, only hoping, praying that somewhere, somehow, Sorcha could feel his warning. All thoughts disappeared from his mind as a playful voice lit up the dark.

"I'm right here, idiot."

He turned from where he stood amidst a pile of rubble toward the source of that voice.

Sorcha stood before him, wearing nothing but a thin nightgown and scuffed up boots, a thin, sad smile on her face. Her hair was plastered to her head, completely unbound, falling to her waist, covering her mostly see-through white slip. The rain soaked them both, chilling them to the bone. They didn't have time to drink in the sight of each other—they had to run.

Kartix's eyes scanned every inch of her for injury. There was nothing lustful about his gaze. It was one any soldier would receive on the battlefield by a medic. His voice was cold and calm as he said, "We need to get you out of here, now."

Sorcha nodded. "Lead the way."

Rain tore at the pair from all directions as they ran swiftly through the dirt-packed street. Before Sorcha had been discovered, there had been some controlled fires, but now the slums darkened as fires were quenched, providing more shadows to hide in. The burnings had not been merciful that night.

The population of those inhabiting the slums for the past few years had been cut in half. Everyone had had a brother kidnapped, a daughter raped by Razan's soldiers.

The pair ran faster, harder. Sorcha's thoughts pounded in time with her steps. Before she had found

Kartix, staring like a bumbling fool at her in the pouring rain, she had checked on the girls at the Assassins Guild. Everything and everyone was alright.

Sorcha had reinforced the space with more barrier spells anyway.

Blocks away, in the western slums, Sorcha felt something wicked, ancient, and evil awaken. It raked claws down the inner barrier of her mind. It wanted to *play,* Sorcha realized.

She sucked in a deep breath. That was captured magik. She knew it. Razan was using it to track her down. Like calls to like, after all.

The black magik howled and bucked on its leash. Razan's leash. It was not the guards that night who stalked Sorcha and her magik—it was the king himself. The bastard that he was.

Adrenaline surged in her veins, awakening her slumbering magik. She could have sworn she felt the creature groaning as it was pulled from its sleep.

This is no time to be dormant. I need you. Now.

At that thought, fire burst through her veins as her magik fully awoke. Sorcha burst ahead, pulling into the lead, Kartix far behind. The male swore as he strained his Fae body to maximum capacity in order to reach his partner. A small part of his magik awoke as well, as if it wanted to play with her powers.

Catching sight of a shadow to their left, Sorcha pulled Kartix sharply into a darkened, small alley to shake off the scent of their trail.

The cramped space hid the pair well. Their wet, labored breathing was the only sound. Sorcha quickly worked a small amount of healing magik over their cuts. Razan's dark magik could smell blood. Patches only held for so long, though. They needed a medic. And soon.

Her leg cramped from the twisted position the small alleyway had forced the pair into. Only a few yards in length, and barely two feet from shoulder to shoulder, Sorcha and Kartix barely fit, but they had survived the alarm. At least their alleyway salvation was not as wet as the main road.

Despite her soaked nightgown, warmth began to leak into her bones as Kartix's body pressed against hers. Her heartbeat pounded in her ears as Sorcha's wide eyes took in the street the two had just escaped from. She could only hope that with his Fae heritage, Kartix would be no closer to hypothermia than she was.

Minutes passed. Then half an hour.

Finally, it seemed that Razan had given up his hunt.

No. He would never surrender—only retreat until his next strike. What his next move would be, though, Sorcha had no idea.

So Kartix and Sorcha waited at least half an hour more until they could be sure the search party had moved beyond the slums.

Alive.

They were *alive.*

Sorcha's muscles screamed in agony. She managed to twist her head, looking up at her partner.

Kartix didn't look any better himself. His black hair was matted, tan skin paled, but his striking features were still, wholly focused on her.

Wide-eyed from the adrenaline rush, Sorcha and Kartix looked at each other. Despite their rain-slicked faces, despite the fact that they had almost been killed, despite the fact that the pair should never have met in the first place, broad smiles slowly began to spread. A chuckle, low and rumbling, rose from somewhere deep in Kartix's abdomen. A gleam in Sorcha's eye informed him that she was also on the brink of losing it completely.

It was only when they were sure that the sounds of their pursuers had faded into the distance that the choked laughter became audible. Sorcha threw up a shield to cover any of the sounds they might make. His smile made her heart ache.

Sorcha's toes curled in her leather boots. Playfully, in a "shh" motion, she brought a rain-slicked finger to Kartix's lips. The motion had been purely automatic. Instinctual. Yet, she couldn't help it as her gaze dipped to his lips, too close to hers.

With nothing else to focus on in the dim space, Kartix couldn't help but to see the trajectory of her gaze, couldn't help the heating of his blood as he realized all too suddenly that this alley was *very* dark and *very* small. Yet, strangely, there was nowhere else he would rather be, Kartix thought with a surprise.

His warm, calloused hand encompassed the finger held to his lips. Kartix gently turned over Sorcha's hand, exposing the soft padding of her palm. He marveled at how small her hands were compared to his. What she had survived. How had she done it with such limited bodily strength? His eyes flashed to meet hers. Ah. Right. Her physical features were a strength on their own. She had used her looks to get into rooms that her lock-picking hands had not been able to gain access to.

Sorcha subtly cleared her throat, her cheeks tinted pink. Her gaze slipped down his face, his lips plump and smooth. She noticed what she was doing and jerked her eyes back up to his, only to realize that his eyes were focused on her lips too. When Sorcha licked her lips, Kartix's eyes were set ablaze.

She whispered, "I think the coast is clear now. We could leave."

Kartix's eyes darkened several shades. "Yeah. We could." But he was still looking at her lips. And—*Godsdamn* her to Hel—she was still looking at his.

She was in such deep, unrelenting shit.

Neither made a move to go. He carefully ran a thumb over her exposed palm. Then again. And again. Kartix noticed as she leaned into that touch. Perhaps it could be from the chill, or the water soaking through both of their clothes in the cold air. They could feel each other's breath against their skin. When did breathing become so difficult?

"Are you hurt?" His voice was rough, raw.

"No. Are you?" *How had she not asked that sooner? How had his lips become a priority before their safety?*

A chilled autumn breeze tore down the alley, whipping strands of silky hair across Sorcha's vision. Shivering, and not just from the temperature, she sharply inhaled. "We should go." Stern. She had to sound stern in order to avoid any suspicion from Kartix that she was losing control around him. Loosening her grip on her inner defenses.

Not that she ever had any defenses up for him to begin with.

Heat pooled in her core. "Let's go," she said, her voice barely louder than a whisper. Slowly, Sorcha slid sideways across the jagged stone. *About ten more paces till the street. About ten seconds by my calculations, several entryway points, two ways of exit—*

Every survival instinct dissolved the moment Kartix grabbed her forearm.

"Who were you with last night?" Kartix's voice was low and threaded with violence.

Sorcha whipped her head around to face him. "How can you tell I was with someone last night?"

Kartix laughed, a thing of dark, cruel beauty. "I can smell him all over you. I didn't know that you had an active sex life."

His dark eyes flashed, rain sending droplets of water down his tan face.

Sorcha gritted her teeth. Of course, Kartix could still smell Adonis. With his heightened Fae sense of smell, Kartix could probably smell the fact that she hadn't bothered to bathe after he had left her sweaty and breathless the night before. After Adonis had left, all Sorcha did was curl up on her bed and feel nothing. "Who I fuck is none of your business."

"When you're one of the leaders of the rebellion, you need to be careful about who you let into your bed. Haven't you realized that, Sorcha?"

She felt nauseous. She swayed on her feet. Had she really been that desperate, that sad, that she'd needed someone, anyone, to share her bed? She was a Godsdamned idiot and a fool. She needed to hit something. She needed to hurt herself. How could she be this stupid? How could she—

"Sorcha. Look at me." Kartix's voice was firm and commanding, the voice of a general assessing his soldiers before battle. "It was not your fault. Adonis is an asshole. And he will pay for this. Somehow, someday, he will pay." And with that, Kartix crushed her against his chest.

Sorcha didn't move, couldn't move, could barely bring her arms around his frame. "We should go." She was trembling, and not from the cold.

"Stay."

This time, Sorcha allowed herself to laugh. "Why?"

Kartix growled, "Stop avoiding this. Stop avoiding me."

She glanced away from the male, barely able to contain her anxiety. She didn't want to think about whether her anxiety stemmed from the question of if they would live through the rest of the night, or from this conversation, one she had been trying to avoid ever since she'd laid eyes on him.

Right before she opened her mouth to respond, a strong voice sounded from behind them. "There you are."

20

Reid and a small, young girl stood at the opening to the alleyway, whole and unharmed, despite the tension etched onto their faces. The girl took a step forward, grim as ever. "We need to move."

Kartix arched a thick brow. "Who are you?"

Sorcha spoke softly, almost as if in disbelief. "Lyra is one of the girls we train at the Assassins Guild. A few nights ago, I killed her master and brought her to live with us. She must have followed me here after I checked in on the Guild earlier tonight."

Reid nodded. "After Kartix managed to sneak out of Senna's bed, I followed him through to the slums. When Razan began to hunt the slums with his dark magik, I sought shelter in an alleyway."

Lyra's eyes flashed as she said, "Sorcha, I heard the alarm from the Compound. I wanted to help you, to get revenge for what Devonshire did to me."

The child bit her lip, then continued. "I hid from the dark magik in the same alley as Reid. I immediately recognized him as the prince's half-brother from my time spent in the Compound."

So that is who this other male before Sorcha was. Kartix's half-brother. Reid.

The child shrugged. "I told him I was trying to find you. To help you, because I thought you might be in danger."

Reid gritted his teeth together before saying, "I knew I had to find you, Kartix, but I couldn't let a little girl go alone out into the slums late at night. She took priority."

Despite Kartix's shock, the prince nodded. "Yes. Getting Lyra back to the Assassins Guild is a priority."

Lyra shook her head, her dark hair matted in the rain. "Not before Kartix explains why he was with Senna last night. Or did you forget to leave out that bit of information, Reid?"

It was as if the whole world froze.

No one and nothing moved for at least a minute.

Sorcha made it out of the alleyway, no longer pressed up against Kartix. She stumbled, putting distance between her and the male. Kartix also bowed out of the alley, coming to stand in front of her.

Sorcha felt sick.

Why were you in Senna's bed last night?

It's a long story.

Kartix desperately sent the thought through the curse bond, but Sorcha had locked him out of her mind, black walls coming down once more.

He took a stumbling step forward, at a loss for words. "Sorcha." Her name—a plea, a question, and a call all at once.

She slowly dragged her eyes up to meet Kartix's. He couldn't tell her. He couldn't face Sorcha knowing about what Senna had done to him, what she did regularly. Kartix's world was swallowing him whole.

How could he tell her? How could he face the shame, the look on her face when she realized how broken he truly was? No one wanted to deal with someone as fucked up as he was.

Cold wind suddenly tore down the main road the four of them were standing on. Lyra shivered and Reid gave her his coat. Sorcha and Kartix continued to lock eyes, but abruptly stopped when a loud howl pierced the air. All the hair on the back of Sorcha's arms stood up. A howl echoed again, but this time joined with a chorus of voices.

The black magik was still seeking Sorcha, somewhere else in Ocyla. It was hunting for her. Despite its retreat from this part of the city, Razan had left his mark on the slums. Fires now burned, lit by the black magik. It was dangerous, too dangerous to stay where they currently were, standing by a broken-down storefront. They were exposed, out in the middle of the road. Sorcha, for once, didn't care about escaping the fires which were racing closer with every heartbeat. Sorcha's entire world was in flames. Burning, burning, burning into nothing. It took a minute before she was able to breathe. Her hollow eyes met Kartix's.

Even from yards away, Kartix knew, in the deepest part of him, that he was so fucked.

It was as if even the fires grew silent as Sorcha, tears blazing down her cheeks, whispered, "You shared Senna's bed?" Tears rolled freely now down her dirt-stained cheeks. The only sound in the alleyway was her uneven breathing.

Kartix thought of last night, how Senna had ridden him into oblivion while tears streamed down the prince's face.

Kartix hung his head. He was too tired to explain his assault to the one woman he never wanted to know about it in the first place. So, the prince didn't explain. He didn't explain the rape.

Kartix had gone very far away from himself. He didn't know if he would ever come back.

"I thought we were *friends*." Sorcha's voice broke on the last word.

Reid slowly stepped in front of Lyra, shielding her with his body. Sorcha's focus blurred, crimson tinged her vision, before she turned back to Kartix. "Why Senna?" she breathed.

Reid gently touched Sorcha's arm, spoke to her as if any extra movement might spook her like she was some type of wild animal. "We have to move. The longer we stay, the quicker they find us." Even now she scouted the horizon, scanning over the ramshackle, clumped-together buildings of the slums. "Razan knows that you have magik."

Sorcha inhaled sharply. The scent of ash alerted her heightened Triumvirate senses to danger—immediate danger. Yet she kept silent.

Reid's swallow was audible, despite the fire raging only a few hundred yards away. "We have to *move*."

Sorcha saw nothing else, nothing but Kartix, the male she had known for mere weeks.

Or had she known him longer?

Memories flashed faster and faster across her mind's eye. When Sorcha had found Kartix in her room, sobbing. When she had formed the curse bond, glowing with light and trust and wholeness between them. When they had met each other's eyes at the banquet, and she had first felt the weight of his stare. When they had all gone back to her rooms after the fighting pits and formed a pact. When Sorcha—

How many weeks had it been since they'd first met? How many nights had Kartix spent talking with Facim, Marie, and Sorcha, only to stumble back to Senna's bed and whisper their secrets in her ear?

As she—

As *they*—

She jerked her arm out of Reid's grasp, then took one lurching step toward Kartix, whose complexion had now paled to the color of parchment. Despite the tears, she managed to bite out, "I don't care who you *fuck.*"

Liar, she thought to herself.

Swallowing back another scream, Sorcha could barely recognize her own voice as she looked at the male. "I care that I told you who I was. Spent *weeks* slowly beginning to trust you. Now I realize I was a *fool* for wanting to build something together." Her voice sounded so small, so far away. She motioned toward Lyra, who was glancing toward the fire mere blocks away. "We were all supposed to stay *together*. Because this was all we had. This rebellion, the Assassins Guild. We only have *each other*." She shook her head, hair matted. She swung her gaze back to Kartix. "But then you shared Senna's bed." Her rain-soaked bare arm flung out in the direction of the main island, to the Compound. "*I thought I knew you*. But you—you proved you're just like everyone else."

How could she have been so foolish? How could she have been so empty-minded? A sob escaped from her throat. She felt like a child as Lyra came up to her side, slid a thin arm gently around her waist, offering comfort, and restraint, if necessary. Sorcha groaned. "You don't have to worry about me."

A pause, and Reid slowly turned toward Kartix, slack-jawed. "What exactly did you tell that slut Senna?"

Reid's words seemed to shock Kartix out of a haze. "You don't have to call her that."

A snarl rippled through the alleyway, which was now beginning to swelter, the fire mere blocks away. "Her reputation for taking advantage of younger men makes me more than a bit anxious for you. Calling Senna a slut would be the biggest compliment a male could give a bitch like that."

A small whimper echoed behind them. Reid and Lyra whipped their heads away from Kartix, having thrown his attention at the now-trembling Sorcha. She looked like a ghost.

Reid stalked up to Kartix, whose eyes were only on Sorcha, could only look at Sorcha.

How could he tell her the truth? That most nights, Senna chained him to her bed and had her way with him?

Reid grabbed his brother by his shirt collar and hauled him closer until the two were inches away from each other. "This is your fault. Sorcha is the final Triumvirate. I've guessed as much, from what Lyra has told me. If she dies, there is no way to take down Razan. Her blood will be on your hands." He growled in Kartix's ear. Thrusting Kartix backward, Reid turned from him and looked to Lyra where she hovered near Sorcha's side. "Let's go."

"Where are we going?" The child's eyes gleamed with fear in the firelight, which was now two blocks away.

Reid grimaced. "Back to the Assassins Guild." He turned to Kartix and Sorcha. "Both of you come *now.*"

Sorcha slowly shook her head. "No," she breathed. She backed up in the direction of the north road, her worn leather boots kicking up hard-packed dirt. "No, I won't be coming with you."

Fire thrashed its way onto the roof of the buildings, now one block away. Reid roared over the sound of the flames. "You have to! Razan has a warrant out for your arrest. You fleeing will only make you appear guiltier than he already sees you. It's best to turn yourself in, and hope he has mercy."

Without taking her eyes off Kartix, Sorcha gently whispered, "Reid, take care of Lyra." And before anyone could protest, the Third Triumvirate turned on her heel and sprinted northward.

Her absence seemed to spark a light in Kartix as his fingers unfurled, reaching out into nothingness. He took a lurching step forward as if he could catch her.

It was at that moment that the building across the street exploded.

21

She ran as far outside the city walls as she could.

Miles of hills and farms and fields blurred before her as she let the pain take over, until she wasn't sure she was wholly herself anymore. Then again, was she ever herself?

Who—who the fuck was she?

So, Sorcha ran until every molecule of her being begged her to stop, until pain was the only familiar comfort left. Pain had been her earliest companion anyway, and hate had coiled itself around her heart until she had come to like the dark. Until she liked being alone. Liked being on dirt paths in the middle of nowhere. Liked that her only friends now were the trees and the moon and the little birds that flitted between forest branches.

Humans and Fae were always a disappointment.

Too many memories still flooded her mind, seethed through her blood, her very soul, refusing to free themselves from her conscience.

So, she pushed her body harder, faster, as the night leaked out across the eastern sky and stars blinked into being. Fireflies illuminated the fields of wheat as she pounded the hard-packed dirt beneath her feet. The north road ran on for miles, eventually passing through Dorm, the third most influential city on the continent. She could spend a few days there, pay for a cheap room. To live in a foreign city would be a much-needed freedom. But the Triumvirate didn't truly get any days off, not when there was a world still in flames.

Sweat poured down her body and she found a stream to quickly rinse herself off. The icy water licked away any ache manifesting in her bones, her body. Not that comfort was Sorcha's motivation. Rather she needed to wash off the scent of her sweat, a beacon for wild animals and whoever else might be around, on her trail.

Paranoia was just a state of being at this point.

The current tangled her hair. Burning. She was still on fire. Could feel Kartix's words skittering over her skin. A shiver tore up her spine, and not because of the stream.

She couldn't decide if it was because of the mileage or what she was running from.

No.

Who she was running from.

Last night, when she'd bedded Adonis, it had been a mistake. Sorcha still couldn't get the look in his eyes out of her mind. Couldn't forget the cruel, twisted look on his face as the truth came out about her magik. To no one and nothing in particular she breathed, "I'm pathetic."

So, she stayed in the waist-high forest stream and sank down to her chin, tilting her head back, glassy eyes barely taking in the night sky, yet focusing more and more as time ticked forward and the water provided more and more of a grounding sensation. It made her remember that, in spite of the numbness, her body was not immune to weakness.

She stayed in the forest stream until she couldn't feel her toes, until she forgot the hounding voice of Kartix. Until she forgot the tears that had run down Lyra's face while she watched them fight. This was all her fault.

She should go to Hel.

She would have gone to the fighting pits. She would have drunk herself into a haze.

Why was she so stupid?

She played with the current, cupping the dark water in her palms as the stars rippled across its surface.

She shouldn't be alone out here. There could be people tracking her movements. Now her cover was blown, and right that very moment, the king had all his guards searching every crevice of Ocyla for her. What they would do to her, she had no idea.

Well. They all knew.

Every Godsdamned last one of them knew about her.

She closed her eyes as one single tear leaked out of her eye.

Fuck.

She needed sleep.

Climbing out of the shallow stream, she blinked at her surroundings. Out here in the country, one couldn't even see the light pollution from the city. She sent out a net of her magik. It laid invisible strands up to ten miles around her. It would act as a silent map, tracking anyone who could track her, sending alerts if anyone who crossed its path had, somewhere in their mind, the intention of hurting her.

It would be easier to walk away from it all. She had enough money to escape to the other continent. To break free of the regime. Forget all about her broken, fractured family. Try to start over. Probably change her name.

But then she remembered the girls at the Assassins Guild. She remembered their faces and names and dreams. She had to go back and face Razan. Or else who would take care of the girls? She couldn't leave Facim and Marie to take care of them alone.

And so, she walked back to Ocyla.

Her stomach growled and demanded food, snarling like some type of wild beast. When was the last time she ate? Not that she was hungry. All bodily

sensations had numbed by then. It was merely the
small logistical part of her brain which, in absolute
survival mode, whispered to her to take care of
herself.

Practically hobbling, legs screaming in pain
and exhaustion, Sorcha approached the massive
outer-city wall well past midnight. When the King's
Guards spotted her, covered head to toe in mud, a
siren suddenly wailed.

Black and red soldiers filed out of the gate,
rushed with spears aimed toward her heart. The men
swarmed her in a circle of death. Black helmets
gleamed in the torchlight.

Sorcha was led, hands and feet shackled, into
the lair of her enemy.

She wasn't afraid of the men.

She wasn't afraid of the torches and chains racing toward her, drawing closer with each breath. She was only afraid for her friends.

Well, two of them.

Were Reid and Lyra alright?

As the shouting grew closer, Sorcha slowly raised her hands above her head. Her body barked with pain. She'd always known that at some point in her miserable life, she would eventually tangle with law enforcement.

But not like this.

The king hadn't sent just a few guards to track her down. He had sent *fifty*. If anything, it was a back-handed compliment. A few soldiers would be an insult to her strength. Sending a whole fucking platoon meant that someone had really pissed Razan off. She guessed that someone was her.

By now, more than Razan and Senna knew about her magik. The only reassuring thought she had was that they did not know precisely how much power she had. It could be a trickle. A mere shadow of power.

To Razan's eye, in a dictator's view, that magik belonged to the state. To him.

He might try to drain her power. He might try to torture her for information. No. No, Sorcha couldn't think like this. It wasn't helpful.

It was a blur of chains as the men swarmed her. She kept her breath even and did not fight. She knew it would be no use. The chains, the horrible, evil shackles encircling her wrists, were as precious as her magik itself—they were made with Mahoun. This precious and rare material had been lusted after for centuries. Only a few prestigious kingdoms had access to Mahoun. Quarries of the deadly rocks were rare. Only a few selected Fae could use it. In Ocyla, it was used in the prisons to keep dangerous prisoners from using their magik. The clamped cuffs were already rubbing Sorcha's wrists bare.

As soon as the shackles were secured around her wrists and ankles, Sorcha felt the cold of the Mahoun sink far down into her blood, trickling her heart to a near stop.

The only thing keeping you alive is your magik.

The voice was familiar, and yet she did not care who might be speaking to her telepathically. Her magik was draining all too quickly. She couldn't feel her legs, and her arms felt like lead.

After half-stumbling across the drawbridge, Sorcha was hauled through the massive oak doors leading to the courtyard. No one was awake. It was the middle of the night, which meant none of the other servants were awake to witness... whatever was about to happen.

At least she had that short bit of luck on her side. The fewer people around to see her downfall, the better.

It stank like burning flesh in the courtyard.

She narrowly avoided falling on her ass when the guard shoved her onto the cobblestone ground. Sorcha spit in the guard's face.

Razan's cold voice boomed across the courtyard. "The deal was to bring her to me unharmed."

The male sneered at his commander. "She didn't go easily."

Razan's head tilted, a lion assessing its prey, the move un-human. Un-Fae.

What is he?

But every single thought and fiber of her being short-circuited when she saw Lyra alone and shivering, strapped to a platform. A whip was brought out.

Sorcha nearly blacked out with rage.

"I'll do anything you want. Just leave her out of it!" Sorcha thrashed and screeched like a wild, feral thing. Nothing about her was human, was logical. All thoughts and feelings and sensations were blinded by the horror. All she could see was Lyra. *How did Razan catch us?*

Sorcha's screaming bounced against the small courtyard stone walls and left ears, both Fae and human, pierced and ringing.

Twisting in the arms of her assailants, Sorcha flung her arm to where Reid, Kartix, and the rest of the King's Council stood.

Behind his father, Kartix had crossed his muscular arms. A golden crown gleamed on the top of his head. His face was carefully neutral, but his eyes were aflame with rage.

"Please!" she screamed and begged through her sobs, trying to get the guards, anyone, to look her in the eye. Lyra's whimper was the only response she got.

"She's a *child."*

"This is what you get for keeping secrets, my dear." Razan smiled menacingly.

"Why? Why do this when you already have me?"

When no one answered her, when silence was the only damned thing in the courtyard, anger began to heat within Sorcha's core. She could not use magik, did not even have her powers. So, she had to fight the old-fashioned way.

It took three guards to hold her down and a fourth one to replace the man she took out with a right hook to his face. But the men were trained. Razan had told them what to expect. He had dealt with her type before.

The hunted. The kind of beings who never go down without a fight.

When binding her hands didn't work, Sorcha's already-bruised face was met with a heavily armored fist. Blood spewed from her mouth, and to his continued horror, Kartix could only stare as her body went limp in the guard's arms.

Was that one of her teeth on the ground?

Dumping her body on the courtyard cobblestones, Mathias, the head guard, bowed to Razan. The massive warrior slowly then backed away, taking up his post at one of the doorways. He shot Kartix a shit-eating grin, smiling wide so that he could see blood in his teeth.

Oh Gods. Sorcha's blood.

It seemed that Mathias remembered Sorcha from all those years ago when she kicked his ass in the clearing, and he wanted revenge.

Kartix turned toward Razan, who was unnaturally still. "Let this be done. I wish to retire, and I am growing bored of this entertainment."

Traitor, traitor, traitor. Kartix had to blend in, had to save what was left of Sorcha and Lyra. Razan could not suspect Kartix had a hand in any of this, so he had to lie, to get away in order to go find a medic.

Razan nodded, agreeing with his son for once. Kartix only hoped he did not appear suspicious, wanting to exit this situation quickly.

He turned and walked away slowly from the king's inner circle, ducking into a doorway to the servants' quarters. Once out of view of those in the courtyard, Kartix broke out into a run. He only hoped he could save the rest of the rebellion, even if its leader might think he was fucking the enemy.

~

Back in the courtyard, Sorcha was coming out of unconsciousness just in time to hear Razan. "You will join my Council."

Her blood went cold.

No.

No.

"You will assist with the capturing and torture of those who hide their gifts from the state." Razan's eyes flashed to hers. "Or we could always hang you."

Sorcha pretended to be afraid, letting her eyes go wide as she met his gaze. She knew her death was an option on the table. It always had been.

"I'll join your council on one condition: Lyra comes with me."

Razan sneered, "I don't really care what you do with the slave girl."

Sorcha's nostrils flared. "You don't care about anything. Not even your own son."

The king's eyes went black with rage. Sorcha didn't know if she was hallucinating from the pain or what, but she could have sworn Razan's frame flickered if only for a moment, revealing a creature of darkness and thorns. She blinked and it was gone. Sorcha shook her head.

His eyes narrowed. "Take her away and throw her in her new quarters. Your first task is tomorrow. You better be ready, witch."

With that, Razan turned, his dark robes swirling around him, and stalked back into the safety of the Compound.

Sorcha could barely breathe. Everything hurt. As the guards hauled her and Lyra, who was barely conscious, away, Sorcha felt dread fill her gut.

She was *so* fucked.

23

She no longer lived in the servants' quarters, but rather in a plush room on the tenth floor. Sorcha took her time dressing in the cool gray light of dawn. When she was done, guards silently escorted Sorcha through the vast hallways, up to the towering center of Razan's lair.

Her fitted golden dress whispered across the pristine, waxed floor. Her hair was brushed and pulled back from her face by two combs, the rest left to fall down her back.

She was unused to such opulence, even uncomfortable in the itchy, showy clothes, the price of which could probably feed the women inside the Assassins Guild for weeks.

Sorcha had wanted to look strong, had wanted to remind everyone she crossed paths with that, although the last time the King's Council had seen her in the courtyard the night before, she'd been a bloody, rotten mess, she was still better than the lot of them. She would give them something to fear. Remind them that she *was* fear.

Last night, Sorcha had been taken up past the tenth floor of the Compound and into the High Court. She'd been thrown in a room so massive it took up the space of two houses. She didn't care for the opulence. As soon as the guards unshackled her, Sorcha's magik had risen up to the surface again. She could tell her powers were aching to be used from all that time spent suppressed within her system.

The next morning, she took a moment to look around her new chambers. She found a sitting room, a massive bathroom, and two bedrooms, in one of which she found the dress. It was golden and held tight against her frame, like the feminine version of armor, except sexier.

As she dressed before dawn, the first rays of the morning hit her dress. She supposed she looked just like a fallen star. Razan had laid out other options for her to wear, but Sorcha had opted for this dress. Only she herself really understood why she had chosen this dress. Women were not allowed to don the same armor as men, so this dress was a subtle version of it. Light refracted in all angles, the fabric moving like molten lava across her frame.

Another type of espionage and warfare: distracting men with her "enhanced" features.

As the clamor of the guards' armor filled the winding staircase Sorcha was now climbing, Sorcha rubbed her chafed wrists. No chains this time—she was a free woman. No longer subservient, no longer deemed only good enough to scrub the floors as Senna leered over her shoulder. No longer a lowly member of Ocylan society.

The marble pillars of the tenth floor stretched high. Her gut twisted. The taste of bile filled her mouth. The amount of money, the sheer volume of resources that went to waste inside this castle, was sickening. Just one pillar had to be worth more than the slums alone. And the cost of hauling it here? Massive.

Probably on the backs of slaves, no less.

It said a lot about Ocyla—who was in charge, what they cared about, and that having a beautiful central point of power, decorating it like it was supposed to be some sort of temple, equated to a strong country. They were more interested in their own self-preservation than actually *helping* their citizens. It was all a facade.

As the guards, only three this time, led her down yet another corridor, Sorcha caught a glimpse of a gold-encrusted bust of an old king.

How many people could just one of those feed if she were to sell it on the black market? If it was her choice, there would be no castle. Why spare expenses on stained-glass windows when there are people dying of starvation in the streets? If she were king, one of her goals would be to make sure that no matter who came into her city, they would be met with a warm bed and kind words.

Why the fuck was that so hard to come by in this day and age? Was she so childish for having hope? Wasn't hope the only thing they had?

Dress caught-aflame in the early morning light, guards in front of her pushed open massive black doors. Her name was announced. Sorcha sucked in a deep breath, her chin high, as she strode into the King's Council room.

It took every bit of strength Kartix had not to look at her, gasp at what he saw. The Sorcha that entered was not the same Sorcha he had seen the night before. She'd been a screaming mess of a woman last night, though justifiably so. Whoever was escorted down the aisle to the middle of the room was a different being altogether. And that *dress*. It looked like golden rays bursting into the dark room, chasing away the shadows.

She was a thousand times more brilliant than the sun.

He thought Sorcha looked like a warrior. She walked into the council room, dressed in that magnificent gown, hair swept back from her face, jaw set and eyes narrowed. She looked like she was ready to ride into battle, to bring down the monarchy, to restore justice to the dark, dangerous world.

A slow smile crept over Kartix's handsome features. He knew why Sorcha had donned that dress.

Sorcha had wanted to look ready for battle. He knew her secret motives all too well at this point.

He glanced across the room to where Adonis stood at attention to the right of Razan. His golden, polished armor matched his curls. Adonis's full lips parted in a sly grin. Kartix gritted his teeth. The bastard was *proud* that he had betrayed Sorcha. As Razan strode into the room and quickly gave Adonis a pat on the back, it was clear why he had done it—to gain favor with the king.

Kartix felt a muscle tense in his jaw as his father came around to face the large chamber. Razan perched on the edge of his chair, assessing the room with dark eyes. The King's Council chamber was a rectangular room with floor-to-ceiling windows looking toward the east. An oblong oak table surrounded by dozens of velvet-backed chairs took up the majority of the space. Seated at the table, with Razan taking a seat at the head, were the rest of the King's Council, gathered from all corners of the kingdom. They were made up of Fae of all heights, ages, colors, sizes, and shapes, and they were all staring at Sorcha as she strode into the room.

Kartix and Sorcha locked eyes briefly as she was escorted to the far end of the chamber, to the seat nearest Razan, but that was the only acknowledgement he got. Sorcha knew everyone was watching her every move, every breath, especially Kartix. She could feel him alert, taut with tension, through the curse bond. She could have sworn she felt something else, however, something gentle and warm, a hand gently brushing through her mind. Sorcha quickly pulled up her mental shields, blocking the curse bond for now.

She wouldn't allow herself to think of him right now, but as she strode to her seat, Sorcha swayed her hips a tad more than probably was necessary. She could have sworn she saw Kartix flinch as she passed.

Kartix wondered if she hated him. He knew Sorcha knew that he was sleeping with Senna. He knew his chances of helping with the rebellion were now down to zero, but he couldn't help but to watch her through lowered lashes. He couldn't help but glance over her figure. Couldn't help but to watch the ass that had tortured him since *day fucking one.*

Kartix shifted in his seat, adjusting his pants. He cursed himself. This was possibly the worst possible time to get turned on, and it wasn't like Sorcha was interested in him anymore. She probably hated his guts after finding out that he had shared Senna's bed.

As she sat down directly across from him, Kartix swallowed. The entire chamber was as quiet as a catacomb. The pop and snap of the logs burning in the fireplace was the only sound. Eyes of all shapes and colors lay their gaze upon Razan, now seated at the head of the table. Razan watched Sorcha with a predatory gaze. "Welcome, my dear." The king's smile was a thing of wickedness.

Sorcha felt a flash of fear radiate through the curse bond. Her eyes flickered to Kartix's. She swallowed at her own nervousness, knowing that he was worried for her.

Sorcha's concentration was broken... she had to steel herself to turn back to Razan and play nice.

She sat up straighter in her chair as she met Razan's stare. She bowed her head, keeping her face carefully neural. "It is an honor to serve you, my king. I am at your disposal."

Kartix felt like he was going to be sick.

His father's smile only widened as his eyes raked over the young woman. "Tell me about your magik. How long have you known that you're Fae?"

Sorcha continued, "I did not know I had magik until yesterday. Something triggered my powers and I erupted." She shook her head, auburn locks tumbling over her golden dress. "I did not understand it at the time. I was afraid." Sorcha's eyes looked up, defiance etched into every feature on her face. "I am loyal to my king."

Razan nodded. Satisfied enough.

Kartix was at a loss for words. Reid, who was leaning against the western wall, only snorted.

Kartix dropped his mental shields and sent a thought down the curse bond, desperate for Sorcha to understand that the situation between him and Senna was complicated.

Sorcha's mental shields were up. She still thought he had been the one to tell Razan of her magik.

A muscle tensed in Sorcha's jaw, the only sign of her annoyance. Kartix's own feelings of irritation flickered through the curse bond. Did she have any idea of the danger she was facing? Did Sorcha know about—

Razan leaned back in his seat. "Well, my dear, although your words are pretty, they mean nothing to me."

Sorcha's blood went ice cold.

Kartix knew before her what was about to happen.

The king tilted his head, flashing Sorcha a feral grin. "Actions speak louder than words." Razan stood. He seemed to swallow all the light in the room. "You have to prove your loyalty."

Sorcha knew she would regret her words as she said, "I will gladly prove myself."

Razan smiled, a thing of horror. "I'd like to see just how strong you are. Prove that I should keep you on as a Council member, and not kill you."

No. *No.*

Sorcha's nails dug into the wooden arms of her chair, but she didn't allow one flicker of fear to show as she slowly nodded. "Whatever you ask, I shall comply." Even as her entire world went up in flames, Sorcha didn't dare say no to Razan. She needed the information the King's Council could provide. She couldn't walk away.

Razan smiled as he waved to the battle arena, which was visible through the large bay windows. "The battle awaits, my dear."

25

The dress had been a bad idea. Within five minutes underneath the southern Ocyla sun, Sorcha was scorched to a crisp, her fair skin not used to this much sun.

As she stood in the battle arena, all signs of strength melted away as Sorcha beheld a pale girl, utterly human, chained to the raised dais in the middle of the battle arena.

Her blood ran cold.

What?

What?

From where he sat on a raised platform to the east of the arena, she could feel Razan assessing her, even at a distance. The nobles occupying the stadium, a rainbow of silks and jewels, reverberating wealth, called out for blood. Razan had declared this event a citywide holiday. Fae and humans alike had gotten the day off in order to attend this bloodbath. Distantly,

Sorcha's heightened Triumvirate senses could pick up individual phrases:

Kill the bitch!

We want blood!

No mercy!

The voices cascaded into a tsunami of wealth and privilege in her head as Sorcha gritted her teeth. She didn't hear the crowd, she didn't even hear Razan's words telling her to begin fighting, all she felt was Kartix's terror through the curse bond. She had accidentally dropped her mental shields. She shut that out too.

She had to kill the girl in order to live herself. She dropped the sword, heavy on the ground. The crowd booed. Sweat washed down Sorcha's temples in an even rhythm. She knew what she had to do. She knew what was going to happen. She knew what the consequences would be. Knew that this human girl would haunt her memory for the rest of her fucking life. She knew she would be a murderer, innocent blood on her hands.

A flicker of comforting warmth echoed through the curse bond. Sorcha had not realized she had lowered her mental shields. She'd practically been shouting her thoughts down the bond.

Do as you're told. Kartix knew he sounded like a general giving orders to his soldiers, but all Sorcha had to do was survive and then they could deal with the repercussions of this later.

I can't. I can't do it.

You have to. There is no other option.

Sorcha swallowed. She picked up the sword, but never once allowed fear to ensnare her heart. He was right, and they both knew it.

Innocent blood has to be shed.

Kartix gritted his teeth. He could only hope Sorcha got on with it soon. Hesitation showed dissent.

Sorcha strode up to the girl, who was chained to the middle of the arena. The crowd fell silent, leaned forward in their seats. She threw an invisible, soundproof shield over them, then went into the girl's mind.

As Sorcha's magik took away the girl's pain, the girl nodded, tears running down her face. The innocent human knew what Sorcha needed to do.

Sorcha whispered, barely moving her mouth so no one would see her, "I am so sorry." She briefly allowed her breath to turn ragged, that rage centering her as tears threatened to spill over. The girl gently nodded at Sorcha as her magik slowly, slowly, slowly made its way through her blood. The girl knew Sorcha did not want this, that her magik was taking away the pain. There would be no suffering, never for innocent victims. In the last few moments, a look of relief passed over the human girl's features, as if she was happy to be free of Razan's reign.

Then Sorcha swung her sword.

As she severed the girl's head, she watched the life drain from her eyes. She did not give her a spectacular death, the one they all wanted. That was the kind of murder that Razan fed off of. She made it a clean cut, the blood spilling out crimson on the sand. The crowd roared in triumph, even though they had expected more of a bloody death.

Sorcha slowly turned around, then threw her sword directly at the king's platform.

26

Her sword lodged itself directly in front of Razan's feet, impaled in the wooden platform. The king just smiled, then walked away, back to the Compound.

Sorcha gritted her teeth. She hadn't even fazed Razan. He was too used to scum like her.

Reid and Kartix dragged their feet as they too returned to the Compound. Being a part of Razan's inner circle often meant they moved when he moved. Kartix threw a glance toward Sorcha, where she stood, panting, in front of the girl's corpse. She was staring, staring, staring, at the slaughtered girl. From where she stood, numb in the middle of the arena, Sorcha slowly turned to lock eyes with Kartix.

Your first council meeting is within the hour. Go to your rooms and bathe beforehand. You look like you've been dragged through Hel. As Kartix walked beside Razan, his spine straight and head up, he sent the message through the curse bond. Sorcha had left her mental shields down, too tired to care.

The nobles who had filled the stadium filed out in an orderly manner, satisfied with the entertainment for their bloodlust. Sorcha was the last one left in the arena. The golden sun reflected off her dress, sending rays of light scattering across the body at her feet.

When everyone finally went inside, when she was the only being left, Sorcha turned her magik on the girl. Silver flames burned higher and higher as her magik burned the corpse. It was the only way she could think of to honor the girl's death. When the body had finished burning, the ashes sailed away on a gentle breeze. Sorcha went somewhere very far away from herself.

She didn't particularly care if she ever found her way back.

~

Bathed, brushed, and groomed, Sorcha entered the King's Council chamber an hour later wearing black leggings, leather knee-high boots, and a white shirt. She had discarded the gold dress the moment she had entered her rooms. To Hel with dresses—she was much more comfortable in pants.

As she strode back into the rectangular room, now warm thanks to the massive fire burning in the hearth, Sorcha couldn't help but notice as Kartix's eyes brazenly roamed her legs, now fully on display in the tight leggings. Kartix shifted in his seat as he adjusted himself. He was seated next to his father, who was currently occupying the head of the table.

Razan turned his eyes to Sorcha as she took her seat amongst the other members. "You did well, my dear." His smile was a dark, twisted thing. "You fought for your spot on this council. You proved your magik has enough worth to the state. Welcome." He gestured toward the other members of the council, who only greeted her with stone-faced expressions. "We begin today by examining the methods of withdrawing magik. But first, the reports." Razan turned toward a Fae woman, who cleared her throat and then stood. Her voice rolled off her tongue thick with accent.

"As we all know, the regime has been successful in tracking down most magik. With Mahoun in our possession, controlling those who still harbor their gifts from the state is more possible than ever."

Sorcha remembered Mahoun, the precious metal that drained one of their powers. She shivered where she sat. Sorcha could still feel the biting cold of the metal as the guards had dragged her into the courtyard the night prior. She rubbed her chafed wrists, where Mahoun had met flesh, and grimaced. If the council was using Mahoun to weaken the Fae and then drain their powers, where was that magik going? Sorcha's ears pricked up as the Fae woman continued.

"Now, the reservoirs of magik are enough to keep both humans and Fae in line. However, the magik has been...reactive the past few days." The woman swallowed, the only sign of her nervousness as she continued speaking to the council. "The magik seems to be calling out for its owners. There have been disruptions from its cell. It's getting harder to guard the trove."

Razan nodded, his calm exterior never cracking.

Razan has an entire trove of magik hidden somewhere? Sorcha practically shouted through the curse bond.

Kartix arched a thick brow. *This is the first I'm hearing of it.*

Sorcha clenched her hands into fists under the table. Even if Kartix had shared Senna's bed, that didn't mean he gave her any information, didn't mean that Kartix had actually betrayed the rebellion.

Sorcha allowed herself to pull on their curse bond, diving deep into Kartix's head for answers about Senna.

When Sorcha entered the prince's mind, sitting across the table from him, she encountered a block in his brain. Well, a block wasn't really the correct term. Sorcha narrowed her eyes from across the table. She could feel a horrible cold creeping down their curse bond. The closer she got to the memory of Senna in Kartix's mind, the colder she became. A horrible chill swept through her and she could have sworn memories of blood and chains came from those memories Kartix had with Senna.

Sorcha's eyes flitted back to the prince. She didn't want to continue diving into his mind any further.

Sorcha had decided that Kartix hadn't given away her secret to Razan, that it had been Adonis to do so.

Kartix noticed Sorcha's distant expression across the table. The prince coughed, Sorcha's eyes flickering back to him, and the present moment.

The Fae woman continued. "We need to send reinforcements tomorrow to the mountain in order to surround the trove of magik with barrier spells. If someone were to break in, to steal even the slightest sliver of that magik, it could be world-ending."

A mountain? Is that where the trove of stolen magik is?

Without looking at her, Kartix responded, *Looks like we have a quest.*

The curse bond flickered with annoyance.

So, we have to somehow locate this mountain by tomorrow, break in, and hopefully restore me to my full power?

Kartix's deep voice rumbled through the curse bond. *Scared?*

Sorcha snickered, the barest smile breaking out across her face. It was quickly replaced by neutrality the moment Razan's eyes locked on hers. "Do you have anything to add, Sorcha?"

Internally groaning, Sorcha plastered a smile onto her face. "I just can't help to think, what if we gave all the power to you? Surely someone of your stature can handle the massive amount of magik."

Why haven't you taken all that power for yourself yet? What are you waiting for?

Razan's face was a mask of cruelty as he said, "We are waiting for the Triumvirates, they have the most magik of all. If I was to try to re-open the portal to Hel, the Triumvirates would try to stop me, and we can't have that." The king turned back toward the other council member, who continued on with her report, but Sorcha wasn't listening. She didn't move. She was chained to the spot.

As her eyes met Kartix's she sent a thought through the curse bond.

We go tonight. To the mountain.

The slightest inclination of his head was all she got in recognition.

Tonight.

Hours later, Sorcha finally made it back to her rooms. The day had been treacherously long. After her slaying of that innocent girl, then the first King's Council meeting, there had been a great banquet that night, which both she and Kartix had to attend. After the council meeting had adjourned, Sorcha had painted and primed herself. This was the first social event in which Sorcha would be presented as a member of the King's Council. She needed to look her best, her strongest.

The banquet had been lively and ruinous. Reid and Kartix had been there, dressed and dripping in their finery. Sorcha's eyes flitted briefly over Kartix's fit frame. He was all muscles and sleek angles. She swallowed as his eyes met hers from across the hall. She looked away.

None of the group of rebels interacted with each other that night. Marie and Facim did not let on in the presence of Razan that they were Sorcha's friends. It was too risky, Sorcha had decided. Caring about people was just a liability. Something for someone to use against you.

After the twelve-course meal, the banquet shifted dramatically. Opium began to perfume the air at the late hour. Sorcha quickly made sure to drag herself away from the thick clouds before it hit her. Kartix and Reid had spent the entire day at Razan's side, so they faked yawns and then retreated to their rooms, claiming exhaustion from a long day. It was a good excuse to exit the banquet early, giving them enough time to plan the journey to the trove.

Now back in her new rooms as well, Sorcha discarded her dress and jewels as she walked. Reid stood behind Kartix, leaning against the silk foyer wall, a dark expression gracing the handsome planes of his face. Kartix's own expression was of equal lethal quiet.

Facim and Marie burst through the heavy oak doors then, disrupting the energy in the room with their brazen entry. "We got your message. What is so urgent?" The two women took in the two males in the room.

Sorcha waved her hand over her friends. "Reid, let me introduce you to Facim and Marie. We three run the Assassins Guild. They know that I'm the third Triumvirate, and, like your brother here, have sworn their loyalty to me through a curse bond. They are my best friends. You will treat them with respect," Sorcha said.

All the Fae nodded. The introductions were short and to the point, then all eyes turned on the Triumvirate.

Kartix's voice was deep when he asked, "Do you want to begin, or shall I?"

Sorcha swallowed. "I can do it. But everyone might want to take a seat first."

~

"A mountain? All the stolen magik of Ocyla is stored in a Godsdamned mountain?" Marie huffed a laugh. "Of course it wouldn't be easy. How do we even find the damn thing?"

The group was now lounging in front of a raging fire, spread out across plush rugs and cushions.

It had taken mere minutes to explain what Kartix and Sorcha had learned in the King's Council meeting earlier that day.

Facim turned to Sorcha, her dark eyes flashing in the firelight. "Good thing we have a direct tie to the trove of magik."

Everyone looked at Sorcha.

Facim continued. "Do you think you can use your magik to find the mountain? Like calls to like, after all."

Sorcha went pale as a sheet, but she nodded. "It makes sense. I've found magik objects before by meditation. So, I suppose I can try to find the mountain."

"But there's a catch," Kartix said softly but not gently from where he sat near the fire.

Everyone held their breath.

He continued, "Tomorrow, Razan is sending more members from the council to reinforce the barrier spells around the trove. Tonight is the best chance we have to steal some—or all—of the magik back."

Facim raised her hand. "Question. If Sorcha's connection to the Gods is based on how much magik she has, does that mean once we steal the magik back, she will be able to connect to the Gods again?"

Sorcha nodded slowly. "That's the goal. But we have only tonight, while everyone is distracted with the banquet, to slip away. Before the barrier spells are reinforced."

Reid agreed, his dark eyes flashing. "We have to dismantle the spells surrounding the trove quickly before we set off any alarms." He turned to Sorcha. "You have to find the mountain. Now. We're running out of time."

Sorcha locked eyes with everyone in the room. She ran her hand through her hair. She hoped no one would notice her hands shaking. "Okay. Okay then." She closed her eyes, sitting up straight. "Here goes nothing," Sorcha whispered to no one in particular, and then she shut her eyes.

The third and final Triumvirate dove deep inside herself, into that core of magik curled around her very soul. She gently, lovingly said to it, *I need to find the trove.*

Her magik stretched as if awakening from a nap. It peered one eye up at her.

I need to find the mountain. Sorcha sent images and pictures of the mountain ranges surrounding Ocyla down into the pit of her magik, showing it where to look, to search. She guided her magik back and forth between mountains in her mind. Her magik wove between peaks, sliding its tendrils over the snow-capped peaks as if trying to feel, to sense for the trove.

All at once, she felt a pull, literally and mentally. She placed a hand on her heart, chest caving in slightly. Everyone in the room sat up straighter, their eyes glued to Sorcha as her eyes flickered back and forth under her lids. Her body shuddered as her magik recoiled inside her.

It had found the barrier spells of Razan's magik.

They were dark and wicked, and felt like something ancient. Cold and cruel magik awaited them at the mountain.

Sorcha's eyes flickered open. She gasped. "I know where it is."

~

Sorcha and Kartix had half an hour to dress in their fighting leathers before they were due to leave for the mountain. Black, skin tight suits fit their frames, allowing free movement. Kartix swallowed his desire as he beheld Sorcha in her gear. She was all curves and sharp angles.

When they came out of their rooms, Marie, Facim, and Reid all turned over their rapiers and daggers and swords to the pair. Dumping the weapons at Sorcha and Kartix's feet, the pair looked up in exasperation. "We have the third and possibly final Triumvirate. You really think we're going to require this much protection?" Kartix cocked his head to the side, his black hair sliding like silk across his tanned forehead.

Facim, Marie and Reid all said at once, "Yes."

Facim cleared her throat. "We can discuss details later. Right now, we have about twelve hours until Razan sends council members to reinforce the

barrier spells surrounding the trove of stolen magik."
She locked eyes with Marie and Kartix from where
she stood, leaning against the fireplace mantle. The
fire cast her in shades of red and gold, flickering over
her dark skin. "Go. Now."

Sorcha and Kartix armed themselves to the
teeth. Once finished, the pair turned toward each
other, nodded, then straightened their backs, chins
held high as they walked to the oak doors which
would surely lead them to their doom.

Kartix looked down at Sorcha, towering over
her with his large frame. "Ready?"

Sorcha grinned wide, her eyes sparkling. "I
was born ready."

Kartix took an involuntary breath in. He had
rarely seen her grin. As the pair made their way to the
tunnels, to the outskirts of Ocyla, Kartix allowed
himself to wonder what he could do to see that smile
again.

28

Wax slowly trickled down the candle, illuminating the cavernous space above their heads. From somewhere beyond the glow, a chilled breeze blew.

Silence.

Rotating in a circle, weapons drawn in each hand, Kartix and Sorcha silently surveyed the underground mountain hall.

Reid had been the one to suggest the two pair off and go together to free the stolen magik. "They're the only ones with magik." Motioning to his bandaged arm, which he had sprained training that day. "I'm in no shape to go on a quest right now." He shrugged.

Marie and Facim were also unavailable. "We have to guard the girls at the Assassins Guild. We don't have extra eyes on them at the moment, so we have to get back to headquarters, make sure they're prepared for tomorrow." The next evening, some of the girls would be introduced into the actual fighting pits of Ocyla. They had trained since they were children for their debut. Tomorrow was the first day Sorcha would let all of Ocyla know that the Assassins Guild was there—and out for blood. So that left Kartix and Sorcha.

And that was that.

Inside the underground mountain hall, Sorcha sent a thought through the curse bond.

I don't like this.

Kartix whipped his head around.

The fun is just beginning.

As they stood back-to-back, she could just make out his wolfish grin over her shoulder.

Brute.

As the two warriors continued their silent survey of the underground lake, Kartix drew in a breath. He pressed harder against Sorcha's leather-clad back. She tried not to enjoy the warmth as it soaked into her suit.

"You remember where the trove is?" Less of a question and more of a statement.

Swallowing, Sorcha nodded in the dark. Although he couldn't see, he instinctively knew her answer. Kartix, satisfied with their thorough sweep of the cavern, turned toward Sorcha, now facing the lake's edge. Though waves lapped gently against the pebbled shore, no sound came from beyond the flickering light of the lantern, which Sorcha softly set between the pair. Shadows and mist stretched out into inky oblivion. A chilled wind swept out from over the water, blowing Sorcha's auburn hair over her shoulder, almost like the lake had felt them and was curious about the pair.

She muttered, "I'm scared."

Onyx hair slid across his tanned forehead as Kartix silently surveyed the woman to his left. A soft drawl drew Sorcha's attention to the male beside her. "You know, for a woman who I've seen survive the most despicable scum of Ocyla, I'd expected my savior to have balls of steel."

Her eyes flitted up to meet the male's unflinching stare. My savior. He'd said *my* savior.

Shaking her head out of annoyance, Sorcha tried to kick out the unnatural thoughts which had started pouring into her head. "This is...different. This time, it actually matters." Face unmoving, she stared across the endless waters. Maybe it was to alleviate some pressure that was building inside of her, the stress of the situation mounting, as she said, "And besides, I don't have balls." A smile tugged at the corner of her mouth.

Kartix was exhausted.

Fuck.

It was harder to concentrate tonight. And with Sorcha's fighting leathers accentuating every dip and curve of her figure, he was having trouble keeping his thoughts in line.

He stared and stared at her.

How he would love to do so much more than to plot and plan and listen to her, the cadence of her voice. What would her lips feel like?

Sorcha whipped her head to his. "What was that?"

Kartix stumbled backward into the biting cold of the underground mountain wall as Sorcha stalked up to the male. She whispered quietly, "What was that, Kartix? I heard you just now. In my mind.

You were practically shouting through the curse bond."

With a sudden shock, Kartix realized he had let one of his thoughts slip into their shared stream of consciousness. His desire had grown so strong, too strong to keep contained, especially when he was exhausted from a long day.

Shit. She knew.

Growling, the male gathered himself to his full height and towered over Sorcha. Two could play at that game.

As terrified as she was from the sudden onslaught of her partner's innermost thoughts, some wicked part of her was fucking *ecstatic* that Kartix felt the same way about her.

Kartix cleared his voice, a blush staining his handsome face. "I'm having trouble keeping my mental shields up. I can't seem to shield my thoughts from you." He sagged against the wall, the truth weighing down his broad shoulders, sagging with…Sorcha didn't know what. Was it relief? At the truth finally coming off his shoulders?

Sorcha glanced back toward the lake, where her magik was calling out for the trove of stolen magik, which was somewhere far, far beneath the dark waters. A shiver ran through her as she focused back on Kartix. They had disabled the barrier spells around the mountain, but they still didn't have much time.

And it was precisely because of the lack of time that Sorcha knew what she wanted to do with what was quite possibly one of her last moments alive.

Sorcha grabbed the lapels of Kartix's black overcoat and hauled his lips to hers.

~

Damp moss pressed against her back as the mineral scent of the rock bloomed into a metal taste in her mouth. His warm lips, at last, met hers, and all at once, they were the beginning and the middle and the end of it all, as if the world itself held its breath, suspended in silence. Words they had wanted to say but never could echoed throughout the precious space between their leather-clad bodies. Kartix's magik rose to play with hers through the curse bond. The light of their powers gently entwined. In the darkness, Sorcha could have sworn she felt a chord being plucked deep inside her chest, something ancient and wicked opening its eye in response to the emotions filling her body.

He took his time with her. A soft nip at her bottom lip had her opening for him. Kartix traced her mouth with his tongue. Sorcha expected herself to move, talk, to do... literally anything but this. Destroying that razor-thin boundary she had so carefully tried to establish and hold in place. Nothing would ever be the same. Not after this. But then again, there had never been any sense of normalcy between the two.

Yet, she just let him hold her against the hard wall. Becoming feverish with expectation, an involuntary, shuddering breath escaped her throat, now tilted and exposed. As his hot breath lingered over her skin, she pulled him against her fully now. What could only be described as a growl escaped Kartix's lips as he searched her mouth in lazy strokes with his tongue. Sorcha whimpered, mouth gasping for air which seemed to evade her even now. As he explored her mouth, she went as fluid as the lake in his arms. Warm, broad hands cupped either side of her face, once more bringing her now-swollen lips to meet his.

As he took his time with her, every other thought emptied from her mind—the mission, the Assassins Guild, Razan—all fading into nothing as he held her in that damp, cavernous space.

But then she remembered who she was. Who he was. There were too many reasons, too many hurdles they would have to face if they were to continue whatever this was. Was it worth it? For just this feeling? She wanted to not care.

Fuck. She was in way too deep.

Flickering her eyes open, a gasp couldn't be stopped as she softly placed her hands on Kartix's broad, muscled chest. "Stop."

And he did. Jerking back, Kartix's scent changed instantly from lust to alarm. "What—"

Her heart clenched at his immediate concern. Sorcha willed her flaming cheeks to subside as she softly met his gaze. "It's not that I don't want it—you. I just— You're flirting to distract me from the Hel I'm about to encounter."

His soft, answering purr had Sorcha arching her back against the stone once again, pressing her hips against his as Kartix whispered in her ear, "And it's working."

With a glance toward the black water's edge, Sorcha quivered, and not just because her body had enjoyed…whatever they were doing, but because of the job which lay ahead of her. "I need something to come back to. If worse comes to worst and I'm about to give up, I need someone to motivate me, to be a reason to keep on fighting."

His stare never left her face.

"And I'd like it to be you."

Another chilled wind swept over the pair as if whatever entity encompassed the mountain was growing impatient.

"I have to go." Tucking her braid back into the collar of her leather suit, Sorcha, at last, met Kartix's obsidian eyes. She held his stare, letting herself be stripped naked, baring her soul to him.

"I didn't mean to—" He started.

"No, it's—" As she ducked under his arm and strode her way across the pebbled beach, Sorcha glanced over her shoulder as she made her way to the water's edge. "Before I go…" She turned toward the great beyond of the underground mountain lake. Her last words were almost swallowed by the fog. "I want you to know that I feel the same."

Just as Kartix registered her words, Sorcha dove deep under the murky water, taking his heart with her.

29

Sorcha wanted to gag within seconds of entering the lake. What a terrible idea this had been, she thought as she swam amidst the reeds and slithering weeds. The water was dark and murky. It slid around her legs like oil, finding every bare crevice of her body. All thoughts of Kartix emptied from her mind. She could focus on hot males later. Right now, she had to keep going. She had to continue so that she could reach the trove.

Sorcha could feel the magik. Somewhere beneath her, further out into the water, was a calming, steady presence, a pressure which was building beneath her skin. The magik danced and sang to hers, calling out to her bones and blood. Encouraging her, begging for a reprieve from its enchanted chains.

Like calls to like.

Invisible and surrounded by a small shield of her own creation, Sorcha focused on the rocky bottom of the lake. Free-diving was terrifying. Horror clenched and cramped in her gut.

The only thing she cared about was staying alive. In order to do that, her small reserve of magik had to be spent wisely. Her magik kept her blood flowing in her veins, and Sorcha was able to breathe underwater thanks to a small bubble of air she had taken down with her.

She swam down for what seemed like hours. The water was dark and thick, cold slicing into her bones. Sorcha could feel other magikal beings in the lake, could feel the dark magik swirling and gathering far, far below her at the bottom. She shivered. The goal was to find the trove of stolen magik and steal it back without disrupting any of the monsters which might guard it.

Her limbs were already burning with exhaustion but her magik kept her awake. It was screaming now, wild and thrashing in her soul. Sorcha winced. The closer she got to the stolen magik, the more trouble she had keeping her own magik on a leash.

It was pitch black at the bottom of the lake. She had taken her time swimming. Sorcha tried and failed not to feel the ever-growing sense of dread in the hollow of her stomach as she swam down, down, down. Deeper even than she had originally thought the lake was.

She realized with a start that there was no bottom. There was no bottom to the lake. Horror overtook her then, her entire body going cold despite the warm blood surging in her veins thanks to her magik. How the Hel was she going to find the trove? Darkness surrounded her. Kartix was back on the surface, which felt like miles away.

So, Sorcha did the only thing she could think of. She dove into her magik, dove into the very pit of her essence. She unwound a sliver of her powers.

I need to find the trove.

Her magik awoke, bursting out of her chest in a stream of light. The magik danced and sparked underwater, in such stark contrast to the darkness surrounding her. Sorcha gritted her teeth.

Very subtle.

Her magik laughed, a soft rumbling sound which settled over her bones. It wanted to play. Sorcha took a deep breath, the bubble of air bobbing with her.

Where is the stolen magik?

Like a spear, a beam of light, pure, unfiltered power, shot out from her body, directly down into the darkness. Sorcha could just barely make out the end of it.

She started swimming, her limbs burning with exhaustion. She couldn't stop now. Not when she could finally see the trove of magik, set into the rocky side of the lake.

A chest, ancient and inset with gold and rubies, rested on a ledge. She could feel, with every fiber of her being, the magik—the *stolen* magik. The magik of the Triumvirates.

How had Razan captured part of her sisters' magik? Were her sisters dead? Was Sorcha the only one left?

She sucked in a deep breath. This was it. This was the trove.

She glanced around, her magik probing every crevice and cranny of the rocky wall. Sorcha tensed. She needed to be on alert. It was quiet—*too* quiet. But time was not on their side. She needed to move, and fast. She swam closer, double-checking the shields around her body. She was still invisible, still unable to be traced underwater. Her magik danced and sang in her chest, flipping over and twisting in on itself. It was calling out for the trove, begging her to touch the chest.

And she did.

Sorcha grabbed the chest, hauled it against her, and started swimming back to the surface. She could feel monsters, their dark magik, in other parts of the lake, but thankfully she had avoided them all.

Or at least she thought she did.

Just as Sorcha was nearing the surface, the trove of magik in hand, she spotted a pair of large, red eyes looking up at her from the bottom of the lake.

30

Kartix stood upon the pebbled shore, black waves silently lapping at his feet. He peered out into the gloom and thick mist obscuring his vision of the lake. Kartix dove deep down inside himself and reached into his own pit of magik. He tapped the curse bond, hoping for any feeling of Sorcha, but her mental shields were up, and the curse bond had gone cold. It was almost as if she had wanted to shut him out of her mind. Kartix wondered if that was because of what had occurred on the beach. How he had accidentally let his thoughts of desire slip through the bond. How she had *kissed him.*

Kartix took an involuntary, shuddering breath. That woman would be the death of him. But all thoughts blinked out of his head the moment he felt a flash of fear, pure unfiltered horror, through the curse bond. Kartix grabbed his sword and started wading out into the black water. *Waiting be damned.* He wasn't about to let Sorcha face the lake alone.

Just as he was about to dive under the water, Sorcha broke through the surface of the lake—*flying*. Black wings with sleek feathers and corded with muscle rose from between Sorcha's shoulder blades. Her face was pale and drawn as she burst out of the water. A wooden chest fell from her hands, empty. Her arms and legs tucked in tight as she soared for the cave ceiling. Rocks and stalactites hung from the top of the cavern, so Sorcha banked right, plunging down to the beach, onyx feathers rustling in a breeze. She looked like an angel. Kartix supposed that she was one, considering the Gods had crafted her and cast her down to protect the world.

Kartix was still standing waist deep in the water—and something was coming right for him. He saw a black fin rise out of the water, several meters tall, swimming directly toward him. He had maybe a few breaths to realize what was happening before Sorcha swooped down and pulled him out of the water with a grunt.

A roar echoed off the cave walls as the pair soared out of the mountain and into the dark night sky. Sorcha shifted Kartix in her arms, holding him closer. New magik, foreign yet familiar, danced in Sorcha's veins as the pair soared higher, now above the mountain range. A few moments of silence were needed. Sorcha was heaving for air, her breath shaky, yet she kept a firm grip on Kartix, her strength never failing.

He gaped up at her in amazement. Her face was contorted in concentration as she steered them away from the mountain. "You have wings."

A nod of her head had Sorcha at last meeting her partner's stare. Miraculously, they had both survived the night. Where that left them, she had no idea.

Sorcha rolled her eyes at Kartix's wide-eyed stare, but a small part of her wondered how he had not yet screamed. He had just taken her in without judgment. He hadn't cringed in disgust, even while they were soaring high above the snow-capped mountain range. She realized with a start that that was not snow she was seeing on the mountains. No, the mountains were ash-capped. Smoke blew in from the east, from Ocyla, drifting in on the night wind to cover the western mountains. There had been more burnings that night.

As they soared closer toward the moon, the only sound was the soft rustle of Sorcha's newly unmasked wings.

"You have wings," Kartix said again.

Sorcha snorted. "Yeah, I fucking have wings."

"You just saved my life and got your magik back, and you're already giving me an attitude?" Kartix shook his head the best he could, given the fact that he was at *least* one mile from the forest floor below. "You're unbelievable."

"You mean incredible." As exhausted as they both were, Kartix could still make out the gleam in her eye.

He snorted. "You get compliments when you put me down on my balcony, safe and sound." Which, by his calculations, wouldn't be far now. Kartix twisted in her arms and shouted over the sound of the wind, "So did you absorb the trove of magik?" He eyed her, taking in the newly formed wings.

Sorcha clenched her teeth, holding him closer to her now than before. "You idiot. Stop moving unless you want me to drop you."

A smirk lit up his sensuous mouth. "I like that you have to hold me closer."

Godsdamn him to Hel. Is he really flirting with me now?

Kartix's pupils dilated as he sensed the change in Sorcha's heartbeat, which was beating more than a bit irregularly.

"Getting a little excited, are we, Sorcha?"

She winced. "Just because of all the exercise. Escaping sea monsters does tend to exhaust the body."

She didn't feel his finger until the shivers already made their way up her spine. Kartix carefully stroked the tip of her ear. "I thought the third Triumvirate didn't get tired. *All that power.*" She could have sworn he was purring.

Sorcha hissed. "Stop that." But the bastard only continued his soft caress of her delicate skin.

"Why?"

A groan nearly escaped her throat. "Because that is very, *very* sensitive."

As they crested the last of the mountain peaks, crisp autumn wind swept up from the valley below. Ocyla, a broken, beautiful kingdom, jutted up in the distance. At least a few minutes flying, give or take. Sorcha grimaced. As exhausted as they both were, they couldn't forget the plan.

"So, what happened? In the lake?"

Sorcha gritted her teeth, carefully choosing her words. "There was a sea monster guarding the trove. My magik did not detect it." Sorcha shook her head. "It was waiting for me as if it knew I was coming." A shudder ran through Kartix's body. Sorcha continued, soaring over a fast field. "My magik was not enough to fight it, so I had to use the trove." She swallowed, shifting Kartix in her arms. He clutched her harder. "I opened the chest, where the magik was stored, and the magik leaped into my body." She was silent for a few moments.

"I escaped just in time. I did not fight, I just ran." Sadness laced through her voice as she whispered, "I'm such a coward. What Triumvirate doesn't stay and fight?"

Kartix shook his head, staring at her. "Pick your battles. Without your full power, you could not have won. Besides, slaying a monster was not at the top of our priority list. Escaping with the trove was. Now that you have the magik back, we actually stand a chance at saving Ocyla, and the rest of this damn world."

The city came into view and Sorcha slid a shield around the pair, masking them from sight and hiding their scents.

She soared, her wings flapping silently in the night, and guided them to Kartix's balcony. Setting them down softly on the alabaster marble, Sorcha unwound him from her arms, gingerly stepping away. She eyed him where he stood, swaying on his feet. "Are you okay?"

Kartix turned toward her with a surprised expression. "I should be asking *you* that! I'm not the one who swam to the bottom of a lake full of monsters and barely escaped."

Sorcha put a hand to her forehead as she dragged her feet, walking into Kartix's room. Stumbling through the balcony doors, she fell on the rug, which was nearly the size of the prince's bedroom, careful to avoid crushing her wings. Gasping, she rolled to face Kartix, his face a mirror of her own pain and exhaustion. "I'm so tired, Kartix."

Kartix gingerly lay down beside her, both their backs pressed against the plush crimson rug. A chilled breeze swept in from the open balcony doors. Sorcha sent a tendril of her magik to close them.

Silence settled around the pair as they lay next to each other on the floor, catching their breaths. It was Sorcha who turned toward Kartix. She was too tired to care as she said, "Can I stay here? Tonight, I mean." She blinked. She choked up, turning her head to look back up at the ceiling. "I don't want to be alone tonight."

That admittance hung in the air between them.

Kartix turned toward her, bracing both hands on either side of Sorcha's head as he bent to whisper in her ear, "You never have to be alone."

269

His words sent fire through her veins. She couldn't feel her limbs as her heart fluttered against her ribs. She sucked in a deep breath, their faces inches from each other. "I need to sleep. I'm exhausted."

In one fluid motion, Kartix stood, pulling her with him, careful not to touch her wings. He swept her into his arms and carried her to his massive four-poster mahogany bed.

She was too tired to care about the consequences as he settled in next to her. She was still fully clothed. The thought of staining the linens made her sit up slowly and look at Kartix. A blush stained her cheeks. "I'm going to take off my clothes, but only so I don't dirty your sheets."

Kartix's scent deepened, muskier and darker. It felt like lightning through the curse bond. Sorcha sucked in a deep breath. His arousal sent thrills through her. *But not tonight. Not tonight,* she had to remind herself. She was too tired.

Kartix seemed to sense that, too, as he nodded, bringing his own jacket over his head. He turned to give her privacy as they both stripped to their undergarments.

Sorcha slipped under the covers, turning to face away from Kartix. She felt him slip into bed. The sheets felt like silk against her skin. Sorcha fell asleep within seconds. Kartix stayed awake for hours, staring at his ceiling. He listened to her breathing, deep, even breaths.

She still had her wings, her magik too depleted to withdraw them back into her body. He turned to look at her in the moonlight. Her alabaster skin was smooth, jawline sharp, and features angular as she slept. He glanced away. He needed to rest.

But how could he sleep when the woman he wanted most was right there beside him?

Reid walked in on a sight he knew he would eventually see, but still was not prepared for: Sorcha and Kartix were fast asleep in his brother's massive bed. His arms were around her, and Sorcha was curled up against Kartix's side, her wings having retreated sometime in the night.

Reid took in a deep breath. He knew better than to react. He had to respond, to think logically about what this implied for all of them. Losing his cool right now was not worth it. If Senna found out what Sorcha meant to Kartix, her life would be in even more danger. There was no telling what Senna could do, not with Razan in her back pocket. She had pure, unfiltered power. Razan had lent her a large portion of the stolen magik. When he'd first spiked the water of Ocyla with Mahoun and gathered all the Faes' magik for himself, he'd bestowed some powers to Senna as thanks for her keeping half of the Compound in line during his siege.

Reid cleared his throat and leaned against the silk-paneled wall of Kartix's bedroom. Kartix immediately sat up, Sorcha rolling off him. The prince, shirtless and seething with rage, flashed his eyes toward his brother. "*Is this necessary?*"

Reid smirked, rolling his eyes as he crossed his arms. "Sorry to interrupt, but Razan knows about the stolen trove of magik. He awoke this morning and received news from his scouts." Shaking his head, Felix's dreadlocks brushed against his lower back. "But it seems you two don't care about today's responsibilities, seeing as you're already... preoccupied." Reid chose his words carefully.

Sorcha groaned from where she lay next to Kartix in bed. "Would it help if I said it's not what it looks like?"

Reid shook his head. "Not a chance."

Sorcha pushed herself out of bed, walking to where she'd left her fighting leathers on the crimson rug. She was about to turn, to walk back to her own rooms, when Reid shut the door behind him. Locked it.

Sorcha went instantly on the defensive. Why had he locked the door? How many exits were there? Her mind flew with a flurry of anxiety.

Kartix raised his brow at his brother from where he lay in bed. "What's wrong?" Kartix's voice was hushed and grave.

Reid met his brother's stare. "She doesn't know about Senna."

Sorcha's ears perked up at the mention of her former overseer's name. She decided that she had to let it go only for now, with the intention of rehashing things with Senna later.

She swallowed. "What don't I know, Kartix?"

The prince slowly turned toward Sorcha. He was now out of bed and standing with his arms slack at his side. He took a deep breath, bracing himself for her reaction. "I'm betrothed to Senna. I have been for months."

Sorcha took a step back, her face paling. "What? How? Why?" She couldn't get words out fast enough as she stumbled to a chair near the fireplace, needing to sit down. The king's council meeting wasn't for a few more hours, so she had the spare time to talk with Reid and Kartix.

Kartix made his way over to the fireplace, leaning against the mantle. His dark eyes flashed with promised violence as he said softly, "I tried to rise up against one of my father's commands. It didn't end well." Kartix lifted up his shirt to expose a long scar running from his shoulder diagonally across his chest to his hip. It was raised and red, in stark contrast to his dark skin. Sorcha sucked in a deep breath as Kartix dropped his shirt.

Reid cringed from where he leaned against the wall, eyeing his brother.

"After I was beaten, I was betrothed to Senna." He shook his head, eyes glazing over with some type of pain. "Razan knows I hate her. It was punishment."

Reid sucked in a deep breath. "Tell her the rest."

Kartix turned toward Sorcha, who was frozen where she sat. "Senna also chains me to her bed most nights. Has her way with me. Discards me the next morning. That first night when you discovered me in

your room when we first met, I was only able to spend
the night since Senna did not request my presence."
Tears threatened to spill over, but Kartix blinked them
away. He couldn't meet Sorcha's stare. He could feel
her eyes burning holes through him, though. He
couldn't imagine what disgust might lie there, in her
gaze.

"So, when Senna called you to her rooms,"
Sorcha tilted her head, eyes assessing every inch of
the prince, "That was not you betraying the Assassins
Guild? Giving away our information?"

Kartix took a step forward, pushing himself
off the fireplace. The fire sent golden rays over his
smooth skin. "No, I did not give away information
about the Assassins Guild."

Sorcha looked to Reid for confirmation. All
the male did was nod this head slightly, pain dancing
in his eyes, his expression closed and quiet. She
looked back at Kartix. He had already given up so
much, had already lost so much. It was in that moment
that she stood up, walked over to him. He stilled, eyes
going wide and breathing becoming shallow as
Sorcha rose on her tiptoes and wrapped her arms

around him. She whispered in his ear, "I'm going to kill Senna, take my time making her suffer." She pulled away, locking eyes with Kartix. "We will make her pay. Somehow, someday, she will pay."

Kartix nodded, eyes hesitant and distant as if exhausted in this admittance. "You have to go. The council meeting begins in a few hours and we both need to bathe and change before."

Sorcha glanced at her dirty palms. "Yes, I suppose I should go. Although I don't know how I'll be able to tolerate being in the same room as Senna without ripping her head clean off her shoulders."

Reid huffed a laugh from where he now stood by the door. "You and me both."

Sorcha's smile was small and didn't meet her eyes as she said to the two males, "Stay out of trouble until I see you at the council meeting."

Reid winked. "We'll try."

But Kartix was somewhere far away from himself, staring out the windows. He didn't notice Sorcha leave, even as she glanced toward him as she slipped out the door. He didn't even hear Reid walking back to his rooms and saying Kartix should also change. All Kartix could feel was the cold of Senna's skin on his, and the clanking of his chains as he was locked to her bed.

Escape was all the prince thought of as he donned his clothing, and rose to meet the new day.

32

Half a day later and Sorcha wanted to scream. She was seated once again in the King's Council chamber. She was nervous and fidgety, along with the rest of the council. *Someone has broken into the underground mountain lake and stolen the trove of magik,* they were whispering.

Even Sorcha and Kartix had to feign worry to avoid looking suspicious. Sorcha crossed her arms and eyed the other members of the council before her eyes rested on him. Kartix looked like a hollow husk of a man. From where he sat beside his betrothed, he gave her a small, sad smile. Kartix and Senna sat next to each other the entire meeting, her hand gripping his thigh.

Making everyone that much more nervous was the fact that Razan never showed up.

Halfway through the meeting, the scouts brought reports that Razan himself had gone to the mountain. Sorcha and Kartix exchanged alerts through the curse bond. They both could feel the string connecting them go taut with tension.

Razan went to reinforce the barriers himself? Sorcha's eyes went wide with fear.

We're fine. We got out undetected. If worse comes to worst, I'll kill my father early.

Sorcha shook her head. She was so tired of war. Of bloodshed. Of horror and ruin and evil. She needed to get away. Needed air, needed space. Not just from Razan, but from everyone and everything. Her mind was spinning, and it could not seem to halt.

At last the meeting adjourned, nothing in particular having been accomplished. Sorcha and Kartix parted ways with a nod. She thought about last night at the mountain, how they had kissed each other.

Cheap thrills, she thought.

It's all just one cheap thrill.

~

Hours after the King's Council meeting, Sorcha wanted to stretch her legs. As she made her way around the Compound, her legs felt better and better with every step.

She rounded a corner, turning into a large hallway. The candelabra chased the shadows away down the vast hallway of the fifth floor. Lush tapestries gave way to hardened rock. Concrete walls soon came into view, a sign that this was an abandoned area. Not even the army cared for this part of the Compound.

Sorcha did not know why she had come here, to the wing that held the Compound's library. Although she adored books, she had not read one recently. Something inside her had begged her to walk toward this section of the Compound.

The library had long since closed its doors for the night. No one was around, not even the guards. No one truly cared for knowledge in this kingdom. That was part of Razan's dictatorship. Beings, Fae or human, took his manipulative words as truths. People would rather listen to lies than read books or learn, understand science, study about other cultures.

That was why the library still had magik. It was technically a living thing, filled with spells and power. Razan had deemed books as only a minor threat, not caring for knowledge, so he'd left this part of the Compound alone when he'd spiked the water supplies and stolen the Faes' powers.

Sorcha sighed, alone in the hallway, unafraid to let her voice echo off the concrete walls.

What a waste, all this knowledge, all these books. Razan had made sure that many texts and scrolls were burned in the great fires. About five years prior, he destroyed all books which did not fit the narrative he was attempting to build with his followers. Discipline and lack of free thought, independent thinking, had given way to Razan's dictatorship.

What else did she have to do? Sit in her room, waiting for the guards to escort her to the banquet? Think about punching Senna over and over and over until blood seeped down her face for what she'd done to Kartix?

No.

She was too wound up to sit alone in the foyer and wait. It all seemed like an utter waste of time when there was an entire kingdom to collapse.

So, she had drifted down the hallways to the abandoned section of the Compound.

She went alone. Her mind flitted between all the choices she had, who could accompany her on this outing. She wanted to be alone. Besides, it's not like she was defenseless. With the magik she'd absorbed from the trove, she could muster a shield if need be. She could use her magik to power her running, away from what she did not know.

Sorcha did not feel alone in the library. Maybe it was the living, breathing books which dwelled inside.

Sorcha used what little reserve of magik she had left to hide from prying eyes. As her frame faded into a blurred reflection of her body, she slid between the heavy wooden doors, into the darkened cavern of the library. That evening, she had found a crimson, figure-hugging dress lying out for her. Chosen by

Razan himself, the uniforms Sorcha and the rest of the King's Council had to wear to the banquet were to be perfect, a reflection of the strength of the government. The King's Council was to appear like a prized possession. The highest chosen members of his staff were deemed to be the strongest representation of the power and prestige of the Compound.

The banquet for the Captain of the King's Guard was in two hours, thus the finery.

Sorcha's tongue was bone dry as she stood alone in the vast space.

Adonis was to be honored before the High Court. Not that his ego needed more attention. She had known that Adonis had been deemed important to High Command. Razan's army apparently adored her former bedmate.

Whatever.

Sorcha rolled her eyes and her shoulders back as she took in the library, loosening her jaw and all the anxiety which had stored itself in her joints.

It had been a mistake to bed Adonis. Sex usually was a mistake with her. She hadn't climaxed, but then again, no man had ever made her cum before, so she didn't expect much.

Sorcha wondered, briefly, what sex with Kartix would be like. She blushed and quickly fixed her thoughts somewhere else.

Cheeks flushing, and not just from the adrenaline of her surroundings, Sorcha slid between the vast rows of books stretching high up into the dark space that was the ceiling of the library. Despite the fact that she was alone, unprotected in the cavernous space, Sorcha felt comforted by the hundreds of thousands of books surrounding her.

That was, until she felt a cold draft drifting in from the basement doors. Descending into an inky black even darker than the first floor, the staircase set into the northern wall of the library led down to the archives. Stored deep underground, sacred texts, ones that had been left behind in the burnings, dwelled there, preserved due to the lack of light.

This wind whispered of secrets and a cold which settled across her bones.

Strange.

Her connection with the Gods had been long since severed, and yet, she could swear voices were speaking to her. Their strange languages bounced off the inner walls of her skull, enticing her, beckoning her from their place far beneath the floor of the library.

Sorcha slowly turned to face the grand staircase, its steps descending into inky darkness.

Here goes nothing.

She could hear the chime of the clock from where it was mounted against the far wall. She had just under two hours before the banquet. Her breathing was shallow and uneven, her heartbeat a wild, reckless thing in her chest. Every instinct screamed at her to run away and not look back. The languages whispered to her from the darkness were warning her of what dangers lurked below.

Another wind, colder than the first, rushed over her skin. The marble steps leading to the lower floors faded down into black, the bottom of which she couldn't see. Sorcha had no idea how far the steps went. She sucked in a breath. It was time she found out.

As her high heels, made of silk and encrusted in rubies, echoed off the stone walls of the staircase, Sorcha couldn't help to wonder what beckoned her from below. The languages were calling out to her, *singing* to her in a voice both young and old, male and female.

She followed the sounds into the dark.

As she wound her way down, down, down the steps, Sorcha knew, the minute she hit the bottom of the staircase, something was off. Coming down here had been a horrible, idiotic move.

The air tasted stale and reeked of a strange smell that coated her nostrils, its oily scent overpowering her jasmine perfume. It was even darker than it looked. Sorcha needed to use up a bit of her magik in order to see in the dark. Even with her heightened Triumvirate eyesight, it was too dark to see unassisted in the archives.

Shaking her head, Sorcha's eyes, with the assistance from her magik, slowly adjusted to the vast expanse of space which stretched before her. Black stacks of books faded into the darkness. Sorcha could not see any walls. It seemed the levels below the library were even more cavernous, more expansive, than the upper levels.

Sorcha sucked in a deep breath, almost afraid to breathe in the stale air. She noticed, out of the corner of her eye, she was leaving footprints. Dust had settled for so long over the stones, evidence of how rarely beings visited the lower levels. But that sickly-sweet wind pulled her forward, down the stacks. She had enough sense, and magik, in her to stay partly invisible. She didn't need to alert any beings to her presence down in this darkness.

The current of air brushed her hair off her shoulders, sweeping past Sorcha to whatever lay beyond the stacks of books.

Two hours until the banquet.

She could be back by then.

So, Sorcha, with what little courage she had, followed those strange voices through the columns of books.

She walked silently through the stacks, her heels leaving soft imprints in the dust.

A minute passed. Then a few more. Then Sorcha lost track of how long she had been stalking the voices. It was a bad idea, but the Gods hadn't spoken to her in years. What if these strange languages were them? She had to know. Had to find out why her connection with the Gods had been severed. Were they still looking down on her from above? Could they even track the progress of her mission? Did they have any magik left at all? When she'd absorbed the magik of the trove, nothing had happened. Her connection with the Gods was still severed.

Scrunching her brow, Sorcha finally glimpsed the library wall, which was, at last, coming into view. Gods, this library was huge. Perhaps she could bring Lyra down here. Perhaps these ancient scrolls might tell them something about her past, where her family might be.

A strange light was coming from just around the last stack of books. As she reached the stone wall, she turned the corner, and was unable to stop the gasp which rose from her chest.

A red leather book was flung open on the ground. It was the Book of Readings.

She recognized its worn pages from all the council meetings. Razan was the only one allowed to touch the damn thing, and yet it had somehow found its way down to the archives of the library. The pages were flipped open to the center, lying flat on its back, the spine of the book resting on the stone floor. A circular orb of light, stretching ten paces in diameter and height, rose from its pages.

Sorcha's knees wobbled, her magik the only thing keeping her standing.

The Book of Readings was an instructional guide on how to open portals to other worlds. Legend says that Razan first used the book when he opened the portal to Hel. Sorcha had never thought it true, not really. But as she gasped, she knew all the stories about the book were real.

That orb of light radiated and pulsed with an energy which made her magik sing. Sorcha realized with a start that it was magik which was calling out to hers.

Like calls to like.

As invisible tendrils of her magik poked and prodded the edges of the light, Sorcha slightly recoiled. It was as if whatever entity was enticing her powers was purposely drawing them closer. Sorcha could see a figure standing on the other side of the light.

No, *inside the light.*

It stood against an outcropping of gray rocks, the sky behind it lit up with lightning, illuminating the creature from Hel which locked eyes with her. The creature had seven eyes, and they all narrowed in on Sorcha's frame. She was quivering in the darkness, on the other side of the portal. Shock was probably written all over her face as she froze, and the creature laughed.

As the creature crawled out of the light which poured from the book, Sorcha decided that she didn't want to know where this damn thing had come from. It had magik, yes. But what kind, she did not know.

Sorcha realized she had to stick around and fight the damn thing the moment the creature touched the library floor, its acidic skin eroding the stones beneath its claws. She had to find out what it knew. Why did it have magik?

Not that it seemed intent on exchanging pleasantries.

The creature was so dark that it seemed to swallow up the light from the portal. From its gaping jaws, bile poured, pooling at its feet—or what could best be described as feet, gauging by the claws and legs which protruded from its lower half. Its skin was stretched tight over its mass, bones protruding against its black, leathery hide. Its bloodshot eyes, all seven of them, focused on her. The air turned to lead in her lungs as she realized the putrid smell had been emitting from this creature. It practically stank up the entire library.

Who are you?

There was that voice again, both old and young, cruel and kind, echoing in her skull as her magik recoiled from the creature. It had not been the Gods then. The stupid fool that she was had followed the voice of this creature, luring her beneath the library.

Sorcha gritted her teeth, and replied, "Who are *you*?" She didn't care to reply in her thoughts. She wanted the damn thing out of her head.

The creature hovered just over the border of the portal, its haunches sitting over the edge of the book. A hiss rattled off its forked tongue. *I can feel your magik. You have it, don't you?*

Sorcha's face remained unmoving. She would not yield, no matter how much she wanted to scream.

I can smell it on you.

The creature's foul breath sent the books on the shelves wilting, their pages and scrolls incinerated, melting into a thick, black mass, ink dripping off their pages onto the floor below.

"Don't touch those." Sorcha's voice was calm, with a thread of promised violence.

She had no idea how to fight the damn thing. Had never used her magik to fight a monster before.

She raised her mental shields, a black wall rising up in her mind. Before she did, she sent a quick message to Kartix through the curse bond.

Monster. Archives.

The creature's magik ran a claw against the inner wall of her mind, scraping, scraping, scraping. Looking for cracks. Sorcha tried and failed to stop the tremors from taking over. It edged closer, and Sorcha took a step back, her back biting into the row of books behind her.

Give me your magik. I know you have it.

Slits she supposed were nostrils were carved deeply into the creature's face, and it inhaled her scent sharply. Great, now that it had her scent, it knew how to trace her. She was so, so, so fucked.

Sorcha planted her feet firmly on the ground. It was either run north or south.

Or...

Sorcha knew her plan the moment the monster launched at her, the darkest shadow against the stack of library books. It moved like lightning, swiping at her with a large hand that ended in razor-sharp claws. Sorcha was faster. She let go a burst of her magik, throwing up a shield around herself while simultaneously blinding the monster with a bright flash of light. The creature stumbled back, all seven of its eyes temporarily blinded. It hissed and recoiled, ready to strike again from where it stood, hunched just over the portal to the Book of Readings. Sorcha threw up another shield to mask her scent and herself from sight. The monster laughed, the sound of stone grating against stone, as it prepared to launch at her again. It was playing with her. They were playing a game of cat and mouse.

Sorcha felt its magik, old and strange, and she recoiled from it, warning her magik to stay away from those dark forces encircling the creature from Hel. It could still feel her. Could still feel her magik, dancing and calling to its evil other half from across the portal.

Throwing up a shield was no use. Shielding her scent was no use. She could only hope to get the damned thing back through the portal and then seal it permanently. Sorcha realized with a gritting of her teeth that she was not strong enough to defeat it, only stall until she was able to close the portal.

The monster's nostrils flared, as if sensing her plan, her hesitation.

I can still feel your magik. I can still sense where it is. Where you are.

Sorcha saw the creature's eyes drift down the same moment she realized what an utter fool she had been. Her footprints. Her feet had left footprints on the dirty, dusty library floor. Despite her shields, she had forgotten that anywhere she walked, she'd be leaving a trace.

The monster smiled, a thing of horror.

Sorcha's magik flared to life, her wings breaking out of her skin, her power coiling around her body in defense as she shot from the floor to the ceiling in one smooth arch. Her wings beat furiously, and she nearly screamed from the pain of suddenly unmasking her wings, but she was no longer on the library floor, no longer too close to the creature. Her shields held firm around her body, and the monster lunged for the empty space she had been standing in not seconds prior.

Sorcha swallowed and banked left, aiming for a bookcase nearest the creature from Hel.

Sorcha whispered to the library, "I'm so sorry for this." Then she thrust all of her magik into one push. The stack of books which faded up into oblivion seemed to groan, to sway with the pressure of Sorcha's request. As she and her magik slammed into the bookcase, the monster looked up, as if just sensing the books which were now showering down in a tsunami of knowledge upon him. Even the creature from Hel was not quick enough to move, to fight, to even bat one of his seven eyes, before the column of books came crashing down on his head.

Sorcha didn't even stick around to find out if the bastard was alive. There was an open portal to another world, another dimension—or was it Hel? She needed backup, she needed more magik. She couldn't close the portal. She didn't know how.

As Sorcha soared between the stacks of books, she heard the monster roar, a sound full of fury and vengeance. It reverberated amongst the stacks of books and Sorcha flew faster. She flew for minutes and minutes, weaving around and between the stacks of books. She could feel the creature's black magik searching for her. She could feel it brush against her inner shields once more.

So she hadn't killed the monster.

Sorcha clenched her jaw. She was in so much shit.

At last, the winding library staircase came into view. Sorcha almost sobbed with relief at the sight of it as she soared up to the first floor of the library. She saw the vast entryway approaching quickly. Sorcha dipped and turned and twisted around desks as she flew with everything in her to the entry doors.

She burst through the doors, slamming them behind her with seconds to spare. So, her magik had lasted. It had let her get through the heavy, wooden doors. Sorcha heard the monster roar once more. This time, it was within feet of the door.

Every hair on her body stood on end.

The creature pushed its entire weight upon the heavy oak doors, but Sorcha was stronger. She used every last drop of her magik to seal the doors, and they held. Sweat dripped down her temples, pounding in time to her heartbeat. Her breathing was rough and ragged, burning as it came out. She could place a seal on this door. As long as it held, the creature would be contained in the library. Sorcha began to set the charms. She stood, arms braced against the doors, head down, concentrating on the seal, for minutes.

"Rough night?"

A soft voice full of quiet humor purred from the shadows, cutting through her thoughts. She opened her eyes and glanced over her shoulder to see Kartix leaning against the neighboring wall of the corridor. His onyx suit matched his hair. The impeccably tailored silk fit perfectly against his large frame. He towered over her, and yet couldn't help but feel incredibly small as Sorcha somehow looked down her nose at him. "What are you doing here?"

A heavy thud echoed against the library doors, and Sorcha gritted her teeth, once more focusing the last few drops of her power into the seal on the door.

"I heard you through the curse bond. The only two words I got were 'archive' and 'monster,' so I came running."

Sorcha shook her head. "Why didn't you help me back there? I could have used the assistance." He noted her annoyance. He tilted his head, a purely non-human move, as his eyes assessed her like a predator assessing prey. "I knew you could handle it."

"I almost *died*."

He looked her over, unabashedly allowing his eyes to roam over her body. Her blood heated in her veins. *Cocky bastard.*

The clock chimed from inside the library, the echoes of the sound reaching them through the thick, monster-guarded doors. Half an hour 'til the banquet. Shit. And she *looked like shit too.*

Fuck.

The thudding eventually stopped. Sorcha backed away from the doors, which were glowing golden given the amount of magik she had used to seal them. She was exhausted. Her shoulders hunched as she sighed and pinched the skin between her eyebrows. The last thing she needed was Kartix distracting her. She met his stare. "I need to send this monster—or whatever it is—back to where it came from." She glanced down the hallway which led to the rest of the fifth floor, now bustling with movement from the banquet. "I don't have time to be parading around like some kind of prized possession for the King's Council."

Kartix followed her stare down the hallway. "If you don't appear and there are reports of upticks of magik within the castle—which there will be, thanks to all your fighting already, and the magik you've dispelled—then it will raise suspicion." His worry for her was palpable.

She sighed again. "I hate it when you're right."

A dash of a smile cut across his rugged features and she couldn't help a small smile of her own. "Kartix." All the amusement slowly faded off her face. "The Book of Readings is a portal. There is currently a monster from another world running around in the library." Her face scrunched up in concentration. "And the books! Fuck!" She turned toward the massive library doors once more, "Kartix, what if it goes after the books?"

Kartix shook his head. "I doubt it cares about the books. I doubt it can even read."

Sorcha shook her head "It spoke to me. In my head, Kartix."

Anxiety shot through him. It was Kartix's turn to scrunch his forehead. "Is that so?"

She nodded vigorously. "And that's why we have to go and close the portal. We can't just let a monster roam in our world."

Kartix crossed his arms, leaning back against the wall of the hallway. "Well, your magik has it contained for right now. Both you and I—and half of the rebellion—is expected at this stupid banquet in half an hour. We'll meet tonight, all of us, and figure out a way to close the portal after."

Sorcha nodded. "Sounds like a plan. I'll send a message to the others." She tapped the side of her head.

Kartix inclined his head. The idea of Sorcha single-handedly fighting a monster turned him on.

"So, what exactly happened back there in the archives?"

Sorcha quickly filled the prince in on her encounter with the monster.

There were a few moments of silence before the prince began, "You know, that was smart. What you did back there with the bookcases? I never would have thought of that."

Sorcha's eyebrows rose. "Is that a compliment?" A smirk lit up her sensuous mouth. "I never thought Kartix would be the one for pretty words."

He shrugged. "You were magnificent back there. And at the mountain with the trove. And in the fighting pits. Would you like me to lie to you? To tell you I'm not in awe of you?" His eyes burned like obsidian fire.

Sorcha took a step toward the end of the hallway, where servants were bustling with movement. "We should go." A blush stained her face. Why had he said those things to her? She didn't know how to process it, so she just numbly nodded her head, not meeting his eyes.

Without another glance at the prince of Ocyla, her enemy's son, Sorcha walked away to get ready for the banquet.

33

She couldn't look at him. Not as she walked away, leaving Kartix slack jawed. Not during the banquet. Not even when the rebellion all gathered in Sorcha's room hours later that night. Why had she pushed him away when he'd complimented her?

Sorcha shoved the thought down as Kartix, Reid, Marie, and Facim all made their way over to the large table in the middle of the room. Sorcha had dragged maps and scrolls over to the table and laid them out, every inch of the wooden surface covered in information. Sorcha had managed to steal the maps from a King's Council meeting earlier in the week.

Facim closed the door behind all of them. "Alright. So, all the information we've received so far is that somehow, *some*-fucking-how, there is a portal to a possible other world or dimension, or even Hel itself, in the library?"

Everyone turned toward Sorcha. She swallowed. Nodded. "This is true. I discovered it before the banquet. It called to my magik, and I followed the call like the idiot I am."

Marie's eyes went soft. "You're not an idiot. You survived a fight with a demon from another world. That's pretty badass, if you ask me."

Reid crossed his muscled arms, assessing the map of the library Sorcha had laid out before them. "Show us where the portal is."

Sorcha put her finger on the westernmost part of the map. "Here. I escaped by toppling these bookcases here." Her finger moved slightly north. "Then I fled. I sealed the library doors with my magik, but it won't last long. The portal still remains open, and I have no idea how to seal it. I tried to fight the monster, but even my magik recoiled." Sorcha shook her head. "Even after absorbing the trove's magik, I still don't have enough to close this portal."

Facim raised an eyebrow and crossed her arms. "So we have to get more magik in order to close the portal?"

Marie asked, "Where do we get magik? The only way to absorb more magik is to drain someone else's powers. Where do we find someone who's worthy of having their magik taken away?"

Kartix answered, "Someone who has taken too much from other people. Someone who was never worthy of their power in the first place." He locked eyes with Sorcha.

"Senna."

The room was silent for a few moments, the only sound the crackling fire in the hearth.

"You want me to drain Senna of her power?" Sorcha asked slowly.

Kartix nodded, his tan skin paling. "*I* want to drain Senna of her powers. It would make sense, since I'm the one who can get closest to her."

Reid and Sorcha winced. Marie and Facim shifted on their feet. Kartix continued, "When she calls me to her bedroom next, I'll use Mahoun to spike her wine. Then, when her power drains out, I can absorb it without her even feeling a thing."

"I hate to say it, but that is a good plan." Facim's voice was laced with sadness.

"You don't have to go back to Senna if you don't want to," Marie chimed in. "There are always other options."

Kartix shook his head, his dark hair shining in the light of the fire. "No. Senna is mine and mine alone to take down."

No one argued with him.

It was Sorcha who crossed her arms and assessed the prince with a cool stare. "If you somehow manage to absorb Senna's powers, how exactly am I supposed to close the portal?"

Kartix shrugged. "We'll have to research that. Luckily, no one goes in the library, so leaving the portal open for just a few nights won't do any harm."

Reid raised a brow. "And what of the monster? What of the fact that there is a fucking creature from another world wandering around in the library?" He shook his head.

Sorcha replied evenly, "The monster isn't in the library. My magik can no longer detect it. It must have returned to the portal once it realized it could not get me."

Marie snorted. "You better be right."

Facim cleared her throat. "So, Kartix, when are you able to drain Senna's magik?"

Sorcha's stomach twisted at the thought of Kartix with Senna. At the thought of him having to drain her magik. At the fact that Sorcha would no longer be in control.

The prince replied, "As soon as she calls me to her chamber next. She has been busy with research for the King's Council, so I have not seen her as of late." He yawned, stretching his muscles. Sorcha swallowed as his tanned abdomen came into view when his shirt lifted up.

Facim agreed. "So, we wait until Senna has called for you."

Kartix nodded. "We wait."

~

The group dispersed hours later after talking about their plans well into the night. Reid and Kartix were the last ones to leave. Just as the males were about to walk out the door, Sorcha turned to Kartix suddenly.

"Thank you. For saying you're in awe of me earlier."

Kartix was unreadable. "It's true. I am."

Reid pretended not to hear their conversation as he waited by the door, turning his back to give the pair privacy.

Sorcha, at last, met Kartix's eyes. "And I'm in awe of you." She didn't let herself say anymore. Couldn't. She was giving away too much already. Had already given too much of herself to this male. Sorcha retreated back inside her inner fortress, shields rising up in her mind once more.

Kartix seemed to sense that as he backed away. "I'll leave you be. Good night."

Sorcha said, without a smile on her face, "Good night, prince." And then she shut the door in his face.

She stumbled to her bed, exhausted. She thought of Lyra, sleeping safe and sound at the Assassins Guild. The child was tired from training in the fighting rings with the women of the Guild. Lyra had joined their forces weeks earlier and had spent all day in the slums at headquarters learning how to fight.

Sorcha collapsed onto her bed, finally settling amongst the sheets. As she closed her eyes, all she saw was Kartix. As she drifted into unconsciousness, his words were on repeat in her mind.

I'm in awe of you.

Sorcha awoke with a start. A man's burly hand was pressed against her mouth. She could feel a large body lying on top of her, leathers and belts and daggers digging into her stomach. She managed, in her first few seconds of consciousness, to send a message through the curse bond to Kartix.

Help.

Her magik flared in response as the stranger whispered in her ear, "Hello, honey. It's been awhile."

As she struggled beneath him, Sorcha hissed, "Adonis, I thought we were finished."

Razan's Captain of the Guard smiled as he eyed her with lust. "You and I? We are never finished." Adonis reached down and hoisted Sorcha's leg over his waist. Her nightgown slipped up to her stomach, exposing her lower half. Adonis gripped her bare thigh in his large and powerful hands as he took her in with a predator's glare. "Now that you're a

member of the High Court, I get to keep you around."
He nuzzled her neck, his warm breath sending shivers
up her spine. Not from arousal.

Adonis's long, golden locks fell in her face as
her magik flared inside her. Adonis had magik too.
His magik awoke and rose to tame hers into
submission. He pressed a dagger to her throat. Sorcha
could not move an inch. She could barely breathe
without her windpipe pressing against his blade.

Then her magik slipped off its leash. There
was nothing, nothing, nothing Sorcha could do as she
watched her magik slip loose of its restraints.
Beautiful golden light leapt out of Sorcha's chest,
knocking Adonis and his knife to the side. A warm
liquid blinded her temporarily. Sorcha wiped her
eyes, her hands coming away crimson red. She
blinked and looked down at where her magik had
flung Adonis.

She screamed.

It looked like he had exploded. Body parts
and limbs were strewn across the room, blood seeping
into the carpet.

Sorcha had killed Adonis.

35

Everything moved in slow motion. All she could see was red. Red on her hands, her nightgown. Her tongue even tasted of steel and bitterness, the tangy, coppery taste of blood clinging to her mouth. She heard someone speaking, but no sounds got through. Sorcha could feel a hand on her shoulder, but her body was not on this earth. Instead, it was detached, drifting somewhere far, far away. Sorcha was unable to move her limbs. A cold settled over her bones. She doubted she would be able to shake it anytime soon.

One moment his hands had been digging into her dress, his dagger pressed against her throat, biting into the delicate skin of her neck, and then the next, a bright flash of light, and Adonis had been no more. His body forever cold on the cobblestones.

Sorcha vomited then. She did again, and again. She did not care who saw.

I killed him.

She had killed before. Remembered the wetness that had coated and slicked her hands. The crimson liquid staining her clothing in the fighting rings after each long night. But she had never in her short, Gods-crafted life killed by *accident*.

A kind voice, full of warmth and soft words, spoke to her, then she bent over, heaving against the silk wall of her bedroom. She could feel the lilt of the voice cut through the gray, a beacon of light to guide her through this Hel. She clung on to that voice, even when grief and shock pulled her from consciousness. Even when her limbs fell out from underneath her, as she slumped to the marble floor of her rooms, Sorcha felt that warm voice, a voice like sunshine on her bare skin.

When the fainting spell took over and Sorcha did indeed drift into unconsciousness, she was left with a faint bit of comfort. Even in her last moments, she felt his warmth beside her.

How nice, she thought. *To have someone here in the end.*

~

After tucking Sorcha into her bed, Kartix went to bury the body.

He chose a spot near the deserted back training grounds, where Reid and his friend Alex liked to train. With the assistance of his magik, digging took mere minutes.

As he dug, Kartix recalled his experience earlier that night. He had been asleep in his own bed when all of the sudden, he'd felt the curse bond go taut with tension. Sorcha was pulling him, calling to him through the bond.

Help.

His magik had instantly transported him into Sorcha's rooms. This time, he'd reminded himself, he would be the one who did the saving, not her. He was tired of standing on the sidelines, watching Sorcha save the day. This time, it was his turn. This time, he would be *useful.*

Kartix had been transported into a scene of gore and horror. Adonis—or what was left of him— was splattered all over the walls, the floor, and Sorcha, who was trembling where she stood against the silk wall. Kartix ran over to her just as she fainted. He caught her just in time, her head inches away from hitting the floor. Kartix lowered her the rest of the way, the cool marble chilling her flushed skin.

Kartix turned back toward Adonis. He quickly used some of his magik to clean up the blood and rearrange the bedroom. Furniture had been overturned by Sorcha's magik. The room looked like a tornado had gone right through the middle of it.

Kartix shook his head as he dragged Adonis's limbs into a burlap sack. The blood seeped through the sack in an instant. Kartix gritted his teeth, checked on Sorcha, and then hoisted the bag of body parts over his shoulder and set out to dig a grave.

The last time Adonis had been in Sorcha's room, he was a jealous mess. Kartix felt protective over her. He still felt that sharp stab of jealousy from deep inside him at the thought of the two alone together. He assumed that he was here because Sorcha wanted him here. Seeing the current state of the room, had Adonis hurt Sorcha?

An hour later, Kartix retreated to Sorcha's room. He watched her as she slept. Her breaths were even and steady, no signs of nightmares. He checked her body over with his magik for any signs of harm. With the exception of a slim band of red at her throat, Sorcha was unharmed. Physically, that was. Her mind had been too overwhelmed to process what was happening. So, she had just... shut down.

She had training in the morning. Razan liked for the King's Council to keep up a proper physical appearance, to "appear strong for the kingdom." So Sorcha had a busy day ahead of her. She needed all the rest she could get.

Kartix crossed his arms, watching her from under lowered lashes. He counted her breaths. There was to be a banquet this night, with Senna. Kartix would be required to sit with Senna all tonight. Perhaps tonight would be the time to drain Senna's magik, to steal her powers so that Sorcha might be able to seal the portal.

As the first rays of dawn burst through the floor-to-ceiling windows, Sorcha awoke to find Kartix, curled up on the couch. She watched him steadily, unsure what to think. He had come last night when she'd called him. She looked around the room, expecting to see Adonis, expecting to see his body. Then she put it together that Kartix had been the one to clean up after her.

Even though he had not been able to stop Adonis in time, he had taken care of the body. He had complimented her outside the library. That night at the mountain where Kartix had kissed her back. In the alleyway where he'd begged her to stay with him.

She liked it. She had wanted it, had started to crave the affection he threw her way. Sorcha fell back against her pillows, staring at the ceiling.

She was in such deep, unavoidable shit.

36

By midday, news that Adonis was missing reverberated through the Compound. Sorcha did her best to keep her head down as she awoke and went through her training exercises. Throughout the day, she couldn't get the taste of his blood out of her mouth, couldn't scrub her hands clean enough. By the time the King's Council meeting rolled around later that evening, Sorcha was drained from keeping her guard up all day.

As Sorcha arrived at the King's Council chamber, she scanned the room for Reid and Kartix. She spotted the latter seated next to his betrothed at the head of the table. Sorcha swallowed and took her seat.

Presentations about the latest upticks in magik began. Later, the Council was slated to discuss the ever-growing presence of war in the Southern Continent. However, all talks halted when dinner was served. Plates were brought by servants, and charts and parchment were swept off the main table as they gathered for a much-needed hour-long dinner.

As the Fae ate, Sorcha felt Kartix go taut with tension through the curse bond. She looked up and found Kartix's gaze locked on her.

Sorcha caught Senna's eye.

It took Kartix every ounce of effort and self-resolve not to sigh. Despite the cold grip Senna had on his thigh, Kartix still studied Sorcha from under lowered lashes.

The King's Council had worked late into the evening. Thick clouds of smoke swirled between a handful of council members thanks to the multiple pipes which were circulating amongst the twenty "researchers." Sorcha waved off the substances when offered. "Not now." What she really meant was, *No fucking way am I ingesting something without inspecting it first.*

Sorcha smoothly brushed her hair over a slim shoulder. The movement caught the prince's eye.

His blood roared in his ears as he watched Sorcha's dress shifting in the light. She looked beautiful tonight, even though she was running on lack of sleep. Kartix could use some sleep as well.

All thoughts of sleep were ripped from his head as a slam of a book echoed throughout the massive council room. Senna's presentation had ended, and another Council member named Brianna had taken her place. The young woman sneered as she threw open an ancient book, bending its spine as she searched for the page she was looking for. Dust swirled out from its pages as Sorcha scowled across the massive center table. Brianna was treating *yet another* ancient text with recklessness. It was the third time tonight that the young woman had broken the spine of a book.

It wasn't worth the energy, but Sorcha was pissed from fighting off Adonis at one a.m. She twitched with anger in her chair. She cleared her throat, assuming the role of a haughty King's Council member. "You will treat the texts with respect." She sent a scathing glare across the table.

Brianna sneered back. "You're interrupting my presentation."

Sorcha shrugged. "We talk of hunting Fae, but you yourself have magik, Brianna. Why don't we hunt you instead?"

Kartix choked on his wine. The table was deadly quiet.

Careful.

Sorcha ignored him. Trembling with restraint, her power broiled beneath her skin. "Break another book and I'll drain your magik myself." Razan wasn't here to hear her threats, thank the Gods.

A glint of candlelight reflected on her hair. Sorcha was commanding, Kartix thought, even when she was pissed to all Hel.

Brianna just grinned as her magik sent all the books left on the table aflame. King's Council members leaped back, several swearing, brushing embers off their clothing. Brianna smiled as she met Sorcha's eyes over the flames. "You were saying?"

Sorcha slowly shook her head. "Fuck this." Whipping her silk napkin onto her seat, Sorcha rose. A heartless laugh escaped her lips. The smile didn't reach her eyes.

Without a glance back, Sorcha walked away from the King's Council.

37

One day later, Sorcha and Facim were running through the Eastern Forest at the edge of the Compound. Facim had nothing to handle at the Assassins Guild, so she had accompanied Sorcha for training.

The dirt track lay between them and the dense forest. The morning air was cool. Autumn was fast approaching.

As the pair ran, their leather boots pounding the floor of the forest, Sorcha's ears pricked up. She came to a halt, no longer feeling safe enough to continue their run. The birds had gone silent, and even the rustle of leaves had stilled as if the entire world was holding its breath.

Facim stopped running. Standing just a few yards back up the track from Sorcha, she asked, "What's wrong?"

Sorcha woke her magik, curled it around her heart, her mind, her limbs, and bones, and blood. "I don't know." She took a step forward, away from Facim. "Whatever is out there, it feels different. It feels like the monster I encountered in the library." Sorcha sent tendrils of her magik floating out on the wind. The magik it scented was all wrong. It was ancient and evil and rotten to its core. Sorcha's powers recoiled at the mere presence of the dark magik.

It was then that the monster crawled out from the brush. Facim screamed, alerting Sorcha to its presence to their left. Sorcha pivoted, throwing a dagger in a smooth arc toward the creature. It embedded itself in the monster's leathery, black hide. The monster rose up on its powerful and sleek hind legs. Its roar was a thing of dread. Black bile, acidic, dripped down to the forest floor. Leaves curled and turned black where the spit landed. Facim ran to Sorcha's side just as Sorcha slid up a shield around the pair. Sorcha's magik awoke, streaming in a line of white from her fingertips as it rose to surround the women. Sorcha gritted her teeth, a muscle flickering in her jaw as she squared off her body, her feet firmly planted on the ground.

Monster in the Eastern Forest. Facim is with me.

Sorcha was just able to send the message through the curse bond to Kartix before the creature from Hel launched at them. Its claws sliced open Sorcha's shields, tearing them like strips of cloth. Sorcha's blood ran cold as she and Facim stumbled back. Sorcha quickly threw up a cloak of invisibility, to shield them and their scents, but it was of no use. The monster scented the use of magik itself. If Sorcha was using magik to fight, then there was no way she would be able to shield Facim. The creature had torn right through her shields as if it were immune to her powers.

The creature hovered over Sorcha and Facim, winding up for one final lunge, when Kartix appeared. He grabbed Sorcha and Facim by their collars and, holding them both, transported them all in a blink of an eye out of the forest.

The women opened their eyes to find themselves dumped in the foyer of Sorcha's rooms, covered in dirt, still in their exercise clothes.

Sorcha scrambled over to Facim. "Are you hurt?" Sorcha's eyes ran over every inch of her friend. When Facim shook her head, she turned to Kartix, breathless. "Thank you." Her eyes went wide as she took them both in. "That was the second monster attack in four days. We need to gather everyone tonight and plan on how to close the portal. Soon."

All Kartix and Facim could do was nod numbly. None of them knew what to say. It felt hopeless. This had been the second attack. Who knew if it was even the same monster? Questions flooded Sorcha's mind, but it was no use, not with the entire day of King's Council meetings ahead of them. Sorcha and Kartix needed to change into their High Court clothes now.

As Kartix made to stand, he eyed Sorcha warily. "In the half hour until I see you again, try not to attract any more demons."

Sorcha rolled her eyes from where she and Facim still were strewn on the marble floor. "We'll try."

Reid burst through the doors with Marie and Facim right on his heels. It was hours later, after a day of King's Council meetings, and the rebellion gathered in Sorcha's rooms. Kartix hovered near the door, leaning against the silk-covered wall panel. Marie and Facim took up two chairs nearest the fireplace.

Reid turned toward Sorcha, wide-eyed. "A second monster attack? In less than two days? Sorcha, we need to close the portal. Now."

All Sorcha could do was nod. "Yes."

"We'll need more magik to seal the portal," Kartix added gruffly from the corner. "The magik Sorcha absorbed from the trove is not enough."

Marie nodded. "The portal is too powerful to be closed with just one Fae's magik." All heads turned toward Sorcha as Marie continued, "We need to drain someone of their powers."

Facim added, "Kartix, now would be the time to drain Senna of her magik."

The prince nodded darkly.

Reid crossed his arms. "We don't even know if her magik alone will be enough." He shook his head, locks brushing against his lower back. "We need to find out more information on portals. How to close them."

Sorcha crossed her arms, shivered. "The library." All eyes looked up at her. She continued, "The library is the only place in Ocyla with enough knowledge. I've looked up portals before. I've found books on it in the back, hidden shelves." Sorcha's blood ran cold as she said, "I can go back into the library. Sort through some books to see if I can find anything."

Reid stepped forward. "I'll go with you."

Kartix quickly pushed himself off the wall, dark eyes flickering. "And I as well."

The three of them looked to Marie and Facim. The latter shook her head. "We can't go tonight to research since the girls need assistance." It was true. Some of the girls of the Assassins Guild debuted this month and had done extremely well in the fighting pits. The women were building a reputation now amongst the burly men of Ocyla. Tonight, more were to be introduced into the fighting pits and the girls needed to be ready.

Sorcha nodded. "Tell the girls I say good luck. I wish I could be there to see them kick ass."

Facim and Marie smiled. "With that being said, we need to return to the slums. We should bid you good night."

Reid and Kartix nodded. "Good night."

As Sorcha watched her friends leave, she couldn't shake the feeling of dread. Sorcha turned toward Reid and Kartix. "Let's go."

As the three of them wound their way through the Compound, Sorcha knew that her friends were all liabilities. Things to be broken. Things that could ruin her if she let herself care about them too much. If she allowed them to take up too much of her heart.

Then again, Sorcha thought as they arrived at the library doors, she had never been good with controlling her own heart.

39

The three decided to split up. Perhaps it was not the best idea, considering that there was still an open portal filled with monsters a level below, but in order to close the portal, the rebellion needed to find out *how* to close it. They would cover more ground individually. As Sorcha, Kartix, and Reid set out among the stacks, Sorcha's magik awakened in her blood. She was alone, not able to hear Reid or Kartix any longer, surrounded by the ancient texts.

She stifled a scream as Kartix's magik whispered against her legs, winding its way through her skirts like a cat brushing up against her in pleasure. Sorcha rolled her eyes as Razan's son came around the corner. "We're supposed to be researching, you know. Not playing tag."

Kartix raised a dark brow, his devastatingly gorgeous face smirking. "Why not have a little fun?"

Sorcha couldn't roll her eyes enough. She turned away. "If you're going to follow me, you might as well help me look for books on how to close this damn portal."

Kartix nodded, his magik retreating from her skirts.

Sorcha and the king's son passed by many bookcases, magik lights twinkling like small stars ahead. One had to make sure you never lost sight of the guiding Reid of light. Gods only knew what types of tricks the library might play on them, or if any more portals had appeared amidst the ancient scrolls and texts in long-forgotten languages. The two had to be careful, on constant alert. Sorcha's magik had awoken and was coiled around herself, ready to strike if necessary.

Sorcha could not make out the tops of the bookcases as they faded into inky oblivion.

As Sorcha tried to find a secluded spot in the library, the stacks suddenly reshuffled in front of them, leading them to a straight path with a slightly glowing column of books. Sorcha snorted. The library was not being subtle at all.

Her eyes met Kartix's.

"Do we go?" Kartix's eyes promised danger.

Sorcha nodded.

So, the pair silently stalked to the nook of books at the far end of the library. Sorcha supposed the library wanted them to reach the column of books quickly, as the pair covered the distance in half the time it would normally take.

Sorcha winced. She did not like that the library knew they were there.

Once they reached the slightly illuminated column of books, Sorcha set about reading the titles along the spines of the ancient texts. As Kartix bent down and brushed against her thigh, Sorcha tried not to shiver at his closeness. She allowed herself to hesitate, to look down at the inky mass of hair which was still, crouched beside her, reading the spines of the books as well.

Find anything good? she asked him.

Not yet. Kartix stood back up, his arms above his head, stretching like a cat. He looked at her then, his inky eyes dimming in the light. *Can you use your magik to detect anything?*

Yes. I can. Sorcha hesitated, then closed her eyes, letting the darkness take over, calming her senses. A blanket of black descended over her and she took a deep breath. Another, and another. Then, like a warm hand guiding her own, Sorcha's magik slowly moved her hand to rest on a single book, slim, about the color of the crimson wine Sorcha had drunk the night prior.

Quickly, without a second thought, Sorcha opened the book, skimming the pages. The library was silent as a catacomb as she read for minutes. As she flitted through the text, her eyes widened.

Kartix came to peer over her shoulder. "What does it say?"

Sorcha swallowed. "That I need to give up every drop of my power to close the portal."

Kartix stilled. "You're power in a shell. Or, that's what you told me a few weeks ago. If you were to give up every drop of your magik, that would mean you'd have to—" He couldn't finish.

Sorcha looked up with such sad eyes. "I have to die."

Kartix stumbled back against a bookcase. He gasped, "There has to be another way. We can gather more magik, drain other people, more than just Senna." His voice broke on the last words. "There has to be another way."

Sorcha shook her head. Laughed. "I always knew why the Gods crafted me. I was only created as part of a weapon to seal the door in the Heavenly Battle. All I am is power in a shell."

The hollowness in her eyes, the guttural emptiness, made Kartix stalk toward Sorcha. She tilted her head up to meet him as he towered over her. "You're *not* going to die." His voice was gruff. "I refuse to allow that to happen."

Sorcha's eyebrows furrowed. "What don't you get, Kartix? I was not supposed to exist in the first place. The only reason I was created was to stop your father for the Gods." She huffed another laugh, crossed her arms. The magik lights of the library cast a hazy glow around her.

But Kartix didn't care about the Gods. He didn't care that Sorcha was just power in a shell. All he cared about was wiping that look of despair off her face.

It was precisely because of that, that Kartix pulled Sorcha against him, and kissed her.

~

The kiss was punishing and savage, a claiming. Being with Kartix was everything Sorcha had dreamed it would be. It was as if the world had stopped and they were the only beings left alive.

At first, she was solid as stone against him, unsure whether the current moment was truly, really occurring. It was only when Sorcha realized Kartix was kissing her with intention that she decided, *What the Hel,* and surrendered. Her body went limp in his arms, as fluid as water against his strong, sure grip on her waist. Kartix's lips were warm against hers and she tried not to sigh. His touch left sparks in its wake as his left hand made to cup her cheek.

She broke away before he did, wanting to continue, but desperately needing an explanation.

"What are we doing?" Sorcha gasped as Kartix brought his lips once more down to claim hers.

"What do you want to do?" His voice was rough with a dark, dangerous edge to it.

"I need a distraction," she answered.

Bookcases suddenly appeared to surround the pair, as if offering them privacy. The magik lights had returned, casting a golden, fiery light over the many books, and provided a warm glow over the pair. Sorcha and Kartix met eyes once more. They were alone for once. There was not even Facim to tease her. No one came this far into the library. What was more, Sorcha cast them invisible to the naked eye and put a shield around the pair, soundproofing them.

She was very, *very* grateful for the soundproofed bubble.

She arched her back, pressing her hips against his as Kartix moaned against her mouth. She wanted to devour him, mind, body, and soul. Leave not an inch untouched, untasted.

The pair sank to the plush carpet. She wondered what Kartix was feeling. If he was only thinking about their bodies. Because right then and there, at that moment, she almost pulled away. She *almost* told the second-most powerful male in the dynasty to—

When he nipped her bottom lip, all thoughts blinked out completely. By then, it was too late. She was already in his lap, pushing *him* down onto the plush carpet, her hands on his chest.

Kartix managed to hook his hands around her waist and gently pull her so that Sorcha was straddling him. A silk wave of her auburn hair shielded the pair, slipping down off her shoulders.

"Wait—" Kartix managed to stumble up and out of her grasp, leaning against the bookshelf. "Are you sure you want this?" he asked Sorcha, who came to stand in front of him.

Sorcha closed the last few inches of space between them, then knelt before him. She slowly unbuttoned his pants, looking up at him through lowered lashes. "Am I your favorite distraction, Kartix?"

He nodded his head, barely able to breathe.

Sorcha laughed as she palmed him through his pants. Kartix moaned and leaned into her touch.

"Do I distract you from every Helish thing in this world?"

Kartix's eyes gleamed with lust. He hardened further under her hand.

"Do you wish you could fuck me?"

Those words became his undoing.

She stroked him again through his pants. Sorcha continued, "I think, you've been thinking about fucking me for months, and if you could, you'd be buried inside me right now."

"Sorcha..." Kartix's breath was full of pain and longing.

She breathed, "Tell me to stop. Tell me you don't want this. Tell me you don't want me."

But he didn't. Instead, Kartix tilted her chin up so her eyes met his. "I love seeing you on your knees." His voice was thick with desire.

"I'd do anything for you," she whispered. "Anything."

She found the last button of his pants. Smoothly undoing every last one of Kartix's inner defenses, Sorcha continued, "Do you want me to suck your cock, Kartix?"

Every single thought disappeared from his head. There was nothing and no one but Sorcha. Nothing but her smooth skin, dark hair, piercing blue eyes gazing up at him from where she kneeled before him, like he was a religion she was praying to. And she would worship him until the end of her days.

Kartix managed to choke out the words, "You have no idea how bad I want you."

But he didn't finish his train of thought. Couldn't. Because in the next breath, Sorcha pulled his pants down just far enough to expose him. Kartix sucked in a deep breath as every inch of himself was bared to this beautiful, terrifying woman. Sorcha's eyes went wide as she took the full length of him in her hand. Her mouth went dry. *Gods, could she even fit him in her mouth?*

She looked up at him, her eyes heavy with lust. "I need to taste you."

Sorcha.

What is it, sweetheart?

Don't stop.

She didn't.

She guided him into her mouth, lips barely fitting around the tip. Kartix moaned, entwining his fingers in her hair, pressing her mouth further down on his cock.

I want to take every inch of you.

It was right then that a book flew off the shelf and promptly smacked Sorcha in the head. Her yelp echoed off the soundproofed bubble. She rolled off the shocked male and hissed, her head in her hands. She moaned, and this time not from arousal. "That really fucking hurt you know." Sorcha sent a scathing glare up to the inky darkness the bookcases faded into.

Kartix quickly buttoned his pants and snorted from beside her. "Did the library just tell us to stop?" They both stared at the book which had fallen from the stacks—*The Man Amongst Monsters,* the golden font on the spine read. Sorcha reached for the book, flipped open its contents after casting a quick cleansing spell. One might never know what might jump out from the pages. Old scrolls tended to have guardian spells cast on them long ago by the author.

Sorcha flipped open to an old, weathered page, worn from years of usage. She scanned the length of the document, her eyes flitting over each page. Kartix's heartbeat increased as he tried to peer over her shoulder. At last, Sorcha took a deep breath, reading from the text, "A man was able to walk through worlds. With this power, he ruled many lands. Cursed generations. Toppled empires."

A cold wind blew through the library. The Fae lights dimmed, as if scared of the words uttered, as if saying them aloud had given them more power.

Sorcha continued, a muscle flickering in her jaw as she leaned over the page from where she sat on the ground. "A weapon, crafted of the core of power itself, opened and closed the portals."

The bookshelves groaned in a wind, swaying slightly. The Fae lights flickered, some sputtering out completely. As Sorcha read, more shelves were plunged into darkness.

Kartix murmured, "Maybe you should stop reading."

Sorcha looked up. The library itself seemed to sway underneath their feet. More lights went out.

Kartix heard Reid call his name from somewhere far away, but a cold sensation was all Kartix could feel. "We should go. Now." Kartix outstretched his hand, helping Sorcha to her feet. She tucked the book under her arm as they strode, hand in hand, back to the main part of the library.

Once there, they met Reid, whose eyes were wide with fear. "Something feels wrong. We need to go, now."

Kartix nodded, still not taking his hand from Sorcha's, and the three exited the library, knowledge in tow.

As they gathered back in Sorcha's rooms to pore over the book, she felt something like dread creep up her spine. Reid opened the book, which rested on Sorcha's desk, and Kartix squeezed her hand, his palm warm against hers.

She looked up at the prince, her eyes at last meeting his. Something fundamental had changed between them in the library just minutes prior, something unspoken. No words were needed to discuss or define what they were to each other now. Sorcha shivered, not from dread this time, but from some emotion. Something warm slowly started to envelop her magik. To calm it, tame it. It wrapped around her soul and sank its teeth into her. It was both a claiming and a yielding.

Kartix seemed to sense just that as his hand tightened in hers. His onyx eyes flared with a mix of understanding and warmth. Of quiet joy.

Reid cleared his throat.

Both blushing, Kartix and Sorcha turned toward the male. "Yes?"

"There is a way to close the portal without Sorcha dying."

Kartix's eyes lit up, like twinkling stars. "Tell us."

"You need to basically kill a fuck-ton of Fae, drain their power, and hope it's enough to compensate for Sorcha's. That is, if she doesn't feel like sacrificing herself."

Sorcha nodded. "I can think of a few who deserve to have their magik drained."

At the mention of Sorcha sacrificing her magik, Kartix took a step forward, her hand still in his. "Sorcha dying is never an option." He challenged Reid in his stare. "Never."

Sorcha's eyes flared, her grip tightening in Kartix's hand. "We kill Senna, see if her magik is enough to seal the portal in the library. If it is, then good. If not, then we hunt more Fae in Razan's High Court. Drain them of their powers."

Reid nodded. "Gods know the bastards deserve it."

Sorcha sighed. It was well past midnight, and there were more Council meetings in the morning. They all needed their rest.

As Reid bid them good night, Kartix lingered by Sorcha's door. He turned to her. Her heart hammered against her ribs. She could only hope that despite his Fae sense of hearing, he could not detect the change in her heartbeat.

Kartix sketched a bow, murmuring. "Good night, Sorcha."

The sound of her name on his lips sent shivers up her spine. She swallowed. "Good night, prince."

He smirked and disappeared from the threshold in a blink of an eye, his magik transporting him back to his rooms. Sorcha inhaled sharply. She needed rest, but as she crawled into bed, the thought of Kartix's warm hand in hers kept her from dreaming. The heat of his palm was seared into her skin. The sheer *taste* of him lingered on her tongue.

Her hand drifted down between her thighs, stroking the wetness that awaited her there. Sorcha swore. Just thinking about Kartix sent chills up her spine. Made her instantly wet.

A few minutes later, she came at just the thought of him. Sweaty and breathless and spent, Sorcha drifted into unconsciousness thinking of the king's son, the one man she should have never touched in the first place.

40

Senna called Kartix to her room the next night. Kartix gathered with Reid and Sorcha beforehand. Sorcha paced back and forth in front of the fireplace.

Reid was hunched over the book Sorcha had found on portals the night prior. "It says that when you drain Senna's magik, it will temporarily be transferred to you, Kartix." Reid raised a brow. "Afterward, since you both made a curse bond, try sending the magik to Sorcha that way."

Kartix nodded from where he sat in front of the fireplace.

Sorcha turned to the prince. "I can give you enough magik to go into Senna's mind, sort through her inner defenses to steal her powers. You have to know a spell to go through her mind undetected, however. You only have one shot at this, so try not to fuck it up, okay?"

Kartix rolled his dark eyes. "Thanks for the vote of confidence."

Sorcha outstretched her hands to him. "Come here. I need to transfer some of my magik to you."

Kartix obeyed, standing slowly. Reid held his breath. As the Triumvirate gently placed her hands in Kartix's, she took a deep breath. "This might feel strange."

"What do you mea—"

A sudden zap of pure, unfiltered power burst out of Sorcha's fingertips. It flowed instantly up Kartix's arms, winding its way around his limbs. The soft sensation felt like silk against his skin as her magik seeped into his pores.

Sorcha took a step back, eyes wary. "Well, I hope it worked. Let me know through the curse bond if it doesn't, and I'll try to send you more magik."

Kartix rotated his neck, bringing a hand to the back of his head, blinking. "I have to go. She's expecting me." Kartix nodded at Reid, bid Sorcha farewell, and walked to the entryway.

Sorcha grabbed Kartix's arm on the way out as he made to turn away as well. "Thank you. For doing this. For going back to her." She swallowed. "I—I know what Senna plans on doing to you. Has done to you in the past. I just— I just wanted you to know I'll be thinking of you. Every second, until you're free." The pain in Sorcha's eyes was palpable, her breathing shallow. Kartix wasn't sure he was breathing as Sorcha whispered, "You better come back."

And it was at that moment that Kartix brought his hands up to cup Sorcha's face and kiss her. For barely a moment, their lips brushed before he pulled away, leaving her lips cold, then turned to the front doors of their chambers. He paused, one foot out the door, and turned back to look at her. "I needed something to come back to."

Just like that, Kartix disappeared down the hall, to meet the one woman he feared the most.

41

She was not stupid enough to ask where Senna had taken him. If he was alright.

Based on the haunted look in his eyes, Kartix was the furthest thing from okay.

It had been days now since Kartix had disappeared into their enemy's chambers. Meanwhile, Sorcha had lost weight, barely eating or drinking.

When Kartix finally reappeared from Senna's rooms, he came straight to the rooms he shared with Reid. Sorcha and Reid were still poring over the book Sorcha had stolen from the library. As soon as the prince staggered in through the doors, they slammed the book shut.

"Are you—" Sorcha's words were cut off by the heavy dragging of Kartix's feet.

He walked to his room, on the far side of the vast foyer, and shut the door without so much as an acknowledgment in their direction. Reid and Sorcha heard the bathwater run.

For several minutes, the two stood there, barefoot on the rug, listening for signs of...anything. Sorcha even unwound a sliver of magik, a small string, to amplify any sounds coming from the bathroom. She wasn't being a pervert—she just needed to see if Kartix continued to breathe.

There was nothing—no sound beyond the infinite pour of water.

Okay.

Okay then.

Sorcha ran her hands through her hair. Rubbed her face.

The candle she had lit prior to Kartix's arrival was now sputtering to a halt, wax dripping onto the plush rug. Sorcha softly padded across the velvet carpet, pressed her ear against the solid oak doors Kartix had retreated behind.

How could she get through to him? Not that Kartix would be sure to welcome her help.

Her shoulders sank. It was a mistake, letting him steal Senna's magik.

She was so, so tired. Bed was the responsible option—sleep, preparing her body for a long day of training. Yet Kartix looked near-dead. And damn her to Hel, she cared.

~

Reid found Sorcha the next morning, asleep, curled up next to Kartix's door.

Reid softly smiled. At least his brother had someone other than him to keep him safe.

Kartix didn't come out of his room the next day.

Or the day after.

Or the day after that.

Reid had attempted several times to reason with him through the door. They both had. On the third day, she began writing him notes.

It began as: *Please come out.*

They quickly evolved into more desperate notes: *Talk to me.*

It had been days since then, and still, nothing.

The rest of the rebellion was listening for Senna to make a ruckus about her magik being stolen. Thanks to the spells that Kartix had placed in her mind, she would not notice for a few more days.

Razan had gone again to the mountain where the stolen magik was kept. The king had been absent for days.

Kartix was still holed up in his room.
Whatever had happened with Senna had devastated
Kartix in a way Sorcha had never seen before.

What had happened?

~

One night later, Sorcha had again resorted to
curling up outside Kartix's room. The clock chimed
midnight. Sorcha leaned her forehead against the
prince's oak bedroom doors. She sighed, alone in the
vast foyer. She allowed a whisper to unfold in the
darkness. "Are you alright?"

A soft caress echoed against her core of
magik, comforting and familiar: *Yes.*

It took every ounce of strength to not jump
out of her skin at the sound of Kartix's voice in her
head. A heartbeat later, she could not keep the
desperation from leaking into her voice as she
begged, *Come out.*

Kartix's voice was quiet in her head when he
responded, *Come in.*

The door handles shot up and out, oak doors instantly parted. Sorcha sucked in a deep breath.

As she beheld the husk of a man who had opened the door, words failed her. Standing in the doorway, she thought Kartix looked as dismal as she felt. Sorcha had to shock him out of this... state that he was in. Seeing him like this tore her heart to shreds.

Sorcha crossed her arms, cocking her head to one side. "I'm not going to ask what happened with Senna because clearly neither of us wishes to talk about it right now." Sorcha swallowed. "If you ever *do* want to talk, one day, about what she did to you, I will be ready to listen, to support you."

Kartix pulled her inside his rooms and shut the doors quickly, before turning toward her, mere feet apart in the darkness of his rooms. His voice was soft as he said, "What she did to me is not important right now. What is important is that I absorbed every single drop of that bitch's magik."

For once, Sorcha smiled. They would talk about what Senna did to Kartix later, when he was ready. She would never force or push him to share.

What was important at that moment was the fact that the prince had absorbed Senna's magik.

When the two joined hands, he transferred all of that power to Sorcha, and she felt something like hope light up her heart.

As every single drop of magik was absorbed into her own body and Sorcha opened her eyes again, it was as if she was seeing the world for the very first time.

That night, after a full day of training and King's Council meetings, the rebellion gathered in the archives of the library.

Marie and Facim stood guard, their backs to the open portal, which still loomed at the back wall. Reid had his sword out and eyes scanning, keeping watch as well.

Sorcha stood in front of the open portal, Kartix hovering just behind her. Through the gaping hole into another dimension, Sorcha could not make anything out besides swirling dark mist which shrouded anything from view. She awoke her magik, curling it around her arms. Absorbing Senna's magik had sent her normal powers into overdrive. They were aching to be used, to be put to work.

Taking a deep breath, Sorcha tensed, outstretching her fingers, pointing them at the open portal. No one moved a muscle as Sorcha allowed her magik to flow out of her in a golden cascade of light.

It poked and prodded the edges of the portal, cringing away in fear. But Sorcha only gritted her teeth.

Close the portal.

Protesting, but eventually caving in, Sorcha's powers began to weave across the portal. Like a spider weaving a web, Sorcha's magik covered the entrance in narrow threads of light. Golden, shimmering, and wonderful, the light chased away the darkness until there was nothing left but an empty book, lying open on the floor.

Sorcha walked over and carefully picked up the book, closing it.

Marie, Facim and Reid all lowered their swords. "Did it work?"

Sorcha looked up at her friends, meeting everyone's eyes. She nodded, a slow smile creeping over her beautiful features. "We closed the portal."

By now the rebellion had assumed that Senna had not realized she no longer had magik, thanks to the binding spells Sorcha had given Kartix to place in her mind. By the time Senna tried to use her powers, there was enough buffer time between when Kartix had absorbed her magik, and Senna's discovery.

Their problem, however, lay not with Senna, but Razan. The next morning after Sorcha had closed the portal, Razan stormed into the King's Council chamber, having returned from his trip to the mountain. The king, meeting everyone's stares, said slowly, "There is a Fae amongst us who has deceived me."

Sorcha's blood went cold. The room was so silent, one could hear parchment land on the floor. Razan continued, "Someone seems to have absorbed the trove of stolen magik and now they are using their powers around the Compound." He shook his head, inky black hair shining in the mid-morning light. The king smiled, a thing of death. "You have given me no choice. Until we find this powerful Fae, we shall be interrogating each and every one of you."

Sorcha swallowed. The woman next to her shifted uncomfortably in her seat.

Razan shrugged. "Starting now." The king pointed to the woman to Sorcha's direct left. Razan grinned softly. "Off with her head."

The woman rose as guards rushed toward her. "No, no, please. I've always been faithful. *I've always been faithful!*" Her screams were cut short by the cut of Razan's blade. As the decapitated woman bled out on the floor, Razan once more looked at the King's Council. Sorcha willed her features into cool neutrality.

"This is what happens when you keep secrets." Razan wiped the sweat off his brow, his black clothing gleaming in the light. "I will kill one member each day until this powerful Fae is brought to me." Razan smiled. "You are all dismissed."

45

That night, Sorcha burst through the doors of the Assassins Guild with Reid and Kartix right behind her. The three marched to the back room, throwing open the curtains which sectioned off Facim and Marie's office. Marie was in the middle of shoving her dinner in her face, and Facim was partly drunk, but immediately sobered up when she read the look on Sorcha's face. "What is it? What happened?"

Sorcha shook her head, "Razan knows someone absorbed the trove of magik. He knows someone is using it around the Compound."

Reid continued, filling in the gaps, "He started killing off King's Council members."

Marie gasped, placing a hand over her mouth.

Kartix cut in. "My father plans on killing one Fae every day until this powerful magik user is brought forward."

"I must turn myself in." Sorcha said quietly.

Kartix immediately stepped toward her. The prince furrowed his brows. "No. That's never an option."

Facim shook her head. "No, Sorcha has a point."

Catching on, Marie nodded. "Facim is right. If Sorcha can distract Razan, we might have a chance at taking him down. We need something the king wants, something that would lure him out of the safety of the Compound. What better prize than the third Triumvirate?"

She looked to Sorcha. "If you reveal your status as the final Triumvirate, then Razan will surely want to capture you."

Facim continued, "Surely the king will send the King's Guard. How do we counter them?"

Marie crossed her arms. "We blow up the slum island, with the soldiers on it. Sorcha reveals her Triumvirate status by using her powers to set the island on fire."

Sorcha raised her hands in defense. "What about the displaced citizens who live in the slums? Where will they live after we incinerate their homes?"

Marie said, "We'll bring them all to the Assassins Guild. The warehouse is big enough to host the few dozen people who are left in the slums. We have enough supplies and weapons."

Reid shrugged. "I hate to say it, but it's a good plan."

Sorcha nodded. "With the amount of magik I've absorbed over the past few weeks, from both the trove and Senna, I actually have a chance at battling Razan." Sorcha swallowed, curling her hands into fists. "I can defeat him. I know it."

Kartix said quietly. "We need to blow up the slums when Razan's army is there. He is nothing without his loyal followers. We take away Razan's strength, his military."

Marie and Facim nodded.

Reid countered, "So, what? Sorcha lights a fire in the slums to get Razan's attention, causing a whole lot of commotion? Then, we can only hope that Razan sends his army to the slums instead of going himself?"

"If Razan himself comes, then I can take him on," Sorcha said.

Everyone nodded. Marie turned to Sorcha. "So, when should we put our plan into action?"

Sorcha took a deep breath. "Tomorrow night. There is a ball. After festivities wind down, most humans and magik users in the

Compound—soldiers included—will be drunk and heavy with good food. Later that night, we'll make our final stand. Right before dawn."

Everyone swallowed. It was as if the world held its breath.

Sorcha continued. "Tomorrow night, I reveal my Triumvirate status, drawing Razan's army to the slums. Once there, we use my magik to blow up the island. Then, once his army is defeated, I go after Razan."

Kartix's eyes were dark, unreadable.

Facim nodded. "We'd better start preparing."

Marie cut in. "Tomorrow night, after the ball, we'll start sneaking the citizens of the slums to the Assassins Guild. Then, once everyone is hiding, Sorcha, you light it up."

The assassin smiled as she looked at her friends. Although the idea of battling Razan scared her to death, Sorcha realized there was no better way she would rather go.

46

The masqueraders were drunk by midnight. The string quartet at the northern end of the ballroom was playing its way through waltzes. As the melodies rose through the air, twisting and turning in time with the dancers, Sorcha practically bounced up and down in her silk slippers.

She had always loved music. Back at the cottage, Meg had taught her to play the piano.

Images of blood splatters on white piano keys flickered across her memory. Razan had taken music from her that day, as well.

Sorcha watched the dancers with envy. How she wished she could get lost in the music, in the notes, lose herself to the rhythm of the night. She was dressed for the occasion, so it wasn't as if Sorcha couldn't blend into the dancers dripping in their finery. She was wearing the assigned colors of the King's Council—red, black, and gold. It separated her from other members of the court. The colors were a sign to stay away, that she, Reid, and Kartix were indeed state property.

Which was fine by her since Sorcha would do anything to avoid the curious glances of males. Nevertheless, she thought she looked pretty, if she could say so about herself. She had taken her time to dress carefully that night. It was mere hours before the rebellion was to put their plan into action. It needed to look like nothing was amiss. Perfect, even.

So, Sorcha had to look completely composed, as to not give off the slightest inclination that something was off.

That night, it had taken help from a woman servant to tame her corset into submission. The golden dress was falling off her shoulders. The crimson and black swaths of silk and chiffon surrounding her legs were not made to fight either. Sorcha was already itching to be back in her black fighting leathers. The diamond choker at her throat was cold against her flushed, pale skin.

Sorcha had come to the banquet alone. Reid, Marie, Facim, and Kartix were busy during the day and would meet her at the banquet later.

She blew out a breath and murmured to herself, "Let's get on with it, shall we?" She wound herself through the crowds, dressed in their finery.

Blood money, all of it. Even the clothes she was wearing.

Sorcha swallowed. Where were her friends? They were supposed to meet her at the champagne fountain—yes, a literal *fountain of champagne.*

Where the Hel were the rest of the rebellion? They were not on time.

At last, Reid and Marie were spotted through the crowd, their heads hunched together, laughing softly as if discussing something incredibly fascinating and important. She didn't say anything, but smiled softly at the pair. "It's about time you showed up."

Felix's dark eyes flashed with amusement. "You look beautiful. Both of you do." He turned toward Marie, smiling softly. "May I have this dance?"

She practically leaped out of her skin. "Yes!" She dragged Reid onto the floor herself, the waltz having begun anew.

Sorcha watched the pair weave and bob through the intricate dance. Marie stepped on Felix's feet half the time, but each time the male laughed, his great voice booming over the violins. Sorcha smiled wide and laughed to herself.

"Well, that's a first. The notorious assassin actually laughs?" A shiver went up her spine as Kartix appeared behind her shoulder. His words were whisper soft, yet his tone was playful as he bowed to her.

A new waltz began. Sorcha and Kartix were now one of the few couples left standing on the outskirts of the dancing. Candles lit the room, the lights casting a hazy glow over the crowd, as if almost enchanted.

Sorcha didn't realize she was bobbing her head in time to the music until Kartix asked, "Since you seem so enthralled in the waltz, why don't you accompany me?" He held out a gloved hand, stepping onto the dance floor. His eyes twinkled as he beamed at her.

Whispers emerged from the crowd as he escorted her to the middle of the floor. Kartix never danced at balls. He preferred to stay silent at the king's side, always. The court was shocked when the prince escorted Sorcha out onto the floor, but she didn't care. He was hers for the next few minutes, no one else's.

As they reached the center of the marble floor, Kartix once more bowed to her, extending his hand. "May I have this dance?"

"Yes." Her voice came out in a breathless rush. Sorcha hoped she sounded stronger than she felt. She wasn't sure if she was breathing.

Kartix slipped one hand around her thin waist, another taking her hand in his. He tilted his head, dark eyes shining, as he took her in. "Let's set the world on fire, shall we?" Kartix smoothly twirled her into his arms as a new song began. Sorcha supposed, as they made their way through the intricate waltz, that Kartix was a good dancer for a reason. He had probably grown up in the Compound, being taught lessons in how to court women. Knowing the steps to popular waltzes had to be a part of his studies as a child.

As they blended in with the other dancers, Kartix asked Sorcha in a low voice, "What are your plans for later this evening?" His tone was serious, a thick, dark eyebrow arched up in a question.

Besides praying we won't die tomorrow? Not much, Sorcha spoke to Kartix in her head. Who knew who might be listening to their conversation, even amidst this celebration.

Kartix was silent as the waltz pulled them apart for a few moments. His eyes had a faraway glaze to them. The swirling darkness of his eyes matched his clothing. His black suit was impeccably tailored to his frame, the threads of the finest quality. Despite Razan being an absolute asshole, Sorcha had to admit he did have fine taste in fabrics. Despite the fact that she didn't want to think this, the thought had crossed her mind that Kartix looked painfully, incredibly handsome.

Colors blurred together as the world spun around them. The music swelled, the crescendo of the waltz nearing. Sorcha didn't want it to end. She wanted to keep going and going and going. Her magik responded to the dancing, wanting to unfurl its tendrils from somewhere deep inside her and come up to play.

Not now.

As he twirled her around, they locked eyes. The dance was intricate, fast, and slow all at once. Sometimes even intimate, given the proximity of their bodies. The rich, dripping in their finery, surrounded the pair, cutting them off in clouds of gold, skirts swirling all around them. Sorcha's hair spilled out of its updo, waves of auburn drifting down, her hair reaching her lower back. The violins and cellos played, but Sorcha could have sworn they were dancing a different waltz completely, one of their entire own language.

The music leapt from note to note with staggering beauty before falling into the final few notes. It was gorgeous. It had been years since Sorcha had heard music this beautiful.

L. Holmes

The crowd mingled as the orchestra took a short break. Kartix's hand remained in hers. "I want to take you somewhere. We should talk."

Sorcha arched an eyebrow, dropping her hand out of his. "About what?"

He shook his head. "Follow me." He led her away from the middle of the floor.

~

"What is it?" Sorcha turned toward Kartix, shutting the study doors behind them. The fire flickered from its spot in the hearth, casting orange shadows over them both. Sorcha's multicolored dress shifted over the oak floors.

An almost pained expression crossed Kartix's face. His voice tumbled out, low and broken. "Do we have a choice, Sorcha, over those our hearts want?"

"Have you had too much wine again?"

Kartix huffed a dry laugh, his black hair slanting over his eyes. "I'm being serious."

Sorcha didn't know where to look, but she said in a low voice, "I used to think we had control over what our hearts wanted, but then I realized, I'm not very good at controlling my own."

The worlds slipped out before she could stop them. Could he hear the double meaning behind her words? That she could not control her heart around him?

Sorcha glanced up from where she stood near the fireplace, flames sending golden streaks through her hair as she looked at him. "Why do you ask?"

Kartix was frozen, utterly still, as he leaned against the wall, arms crossed. His dark eyes were wide and focused on hers, his breathing ragged in his chest. His soft, onyx curls fell in his eyes as he tore his gaze away from hers. "It is not safe for you to be around me."

"Tell me something I don't know."

"I mean it, Sorcha." Kartix pushed off the wall and stalked toward her. "I put you in danger. I put all of you in danger. It would be best if I left. After we kill Razan, I won't bother you again."

Sorcha was stunned. "I don't understand. I thought you wanted to help the rebellion."

"I do. But I realize the best way to help is for me to do this alone. Let *me* face my father. I could not live with myself if something happened to you, to any of you."

Sorcha shook her head, her wavy hair brushing against her lower back. "My life is mine to give. This is what I was crafted for—I'm the martyr. I have always been the one who was supposed to be sacrificed for the greater good. That is why the Gods placed me on this earth, to protect magik. Not you. It is not your responsibility."

Kartix took a stumbling step forward. "I don't want you to sacrifice yourself. Don't you get it? *I* would be better off dead, not you."

Sorcha sucked in a rattling breath. "Shut up. Don't you ever say that again."

But Sorcha could see it now. The desperation had lit up Kartix's eyes, a certain type of hunger and pain taking up residence. This male actually believed that he could stop his father, alone.

Sorcha closed the last few feet between them. "Do not ever think, for one second, that you need to fight this battle alone."

Kartix took another step forward. "Says you. You would rather destroy yourself than live."

Sorcha's eyes lit up with rage. "What is the alternative, Kartix? We read it ourselves. The only way to seal *all* the portals is to give my magik back."

"Can't you save a drop for yourself? To keep yourself alive?"

Sorcha shook her head. "If it takes every ounce of my power to keep this world whole, then I would gladly sacrifice my own life. It has always been my purpose, and always will be. No matter who or what tries to change that."

The words came out before he could stop them. "I don't want you to die. You can't die." His voice broke on the last few words.

Sorcha paused, her anger receding. "Why do you care if I die?"

Because I love you. I can't stop thinking about you. Every moment I'm near you, it hurts.

Kartix didn't send his thoughts through the curse bond. How could he stop her from saving the world? How could he be so selfish?

"Then go. Leave me alone. Make your own decisions. I don't care. But don't for one second try to get in my way. My father is my kill, and my kill alone."

"Why didn't you speak up about this when we were all planning earlier?"

"Because I knew you would say no. I can't let you control my choices." Kartix said.

Sorcha narrowed her eyes. "You're an arrogant bastard."

"And you're a vain sorceress. We're evenly matched."

Sorcha's anger flared inside of her, her magik responding, nearly slipping loose of its grasp. "Whatever you say, *prince.*" Her voice dripped like poison from her lips, staining Kartix's very soul with its bitterness. She was being mean, but she didn't care. Sorcha turned away from him, spine straight, head held high. She wouldn't let him embarrass her.

"Goodbye, Kartix."

As she moved past him toward the door, he almost turned, to catch her by the arm.

But he didn't. He just stayed there, locked in permanence and perpetual fire as the one woman he revered most walked away.

She was drowning.

Sorcha knew that much.

Tangled in the weeds, she was pulled beneath the surface of the lake, the current carrying her far beneath the dark waters. The air had been ripped out of her lungs. The water felt like velvet against her skin, beckoning her into deeper waters. The cold tore at her body, her soul, her *magik*.

The fucking Gods were nowhere to be found. They had crafted her, cast her out into oblivion to save this planet for *themselves*, and when she needed them most, they had vanished.

Greedy bastards.

From her last moments alive, Sorcha was just able to make out a figure above the surface: a man looked at her from shore, a witness to her death. He was an older man, white hair and a weathered face, and he smiled as she was pulled under the water. She shivered, and not just from the current. Sorcha knew to be frightened of him. Something inside her warned of escape. The waves swept her under once again.

Then, coldness greeted her, and Sorcha knew she was dying.

A shock went through her body, her heart rate spiking and her eyes shooting open, suddenly aware that she was no longer unconscious. As quickly as the dream had come, it dissipated the moment Sorcha shot up out of bed, screaming, her voice echoing against the walls of her bedroom. She was covered in sweat, the hot liquid beading between every crevice of her body. Her heartbeat was a wild, thunderous thing in her chest.

Just a dream, just a dream, just a dream.

Sorcha was sobbing, hot tears running down her face.

Why did this happen?

She wasn't sure she remembered how to breathe. It was the fifth time that week that she'd had that same nightmare. She was afraid to sleep by this point, afraid to truly believe that she was awake. That she was indeed safe.

The rebellion had been up all night planning. Just after one in the morning, she finally had an hour alone to collect her thoughts after the rebellion had left her room. Sorcha had not meant to fall asleep.

A loud knock sounded at her chamber door. Panting heavily, she didn't move. She didn't yet trust that this world was, in fact, real. That she wasn't still stuck in yet another night terror. The door opened then, and Sorcha tensed her entire body, cowering back against her pillows, ready to cast herself invisible if there was indeed an intruder. She wasn't in the mood for a fight. Wasn't sure she even remembered how to use her legs. If someone was to indeed attack her, she needed—

Kartix's head of curls instantly calmed her thoughts the moment she laid eyes on the male, who was standing with quite the alarmed expression in the doorway. "I heard you screaming through the curse bond and I—" Kartix lost his voice looking at her then, cowering in her thin nightgown against the gray silk pillows. Her auburn hair had spilled out of its braid during the tossing and turning of the nightmare.

His black shirt was cut to his frame. His hair was tousled. Sorcha could tell he had awoken suddenly and ran straight to her.

Fuck modesty, he thought. Kartix had heard her screaming in the middle of the night, crying. He had jumped out of bed to come to check on her. He'd be damned if he let Sorcha push him away like she did anyone else who tried to help her.

Standing at the foot of the bed, he towered over her, his dark eyes flashing in the moonlight. Sorcha was beyond embarrassed for Kartix to see her like this.

The visions of her nightmare, the man standing on the riverbank, sent sudden tremors up her spine. Tears still streamed down her face. Was she dead? How pathetic she must look to him, Sorcha thought.

Cowering.

Weak.

Frightened.

Little did Sorcha know that Kartix thought she was the most beautiful thing he had ever seen.

She hadn't the faintest idea of his feelings for her as Kartix took her in. The male shook his head at the barely conscious woman before him, still swaying where she sat.

"I'm not going to ask if you're okay." He moved to sit down on the edge of her bed, but then hesitated. "May I?"

Sorcha was thankful he asked.

She nodded, and the male gently sunk into the soft linens of the end of her bed. Sorcha was relieved it was Kartix who her screams had awoken, instead of Reid, Marie, or Facim. She didn't think she could handle being around anyone but him at that moment.

"I won't tell anyone, if that's what you're worried about." His voice was soft and low. Kartix spoke to her as if she was a wild animal and he might spook her any second. His presence already was calming her wild heartbeat.

Sorcha's voice came out broken, scratchy as she said, "I'm not concerned with my pride. I just—" Sorcha looked out her window then, toward the distant snow-capped mountains. "I just want to sleep." She looked back at Kartix. "I just want to sleep

peacefully without dreams of this fucked up world."
She sat up, closer to him now. "Is it too naive to
believe in a better world? To hope that people can be
good just for the sake of being good?"

Kartix took her in, her skin glistening with
sweat, chest still heaving for air. Her body still had
not calmed down physically from the night terror. She
quickly unbound her braid, her hair loose and flowing
around her.

She was so beautiful.

Sorcha continued, unaware of his thoughts as
she rubbed her wrists. "Sometimes I get these...
attacks, I call them. I can't sleep all night since my
mind will torture me with horrible, terrible
memories."

She wished she had the courage to ask him to
come closer. She was trembling and couldn't stop.
She needed someone to calm her. To quiet her mind.
Was that too much to ask? Why would she think of
using *Kartix* as a possible distraction? Would he even
want her in that way? She didn't want to cut herself.
What she was feeling was not that type of destruction.
She didn't have any root to smoke to calm her

nerves—Marie and Facim had used it all the night before, when they had gotten high in her room. And alcohol was out of the question.

She needed *something*.

Through the curse bond, Sorcha asked, quietly, for just that.

Kartix met her eyes, his dark stare glowing with a simmering mix of yearning and pain. A muscle tensed in his jaw. "Tell me what you want, Sorcha."

Say it out loud.

Kartix brushed against her mind, the inner wall of her thoughts, begging to be let in. The gates to her mind were sealed shut, but she opened them just a crack for him. Only for him, would she allow her mind to be seen in this vulnerable state. Their invisible bond glowed brighter between them as Sorcha opened her mind, letting him see each one of her desires laid bare for him.

Kartix examined each and every one of her thoughts. She let him pick and comb through her mind. She didn't give a damn about the consequences. It was a first for her, letting someone inside. Sorcha was so used to being the one deciphering someone else's thoughts. It was refreshing not to be alone in her own head, for once.

As they sat there on her bed, silently staring at each other, Sorcha finally closed the connection. She pulled him out of her mind, shutting firmly the gates to her thoughts once more. Her shivering had receded, but Sorcha was filled with a sudden cold.

It was Kartix's turn to tremble now. Sorcha had shown him what she wanted, and he wanted to give it to her.

Gods, he wanted to give her *so many things*.

Sorcha bit her bottom lip, unconsciously sitting up even more, the covers sliding off her lap, exposing her bare legs. Despite her best intentions, the pale blue nightdress she wore was the furthest thing from modest. In her defense, Sorcha had no idea when she had fallen asleep earlier that a male would be standing in her room half an hour later. She *would* have dressed more modestly.

Sorcha was all too aware that Kartix was trying painfully hard to disguise the fact that he couldn't take his eyes off her. His pupils dilated and she could have sworn Kartix's breathing hitched as he beheld her bare legs.

Now he could see every dip and curve of her body, and he hated himself incredibly in that moment for the thoughts racing through his mind, heating his very core.

Kartix did not know how long he could stand this game they were playing. One of them had to win eventually.

The moonlight slanted in through the floor-to-ceiling windows, illuminating her bedroom. Kartix was suddenly very thankful he had remembered to close the door.

The tension in the room grew to be too much for Sorcha. From where she sat, avoiding his gaze, she wondered if she should be the one to break this silence.

Could she walk across that razor-thin line?

She wanted to.

Gods, how she wanted him—no, *needed* him. In a way she had never felt before.

Kartix choked the words out before he could stop himself, "Forgive me for how I acted back in the study." From where he sat on the edge of her bed, Kartix had a pained expression on his face.

To Hel with boundaries, she thought. *"Come here."* Her voice was soft and commanding all at once, with a touch of longing.

Kartix slowly stood from where he sat at the end of the bed. Never taking his eyes off hers, he silently came around to the side. She moved over to make space for him to join her, beside her, but Kartix hesitated. "What do you want, Sorcha?" His voice dripped like honey from his lips.

Sorcha breathed, "Just get in before I change my mind."

Who was he to argue with that?

The sheets settled around them in a cloud of silk. It felt whisper soft against Kartix's tan skin, as he lay there next to her. The rebellion was due to resume planning in an hour, and Sorcha dreaded the rest of the night.

"I need sleep, but I'm too afraid to dream," she admitted in the dark.

Kartix was lying on his back, not facing her, but with that sudden admission, he turned on his side to meet her stare. It was purely instinctual for his hand to rise up to brush a stray strand of hair from her face. She moved closer, leaning into his touch.

There was no going back now. He was in her Godsdamned bed. Sorcha realized at that moment, if she was going to Hel, it would be worth it. She didn't give a damn anymore. With every moment that ticked by, Sorcha realized that she wanted him. She wanted him *so bad*.

Their bodies were only inches apart now, despite the size of her bed. Sorcha was still trembling, not having shaken off the horrors of the night terror. Memories of blood and children screaming, of flames and ash filled her mind, stained her very soul. "It was horrible." she whispered, her breath nearly catching in her throat. She met his eyes, then, in the dark. "And the worst part is that my nightmares are no different than reality, than what we are facing, the rebellion, this city, all of us."

She knew what he was going to ask before the question even formed on his lips. "I want you to stay, yes."

Kartix nodded, his massive frame already having taken up her bed at this point.

Sorcha managed to huff a dry laugh. "You're taking up most of my bed, you brute."

Kartix shrugged, the movement alone sending her silk sheets swirling. "Then tell me to leave." A few moments of silence ticked by. They both knew she would never tell him to.

What are we doing?

Kartix's gaze refused to leave her face.

I think we both know.

Sorcha briefly closed her eyes.

It was at that moment that Kartix realized what Sorcha was asking for. "Do you want a distraction?" He tilted his head, searching her eyes for the answer, his black hair slanting over his face.

"Yes," she breathed, barely able to contain herself now that they were in such close proximity. "Yes, I do."

A wicked smile curved his full lips. "Sorry to disappoint, but I'm realizing that this bed is not nearly big enough for me to fuck you in."

Sorcha's toes curled underneath the covers. "Is that so?" Her voice was soft and slow. Yes, this distraction was working. Although she could still feel the weeds dragging her down, down beneath the waves, the coldness of the waters choking her, Sorcha felt... better.

"Hey, where'd you go?" Kartix took in the blank, distant expression on her face.

Sorcha blinked. "Sorry, I—I was just thinking about the nightmare. Sometimes they can turn out to be prophecies or visions from the Gods." Sorcha shook her head. "But they have cut me off. I haven't heard from them in years. Why would the Gods send me a vision of my own death? If the nightmare was, in fact, from them."

Kartix swept his hand up her back in comforting, broad strokes. His hand was warm, and it was calloused in all the right places.

Sorcha wondered how those callouses might feel on different parts of her body. Her cheeks heated. Why did she always think such treacherous thoughts? This was not her purpose. She locked eyes with Kartix then. They were both laying on their sides, the moonlight the only light in the room. "I can't sleep."

Will you stay?

Kartix moved closer to her, the heat of his body settling over her bones. Sorcha hadn't realized how cold she was until Kartix had gently come even closer. His black cotton shirt had shifted up during the process of getting into her bed, and exposed his midriff. His dark skin showed the hardened muscle underneath, and it was all Sorcha could do to not look. She swallowed, trying not to show her sudden desire. She was having trouble breathing, and this time, it wasn't because she was afraid.

"This wasn't supposed to happen, this thing between us." Sorcha's voice was soft and full of longing.

Kartix took her hand and brushed his lips across her exposed palm. "I know, but thank the Gods it did," he murmured against her skin, his hot breath sending chills up her spine. He smiled as she managed to move even closer to him under the covers. She was burning up, burning alive at his closeness. The bed was soft and enveloped them in its sheets. There was no one to stop them now, Sorcha realized. No one was awake. No one would come in. No library to throw books at them. The best of all? No one would know.

Kartix, too, had seemed to catch on to the fact that the two of them might set the world on fire—literally and figuratively—if they weren't careful. Sorcha did not know if she could handle the release that she knew he would give her, if she would be able to keep her magik on a leash if he did bed her. She might explode her dresser or send the curtains up in flames if she wasn't careful. Gods only knew how he could make her lose control.

A nightgown strap had fallen off her shoulder, Sorcha's clavicle now on full display. Her pale skin glowed like a diamond in the moonlight in contrast to the inky night sky that was her dark hair.

Kartix thought she was the most beautiful woman he had ever seen.

Sorcha lifted her hand to run it through his onyx hair, like silk between her fingers. He leaned into her touch, their breath now mingling.

Sorcha did not know how much time had passed since the nightmare. It could have been ten minutes or ten hours. All time was irrelevant when she looked at Kartix.

Bare inches separated their lips and Sorcha could not remember how to breathe. She could not think, could not fathom the position in which she found herself, her thin frame almost pushed against that of the most handsome male she had ever seen.

Just fucking kiss me already.

Sorcha wanted to let him back into her mind just to tell him that, but she was so scared. Too frightened. What if Kartix said no? What if it went to waste and it was all just—

Every single thought blinked out of her head as Kartix slipped one hand around her waist and pulled her against him. Her entire body was pressed up against him now.

Not for one second more did Sorcha regret having that nightmare.

She slipped her arms around his neck as they locked eyes.

"Tell me what you want, Sorcha." Kartix's voice was soft. His expression was almost painful as he took her in with wide eyes, as if he was trying to memorize every inch of her features. As if he might never be able to be this close to her ever again. His thick, dark lashes brushed his cheek. He was so devastatingly gorgeous.

"I want you." The world hinged on those three words.

Sorcha's blue eyes met Kartix's dark ones. She was lost in his gaze and never wanted to find her way back. To Hel with the rest of the world. It was someone else's turn to be the martyr for the Gods, for once. Right now, Sorcha didn't care about anyone or anything else except the two of them. It felt good to not care. To be selfish, greedy almost, in what she wanted. To not have to think about the consequences of her actions.

Sorcha pressed herself against him. Kartix could feel every dip and curve of her body. He sucked in a deep breath, his eyes wild and hot and filled with a type of darkness Sorcha wanted to fall into.

She took a deep breath, "We're not meant to be—" but she got no further. A moment later, Kartix's hand cupped the back of her neck, closing the last few inches of space between them carefully. But Sorcha didn't want careful. She wanted flames to devour them both, wanted to take him somewhere far, far away and never give him back.

You're mine.

The words echoed in her mind. She didn't know who had said it. It didn't matter, and she didn't care. All Sorcha knew was that Kartix was kissing her, gloriously, gloriously kissing her. His lips were so soft, and he tasted of spices and sweetened wine. She didn't know if this was real, another nightmare, or more of a dream. But it didn't matter. Nothing mattered except the way he was kissing her. Gods, it was so devastatingly *good.*

She wrapped her arms around his neck, arching her body up against his, her fingers sliding through his raven-dark hair.

Kartix rested one forearm on the sheets, raising himself slightly. He was so much taller than her that the shift in stance alone sent him hovering over her, Sorcha now beneath him entirely. Gods, how she liked it.

She opened her lips against his, and he cupped the back of her neck, deepening the kiss. Her magik awoke inside her, wanting to play.

Not now.

Sorcha almost groaned at the interruption, but Kartix only huffed a laugh against her mouth. "It looks like someone wants to play."

A near growl escaped from her lips. "Play later."

"Indeed."

Sorcha was swimming in dizziness.

She felt Kartix run his hand in broad, sweeping strokes up and down her curves. He was touching so much of her and yet not nearly enough. She ground her hips against him and Kartix couldn't help the moan that escaped him. Sorcha captured the sound with her lips, wanting, *needing* to have more of him. To taste more of him.

Kartix's lips were firm and sweet, taunting, as he hovered above her, taking his time with his hand as he caressed her body. Sorcha tried to deepen the kiss by rising up on her forearms, but Kartix only pushed her down, his soft laugh sending shivers down her spine. "So greedy."

Sorcha pulled his head down to hers, one hand in his dark hair, the other wrapped around his waist. His shirt had ridden up and his abdomen was on full display. His skin was tanned with decades of hardened muscle underneath. Her hand slipped underneath his shirt. She shivered in amazement. She was touching his skin, his bare skin. He didn't pull away. In fact, Kartix leaned into her touch, and she explored more of his body. Sorcha played with the hem of his shirt. "You should take this off."

His dark eyebrow arched. "Only if you take yours off."

"But this is all I have." The thin blue nightgown was, in fact, all she was wearing.

"Is that so?" Kartix emphasized his question by slowly running his hand down her side, bringing his hand underneath her nightgown, just above her knee. He rested his hand on her bare thigh. "You're not wearing anything but this?" Kartix's breathing had gone ragged, his eyes burning, his pupils wide and black.

Sorcha's eyes silently begged him to move his hand higher, higher, on her leg.

He did.

Slowly, all *too* slowly for her liking, Kartix slid his hand up the very center of her. Sorcha gasped as he beheld what wetness awaited him there. Kartix sighed, needing to feel more of her. He stroked her then, coaxing moans out of Sorcha with his fingers, which Kartix then brought to his lips. "You have no idea how long I've wanted to taste you."

She whimpered softly. She could die from this, from wanting him.

Kartix pinned her down with both of Sorcha's hands over her head, as he kissed her cheeks, her neck, her chest. Sorcha was burning, burning, burning, and she didn't care about anything else but them at that moment. This was dangerous—*they* were dangerous. She loved it.

Kartix pressed himself against her, the full length of him along her body. He was massive compared to her small, thin frame. She was dedicated to showing him just how much she could keep pace with him. His hands found the bottom of her nightgown, taking it off her in a second, and Sorcha sat up, bringing her arms above her head to help him.

What he saw made Kartix nearly die.

She was so beautiful, her pale skin glowing in the moonlight, hair spilling out of its braid.

She lay back down, her eyes begging him to be on top of her once more.

He obliged her.

Kartix captured a generous breast in his mouth, and she cried out as his tongue swirled and found all the right spots. For once, she didn't want to get lost, to lose herself. Instead, she wanted to remember every single moment, memorize every inch of him. His dark skin glowed in the starlight, and she thought she would cry of happiness.

Kartix trembled as he kissed his way down her navel. Then further down, down, down until he reached the apex of her thighs.

Then, she exploded.

In Sorcha's defense, she hadn't had anyone go down on her in *years,* so she wasn't entirely surprised when her bedsheets went up in flames. The blue and white fire did not burn the pair, or hurt in any way at all, for her magik knew friend from foe.

Kartix laughed as the flames illuminated them. "I can finally see all of you," he whispered from where he lay between her thighs.

She moaned as he kissed her then, running his tongue over that sensitive, *sensitive* spot. For minutes he feasted on her, and not once did Sorcha feel guilty about riding the edge of pleasure.

You're so beautiful, Kartix whispered in her mind, brushing up against her inner wall, begging to be let in as she cried out. Sorcha didn't know if she was calling out his name or not. She arched her back as she ran her fingers through his hair.

The world ceased to exist. She had no words for it. Nothing and no one had ever felt this fucking *good.* His magik swept over her in a wave of inky night sky. The only thing she could see was his stars and her fire, their magik entwined in the night. There was no end and no beginning. It was everything. It was nothing.

Was this nothing? Was she nothing to him? Was all this a game to him?

But his magik soothed her muscles, winding their way through her body in comforting strokes. "Come for me, sweetheart," Kartix murmured against her skin.

She did.

Sorcha tipped over the edge of pleasure and fell down, down, down, into somewhere very far away. She cried out in ecstasy as her flames burned higher, brighter around the pair, her magik responding in its own pleasure. Everything was on fire but them and she didn't care.

She didn't fucking care.

Kartix smiled and kissed her inner thighs. "I've waited so long for this. You have *no* idea."

Only then, after her climax, did Sorcha realize how tired she was. How badly she needed sleep. Kartix seemed to sense just that as he kissed his way up her body once more, his soft lips making her want to start all over again. His mouth met hers and Sorcha pulled her body once more against his.

Stay.

She was not above begging.

I never planned on leaving.

Sorcha dared let a hint of a smile show.

Kartix gently lay down beside her, pulling her against him. His chest leaked warmth into her back as Sorcha curled up beside him. As she drifted off peacefully in his arms, the flames around them faded out, her magik now cooling the room into a drowsy aura.

All through the night Kartix held her, and not once did she have a single nightmare.

48

By the time Sorcha awoke, Kartix was gone. Sorcha had only slept an hour. There were still four hours till dawn. She needed her rest in order to use all of her magik.

Kartix and Reid were preparing with Senna and Facim at the Assassins Guild. It would take only half an hour to gather the few dozen people still left in the slums. The plan was as follows: once Marie and Facim had gathered all the citizens in the Assassins Guild, Sorcha would light the main section of the slums on fire, using her magik. This level of power would expose Sorcha as a Triumvirate, making her the most highly prized possession in the entire damn Northern Continent. They could only hope that Sorcha would be able to blow up the island and every single one of Razan's soldiers along with it.

Sorcha slipped out of her bed, dressing quickly in her fighting leathers. She braided back her long, brown hair. She looked at herself in the mirror.

Sorcha barely recognized herself.

~

Hours later, when dawn was just about to break, Sorcha stood in the courtyard of the slums. She flexed her fingers. Her friends had gathered all the citizens of the slums. There was no one left on the main part of the island now, they were all safe and hidden at the Assassin's Guild. Thank God that part of the plan had gone accordingly. Now it was all up to Sorcha.

Sorcha walked to the slums through the tunnels, feeling the flames already dancing in her hands, ready to go. Once she reached the main part of the slums, far away from the Assassins Guild, she planted her feet in the dirt road facing the mainland. She could spot the Compound in the swirling mist of dawn.

She took a deep breath, unfurling her magik, allowing it to bubble to the surface. It wound itself along her skin, her bones, her blood as it powered its way through every molecule in her body. The magik was light, pure, and good. Sorcha gritted her teeth, remembering why she was here. Remembered Meg's face as she was dragged into the carriage and carted away, all those years ago from their village. Sorcha remembered the fact that she still had not found her sister, that Meg was still a slave—if she was even alive.

Marie's words echoed in her mind.

Light it up.

It was with that thought, those feelings of rage, that Sorcha unleashed every drop of magik upon the slums, watching it all go up in flames.

Broken down storefronts were covered in fire within seconds. The blaze grew stronger and higher with each passing minute. Sorcha kept lighting fires as she walked through the empty streets. After five minutes, she hid in an alleyway she had not yet set aflame. She could see the soldiers running to the slums, armor clinking, as the fire glinted in the distance. She could hear the soldiers screaming as flame enveloped them. A few men came too close to where she was hiding, so she allowed her magik to boil the blood in their veins. Once they dropped to the ground, dead, she turned back to see Razan's army burning. Sorcha watched from the shadows, a smile on her face. Ash and smoke billowed around them.

Sorcha then gathered her power, and she exploded the main part of the slums.

49

The main part of the slum island exploding had to be one of the most beautiful sights Reid had seen in years. He and Kartix stood on the edge of the mainland, where the rich liked to gather overlooking the Sea of Discontent. The water reflected the flames, as it had for months, but this time, it was different. The flames glowed brighter, burning hotter than any of the fires Razan and his army had ever set. One could hear, for the first time, the screams of the dying from the mainland. This time, however, it was not the screams of the innocent, but the damned. Soldiers burned better than tinder.

As Reid and Kartix stood on the edge of the sea, looking out into the now-cleared horizon, something like peace washed over the two males. Sorcha had done it. She had lured the king's army to the slums. Once all the soldiers were gathered, attempting to take Sorcha down, she had blown up the island.

That was the first half of the plan. The second half had barely begun. Kartix and Reid now had to make sure Sorcha was safely escorted to the compound through the tunnels so that she could battle Razan while the rebellion still had the element of surprise.

Reid turned to the prince, smiling softly. "She did it. She actually blew up his army."

Kartix returned his half-brother's grin. "She's magnificent, isn't she?

A cold wind blew in from the north, sending goosebumps over the prince's skin. He felt his father's power before he saw him. Kartix only had a few moments of breath before he realized Razan was behind him, dagger pressed up against his tan skin. His father hissed in his ear, "You will come with me, boy."

The prince shot his eyes towards Reid, every muscle in his body frozen. Reid was helpless. Razan's magik held him as if in perpetual stone. He could not move to help his brother. He could only watch with fear as Kartix was dragged away by Razan.

A collar of Mahoun was strapped around both the Fae males' necks, draining their magik to a near trickle. The pair was dragged through the empty streets of Ocyla and thrown into the main square. The old theatre overlooked the large space. As Kartix was hauled to Razan's side, the dagger still pressed against his throat, he looked to Reid, who had been forced to his knees by a guard.

The prince thought of Sorcha, the woman he loved. He thought of how she had succeeded, how she had blown up part of the slums, and most of Razan's army.

As the king looked down at his son and spit in his face, Kartix didn't even flinch. All he could think of was Sorcha. His partner. His equal in every way.

But the worst part was, Kartix could no longer feel the curse bond.

50

Sorcha ran as swiftly as she could through the underground tunnels. Kartix and Reid had not been at the entrance to the tunnels in the slums. Had something happened to them?

Sorcha had sent a message to Kartix asking where they were, but the curse bond was a cold—almost dead—thing in her chest.

Panic laced her veins. She ran faster.

Her right heel ached, and she was pretty sure she was bleeding from her left bicep, but whatever. She had been crafted to destroy herself for others. She was sure that the Gods had pictured her death differently. Surely they had meant for her to die protecting magik, not a few dozen people, selfish bastards that the Gods were.

One person or one thousand, it didn't make a difference to her. Sorcha was thankful, for just one moment, that the Gods had been cut off. They couldn't tell her what to do, or where to go, or who to see. She had lived for so long, trained, studied, learned everything there was about this stupid fucking world, and now that she had become a living breathing *being* of this inexplicably human realm, she realized she loved this world.

She truly, honestly loved this world.

And wanted to save it.

The Gods would be furious. They would have forbidden her to get attached and would have probably drained her powers and given them to another woman. But Sorcha understood then that she would willingly give up her magik if that meant saving others.

Sorcha wanted to live.

Not just survive.

But to *live.*

She could hear the clamor of battle breaking out above her head, the tunnels now winding their way beneath the main courtyard of the Compound. A few dozen citizens of the slums had chosen to assist the rebellion in fighting what was left of Razan's guards on the mainland.

Sorcha was running behind schedule.

She ran as fast as her body would allow without magik. Sorcha wished she could run with the assistance of her powers, but she needed to store up energy, to dive deeper into that vast, expansive space inside her, where her magik lived. She couldn't waste one single drop of power.

Once she saw the light at the end of the tunnel, she almost gave a sob of relief, her legs trembling beneath her. Despite the theatre's having been closed years ago, the rebellion had managed to repair it and turn it into a second base.

When she emerged in the theatre, she immediately had her magik up and forming a shield around her. The citizens from the slums were engaged in a bloody struggle with the remaining army, who were, admittedly, winning at the moment. Screams were silenced by metal swords. Most of the citizens were humans, unable to fight with magik. People were running, toppling over each other in an attempt to outrun the army.

Sorcha panicked, and before she could stop herself, her magik had slit the throats of several of the guards. Gasps echoed around the theatre as Sorcha raced down the main aisle, heading straight for the front doors. As she jumped over dead bodies, she noted the change in battle. The citizens were winning now, Sorcha having killed the majority of the guards. People cheered as she rushed by, and just for a second, Sorcha dared to allow a hint of a smile to form on her blood-stained lips.

As she emerged from the theatre onto the main street of Ocyla, she halted in her tracks.

Razan stood in the middle of the clearing, a dagger pressed to his son's throat. Kartix was kneeling on the cobblestones, fear, dread, and something else lighting up his eyes as he saw Sorcha. A chain of Mahoun encircled his neck. Kartix's powers had been completely drained.

Reid, Facim, and Marie were all on the outskirts of the circle of citizens, watching from under lowered brows, guards holding swords at their throats.

Razan hissed through clenched teeth, holding Kartix closer to the dagger. "I always knew it was you."

Sorcha arched a brow. "Here I am, your highness."

Razan cut right to the point. "I'll trade his life for yours if you put this collar of Mahoun on. It is that simple, my dear."

Marie cried out from where she was being held. "Sorcha, no! It's a trap!" She was shut up as a guard promptly hit her across the face.

Sorcha only turned slowly to meet Razan. She slowly nodded. "Free him first, and then I'll put on the collar."

Razan's magik hit her before she could brace herself. A dark, swirling cloud of horrible, evil power rolled over Sorcha. She felt something tighten around her neck. She could barely breathe, barely think, as Razan strapped the collar of Mahoun to her neck.

Sorcha fell to her knees, her magik swallowed up completely.

She didn't have time to say goodbye. All she could see from her blurred vision was the outline of Marie's frame where she crouched, screaming Sorcha's name over and over. No sounds got through. She was completely numb. Sorcha felt a hot tear stream down her face. She'd never had friends before, friends who would willingly go out on a limb to save her life.

I'm sorry, was what she wished she could say.

I'm sorry for failing you.

She heard everything as if she was underwater. Sorcha knew she had been weakened, Razan's collar having swallowed up her magik thoroughly at that point. Her body gave out under her. Now she was nothing but a shell, an empty husk of a host.

What would the Gods think of her now?

Even though she knew better, all she cared about was the crumpled body in front of her. While Razan had strapped on Sorcha's collar, he had stabbed Kartix. Their bargain was no more.

Sorcha knew she was begging for his life, but no sounds pierced her ears. She knew she was on her hands and knees, crawling toward Kartix, utterly pathetic, but she could barely feel the stones as they scraped open her skin. All she could hear was Kartix's cry of pain as he fell to the ground, his white shirt stained with blood. It had been her idea to wear white under the black fighting leathers. It was easier, she said, to identify when and where they were injured in battle that way.

All she could see was Razan's blade buried deep in his side. Kartix's usually tanned face was now ashen white, the color leaching from his skin with every drop of blood he spilled.

Razan shoved Kartix, his *son,* across the cobblestones, sending him tumbling her way. Sorcha rushed to meet Kartix as he stumbled, his legs giving out from under him. It was only when she caught him in her arms that she felt the wet warmth spreading against his side. The blood was pouring too quickly from the wound. She examined the dying male before her, and she noted how shallow his breathing had become.

Razan brazenly took in the pair. "You may collect his body." His tone was casual, completely neutral, as if nothing had happened at all. As if he hadn't just stabbed his *son.*

She did not notice Reid and Facim rushing to their sides, freed at last by their guards. They collected Kartix's body and brought him back several yards, to where a medic could properly assess him. Sorcha was still kneeling on the ground in the pool of blood.

She was so, so tired.

Razan stalked to her. He grabbed her by the throat and hauled her up to meet his blackened eyes— eyes that were the dark mirror image of Kartix's. An inky, horrible reflection of the male she—

No.

She wouldn't allow herself to say it. Refused to allow such hope into her heart.

Razan's nails dug into the delicate skin of her neck. "What a pretty little prize I have." His voice was like gravel. There was nothing warm, no light in his voice. He was darkness while Kartix was light.

Sorcha managed to glance at the sunlight one last time. Gods knew, it could be the last time she would feel the sun on her skin. Golden rays illuminated her bloodstained fighting leathers. With Razan's grip on her neck, she knew she would be dead soon. No one would be coming to save her.

Not that she wanted them to.

Sorcha had whispered to the group of rebels the night before, "If the worst happens, go as far away from Ocyla as you can." She told her friends where the Assassins Guild vault was, how much gold awaited them there if she did not return. It comforted her, in her last moments, to know that at least the rest of the rebellion might make it out alive, even if she didn't.

That was what she had been crafted for, was it not? To ensure the survival of magik? To sacrifice herself?

She couldn't even do that right.

Razan's strong fingers dug into her thin skin. *"You're mine."*

Sorcha shivered. Mere hours earlier, Kartix had been in her bed, whispering the same thing in her ear as she came for him. But now those words came from his father.

Razan's breath was hot against her cheek. Sorcha kept crying, kept fighting, and scratching Razan's arms. He had taken her magik. Now she was fully human.

Soft.

Weak.

And Kartix was *dying, and she couldn't do anything to stop it.*

She kept calling Kartix's name, and Razan tolerated it until he didn't. With a smile, he swiftly hit Sorcha across the side of the face and dropped her on the cobblestones when her body went limp. It was of no use, trying to escape. Her head swam with dizziness. Razan had her magik. He had *her*.

It didn't matter now.

Sorcha felt utter despair over the rebellion's plans falling apart. Sure, they blew up the main part of the slums and the majority of Razan's army, but how will the Assassins Guild continue to save girls without her, Marie, or Facim to run the place?

A small remaining kernel of magik, what was left of the curse bond, kept her grounded. She grasped it, desperately clinging onto it. Even as unconsciousness slowly took her under, Sorcha tried to crawl toward Kartix through the blood. She reached for him as if she could still save him. Sorcha could feel the curse bond slowly starting to fade deep within her chest, thinner and thinner as the life inside Kartix started to expire.

Then, the light of the bond dimmed.

And went out completely.

Sorcha felt something like death, right then and there, and she screamed. She screamed at the sudden hollowness inside her chest which weighed upon her. She screamed when a pain like she'd never felt before shot right through the core of her, right down to her soul. She screamed at the loss of what had been hers, yet another person taken from her. Where there once had been a bridge between their minds, there was a burning emptiness, one she would never recover from.

"*Please*," Sorcha cried, begging from the ground. "Let him live."

But was he even alive?

Razan pulled her up by her arm, nearly dislocating her shoulder. He brought Sorcha against him, one hand on her neck, another around her waist. She did not realize before how much taller he was than her. His breath was hot against her lips. "Let's play." He cupped her face in his hand, smiling softly as his fingers dug into her fighting leathers.

Sorcha suddenly knew what awaited her back at the Compound—not a prison cell underground, but Razan's bed chamber. For the rest of her miserable fucking life.

She allowed a single tear to run down her cheek. Blue eyes met black as she nodded. "As long as he lives."

Razan huffed a laugh, and she tried not to wince. "Foolish girl."

"I'm a *woman*," Sorcha managed to choke out before he hit her across the face once more. Her cheek sang with pain, but she tolerated it. Better get used to the sensation.

A woman cried out in the crowd before she was silenced by one of the guards. Razan shook his head. The courtyard was dead silent. "Such a lovely pet."

Sorcha tried to twist around to look at her friends one last time, but Razan pulled her against him once more. He whispered in her ear, "I like it when they struggle." He grabbed her hair, having now slipped loose of its plait, yanking Sorcha's head back and bringing tears to her eyes. What was left of the army surrounded the courtyard, bows and arrows at the ready. There was no escape. For any of them.

As Razan dragged Sorcha by her hair through the gates, she kept twisting back to look at the group of rebels she had come to know as family. The last thing she saw was Kartix's body, crumpled on the cobblestones. She could have sworn he was reaching out to her, one arm extended through the blood.

Reaching, as if he cared.

As if he could save her.

L. Homes is the author of the *City of Flame and Ash* series. She has four years of college from Hampshire College and the Moscow Art Theatre. A Connecticut native, Lily lives with her husband and two cats near North Carolina. *City of Flame and Ash* is her debut novel.

Acknowledgements

First and foremost, I want to thank my husband, Leland. Not enough books in the world would be enough to express how thankful I am that you're in my life. You held my hand every step of the way through this process, and never once let go. You are the brightest light in my life. I love you so much.

To my Mom and Dad: You are the best parents in the world. Thank you for supporting and believing in me even when I didn't think I could do it. I can't wait to repay you for everything you've done for me. I love you.

As for the rest of my family, your support means everything to me. I love and miss you all so much.

To my fearless editor Jessica: Thank you for taking my first book and polishing it into perfection. I could not have published without you; You are truly a master. I can't wait to share my future books with you!

To James Barry: Thank you for saving me countless times, and for cheering me on from the sidelines. I love you.

To my publisher, Nate Crew and his wife Amanda: Thank you for taking a chance on me. I was so nervous when you said yes to signing me, and I'm so proud of how far we've come. I'm so excited for what the future has in store for us all.

To JN James: You were there from day one, cheering me on. I annoyed you with many emails, frantic messages about plotlines, and way too-many office visits. Thank you for the memories.

To my artists, Kelly Ritchie, Madison Gilmore, and Samuel Swap: I adore each of you so much. Thank you for your work and time on CoFaA. I could not have published without you all.

To my best friend Shauni: I don't tell you this enough, but I love you. Thank you for the endless hours of listening to me vent about the book, and always having a safe space for me to come to.

And lastly, I want to thank my readers. Wow, what a journey this has been. I could not have done this without you. Whoever you are, wherever you are, I want you to know that you are so loved; You are loved more than you can ever know. I wish I could hug each and every one of you. But for now, just know that I'm thinking of you. From the bottom of my heart, thank you.

CITY OF KINGS AND KILLERS
Coming soon

CITY OF DEATH AND DISCONTENT
Coming soon